PEAKS AND VALLEYS

A SHENANDOAH ALBUM COLLECTION

EMILIE RICHARDS

CONTENTS

PROLOGUE TO PEAKS AND VALLEYS

Helen Henry had lived alone most of her eighty-nine years. Yes, she'd been married for a short time, until her husband had died at Pearl Harbor. Then she'd had her daughter at home while Nancy was growing up, but they hadn't been close. Nancy had been a flighty child who needed people in a way Helen never had.

Now Helen understood her daughter better, even glowed inside when Nancy and her family were visiting. But back then, Helen had been plain overwhelmed just trying to keep food on the table. Their new intimacy was a gift which had helped lift away her loneliness, as had the companionship of the young Claiborne family who now shared her house.

Another gift was even more surprising. The ladies from the SCC Bee, the church quilting bee, had become friends, good ones, when she'd been sure she was too old to need them. Helen had grown up with women who quilted together. She could still remember sitting on the floor under a quilting frame lowered from the ceiling so that family members and neighbors could gather around it and make shorter work of a long project. But after her family and neighbors had died or dispersed post-war, she had quilted alone. She hadn't expected anything else. Life was different, and she'd had a daughter to see to. There had been no time for friends, for socializing with the new people who moved into old houses or staying to chat after church.

She guessed she'd just gotten used to being alone.

Then one morning she'd been dragged to the church quilting bee, not a bit glad about it, either. For some reason, since that time, she'd never put her foot down and told them to leave her alone.

That was how she'd gotten herself into this mess.

At the moment Cissy Claiborne, who was holding on to Helen's arm, held it a little tighter as they stepped over particularly bumpy ground. The girl had insisted on going for a walk, even pretending she needed the fresh air when they both knew that what Cissy really wanted was for Helen to get a little exercise.

"I guess you don't want to come up with anything real ordinary," Cissy, said, continuing a conversation that had begun a few minutes ago. "The other quilters are expecting you to come up with the best idea, even if they put other ideas forward themselves."

Helen wanted to tell the girl that she didn't need all this hauling and guiding, but she figured Cissy thought she was helping, and she didn't want to hurt her feelings.

She lifted her feet high to show that she still could. "Who knows? The whole bee might be as stubborn as all get out."

Earlier Helen had confessed that she planned to come up with the perfect pattern for next spring's raffle quilt, which would be used to raise money for the church's prison ministry. The quilters would vote their choice of designs, and Helen had to admit she wanted them to vote for hers, whatever it was.

"Everybody thinks they can do a raffle quilt," she said. "I saw one up at the bank a few months ago. Nine patch blocks so stretched out of shape there's not a bed in the whole world that quilt would cover. And somebody stippled the whole thing in black thread. Looked like a bunch of dying spiders thrown on top."

"Mercy. Did you buy a ticket?"

Helen hated to admit she *had*. Unfortunately, the quilt had been for some cause or other that she'd wanted to support. "I made up a name and phone number," she said. "Just in case my ticket stub got drawn."

When the weather was nice, the way it was today, Cissy always managed to come up with an excuse to get Helen outside. Usually Reese, Cissy and Zeke's five-year-old daughter, came with them, zipping ahead to find stones to throw or sticks to take home and weave through the fence around the vegetable garden. Today the little girl was eating dinner at a friend's house, and Cissy and Helen planned to pick her up after their walk.

"So you're looking for something original, but something quilters in the bee can do with their varying levels of skill," Cissy said.

"You got that right."

"You want a traditional pattern?"

"I thought about houses, maybe everybody using their own fabric stash and imagination with the old-fashioned school-house pattern."

"That would be pretty."

"But a quilt like that? It could be from anywhere. I'd like a quilt that says something about where we live."

"So something about the Shenandoah Valley. Original then."

They stopped at the end of the path. They weren't far from

Helen's farmhouse, but neither of them ever got tired of this walk. It was a gentle slope uphill, bordered by trees with foliage that changed with the season. The view at the end was the real reward. The clearing looked over a lush green valley and beyond it to the west, distant mountains. This evening the sky was beginning to turn salmon pink as the sun sank low behind the peaks. Helen knew they'd have to start back in a little while or risk walking home in the dark.

"It's so peaceful here," Cissy said. "When I'm standing here I always feel like whatever's wrong in the world, maybe it's going to be okay."

Helen was feeling unnaturally philosophical tonight. "Like looking at life's ups and downs. Mountains, valleys, mountains, can't have one without the other." She turned to Cissy. "My mother had a pattern she used a time or two. Something about mountains." She considered. "Moon Over Mountain. That was it."

"Maybe there's your idea."

But Helen was thinking ahead. She wanted something with more room for creativity. Her mother's pattern had relied on a circular moon, and she wasn't sure she trusted the new quilters in the bee to stitch a circle that anybody would want to see.

"I'm going to think on this," she said.

"Could you work in the sunset? I mean, behind the mountains, it's so beautiful."

Helen's mind was spinning and suddenly she was aching to get back home to her sewing room. "We'd better go pick up that little girl of yours."

"The prisoners this quilt will help have had a lot of ups and downs in their lives, I bet," Cissy said.

"Brought it on themselves," Helen said, but she softened.

"Not always, I expect. And I guess most everybody deserves another chance."

"Sun goes down every single night, but the next morning, there it comes. Back up again. Nothing can keep it from doing what it's supposed to."

Helen took Cissy's arm. "We better get going, or pretty soon we'll be looking at tomorrow's sunrise."

They started down, walking slowly, and Helen didn't speak until they neared the house. "I used to go up to that spot and look at those mountains when I didn't think I could look at one more day. Just me by myself. Back when I was alone, and there was nobody to walk there with."

Cissy moved a little closer as if she understood that Helen was telling her walking with *her* was better, even if she couldn't say it out loud. "I'm glad to be walking there with you now. If it wasn't for you showing me, I wouldn't even know that view was right there waiting."

"Sometimes things work out."

"The quilt's going to work out, too," Cissy said.

"Maybe it will."

Cissy squeezed her arm. "You know what? I'd be willing to bet on it."

STEPS TO THE ALTAR
BY EMILIE RICHARDS

A Shenandoah Album Collection
Peaks and Valleys, Book 1

CHAPTER
ONE

"Recovering from a broken heart takes time, dear."
Rebecca Patterson stared at her mother and struggled for a polite response. Glenda Albritton had a seemingly endless repertoire of inspirational one-liners. Rebecca was tired of all of them, particularly *that* one, followed closely by: "Everything happens for a reason," and "Someday you'll look back at this and smile."

She couldn't tell Glenda that she thought any woman who looked back on the worst moment of her life and found *anything* to smile about was crazy. When she was a hundred–if she was doomed to live that long–she would not find anything humorous about having her wedding cancelled just hours before the ceremony, by the man she loved. In fact, she wasn't sure she would *ever* smile again.

She couldn't say that, though. Glenda despised criticism. Instead, Rebecca straightened her shoulders and gave the vaguest of nods. "As long as this quilt is staring at me, I'm not going to recover from anything. I'm taking it back this morning before the bee gets started. Dovey Lanning will be at church now setting up, and I'm sure she'll understand and explain to the others that I can't keep it."

Glenda stood silently as Rebecca refolded the quilt, carefully matching the edges, doubling and redoubling until the quilt was a bundle that fit under her arm. "You don't need to be embarrassed," Glenda said at last. "None of this was your fault . . ." A pregnant pause followed. "Except for your choice of boyfriends," she finished.

Rebecca had known that zinger was on its way. From the beginning, her mother hadn't approved of Connor O'Keefe, and even when Glenda had seemed her most accommodating, her dislike of her future son-in-law had been obvious. Connor wasn't good enough for Rebecca, something Glenda's second husband had agreed with. Of course, during the first weeks of his marriage, the astute Herb Albritton had figured out that agreeing with Glenda was the only way to maintain a happy home.

She averted her gaze from her mother's sympathetic smile. "I'll be sure to come back in time to see you and Herb off to the airport." She didn't add that she would calculate her return to the minute, so she could avoid more platitudes.

Glenda glanced at herself in the mirror in Rebecca's hallway and swept her blond bangs back from her forehead, patting them into place. "I'll be glad when you're settled in Philadelphia, and I don't have to visit you *here*."

Rebecca and Connor had found that mirror in an antique mall in Strasburg, the next town over. He had stripped the frame and painted it a bright blue to match the equally bright photo frames on the wall around it. Rebecca doubted that her mother noticed anything except her tanned good looks. The photos were of Rebecca's father, of the Patterson family before her father's death, of Connor with his grandfather Harry, of Rebecca with Connor.

"It will be months before I finally get to Pennsylvania." Rebecca turned away from the photo of Connor with his arm draped over her shoulders. "It will take me that long to pack and make arrangements to sell this house."

"A shame, isn't it? You won't find a teaching job that late in the summer. You could stay with us in Colorado in the fall, instead of with your sister, and save money until the timing's better."

Rebecca was doubly glad her sister had thrown her a lifeline. "No. Sandy is expecting me, and she wants me to come. Maybe I can sub or find something else in the fall while I get my certification."

"If you refuse to move to Denver to be near me, at least you'll finally be somewhere with a decent airport." Glenda gave her bangs one more swipe, then leaned forward to check her lipstick.

Rebecca squeezed past her. "I'd better get going."

"Herb and I are going out to breakfast. We'll see you when you get back." Glenda smacked her lips and waved the kiss in Rebecca's direction.

Rebecca was a mile down the road before she released a deep breath. In her own way, her mother was trying to be supportive. For the most part Glenda had even managed to hide her relief when, on the eve of their wedding, Connor had announced he couldn't go through with the ceremony. Glenda had helped her call all the wedding guests to let them know the news, and she had dealt with the caterer and the photographer, too. She wasn't perfect, but she loved her two daughters and tried her best.

Rebecca knew she was avoiding the real issue by dumping silently on her mother. Thinking about Glenda was easier than thinking about Connor or the upcoming humiliation of returning the quilt that the women of the Shenandoah

Community Church Bee had made for the wedding-that-wasn't.

The Steps to the Altar quilt had been Rebecca's favorite wedding gift by far. Connor had loved it, too, although he had been mystified that anyone would take the time to piece and quilt such an heirloom for a young couple they hardly knew. Of course, Connor was always surprised when people were kind to him.

Not something he would have to worry about for a while.

Returning roasting pans and spatulas was one thing, but a handmade quilt was different. The Steps to the Altar quilt was like a living thing, infused with the spirits of the women who had created it. The women's hopes for the Patterson-O'Keefe marriage had been quilted into every stitch. Now Rebecca could almost hear the quilt groaning with disappointment.

She arrived at the church too quickly, although she knew that finishing this sad business was going to be a relief. In the front parking lot, with the quilt folded against her chest, she tossed her curly blond ponytail over one shoulder and slunk toward the front door which was cheerfully flanked by blooming yellow daffodils. She'd had daffodils in her bridal bouquet, tulips, too, and lilacs, of course, because a spring wedding needed them. The bouquet had arrived at her house by delivery van just minutes before Connor's announcement. After that she'd fed the flowers, one by one, down the kitchen garbage disposal.

The quilters arrived in half an hour for their weekly session, and she didn't want to confront more of them than she had to. She had written a note to be passed around or read out loud explaining how grateful she was for the gift, even if she couldn't keep it. These were good women. They would understand why she wasn't ready to face them in person.

Inside, glad to find nobody was nearby, she followed the

hall to the basement stairs and took them quickly. Outside the room the quilters called the Beehive, she heard Dovey's voice and realized another woman must be inside helping her set up for the meeting. With a hand on the doorknob, she reconsidered her plan, but she had come too far to leave just because someone else was there, too. She opened the door and stepped inside.

Almost two dozen heads turned in her direction.

Rebecca stood frozen in the doorway. Dovey Lanning, an older woman in her eighties with a tight bun and an unwavering voice, had her back to Rebecca, and without turning she finished what she had been reading from a notebook held at nearly arm's length.

"*The Steps to the Altar quilt for Rebecca Patterson and Connor O'Keefe was carefully wrapped in archival quality tissue paper and tied with pale blue ribbon to match the blue used in the quilt. As expected, there was an argument about who would deliver the quilt to the happy couple, and for once Dovey Lanning won, an occasion so surprising that afterwards, she considered visiting her physician to be certain she hadn't passed away during the meeting without realizing it.*

"*The meeting ended after Helen Henry suggested that we convene an hour earlier this week so the Log Cabin quilt can be finished and taken off the frame. She also suggested—and I use that word loosely—that today we look at all the options and get down to figuring out which pattern we want to make for the prison ministry raffle. Those motions passed with no objections, because Helen was at her most formidable and one argument per session is more than enough.*"

Dovey lowered the notebook as she finished. "*Sincerely, Dovey K. Lanning, permanent recording secretary because nobody else will take the job.*"

Rebecca considered turning and walking away, but wasn't

that exactly what Connor had done? He had walked away from a life with her, walked away from any hope he would ever again be respected in Shenandoah County. Walked away from all the promises he had made.

She stepped into the room and closed the door behind her. "I'm sorry. I didn't mean to interrupt."

Dovey faced her, and in one glance seemed to read the entire story unfolding in front of her. "You couldn't be an interruption if you tried."

"I just—"

Helen Henry, as old as Dovey and twice as large, labored to her feet and interrupted as the other quilters continued to stare.

"Well now, I've been telling you for practically forever that you need to come exercise your needle with us, young lady," Helen said. "We don't have near enough young folks in here. And here you are this morning when we need help the most. You come on in, and we'll get you set up at the quilt frame. I'll supervise you myself."

"I'm just here to—"

This time Dovey interrupted. "To show us how much you love that quilt we made for you. We're so glad you do, because you know, it's yours to love, Rebby. It was our pleasure to make it, and we know you will treasure it through thick and thin for the rest of your life."

Tears clouded Rebecca's vision. She tried to speak and couldn't. Somehow that didn't matter.

Dovey was beside her in a moment, her arm around Rebecca's shoulders. "So you come on in and get settled at the frame. We'll spread that beautiful quilt of yours out for everybody to admire again, before we fold it up so you can take it home once you're finished today."

Helen lumbered up to stand on Rebecca's other side. "Of

course, just so you know. We can't go easy on you, even if quilting's new to you. There's quilt stitches and quilt stitches. We'll expect yours to hold up for a century or more. It takes a long time to learn to do most anything, but practice makes perfect."

"In quilts, just like life," Dovey said.

Rebecca thought there were some things that all the practice in the world couldn't set right, but she knew better than to say so. "I can't stay long. My mother and stepfather are leaving soon."

"An hour'll do," Helen said. "Your fingers will be sore as it is. Next week you can stay longer."

The other women were chatting now, or heading toward the coffee pot, as if nothing unusual had just occurred.

Rebecca tried one more time to be clear about her reason for being there. "I really wasn't planning to quilt."

"Ain't that the way?" Helen asked. "We make plans, and just like that, things change, and sometimes for the better, even if we can't see it. We're just glad you're here anyway. Right, Dovey?"

"Helen will teach you to quilt whether you want to learn or not," Dovey said. "Sometimes it's just better to go along with fate and see what happens next."

CHAPTER

TWO

Connor O'Keefe woke up on the floor beside his bed, although it took him more than a minute to piece together enough information to identify his surroundings. He recognized the embossed metal ceiling tiles above him, the rug below, and the comforter he had somehow managed to tug off the bed and cocoon so tightly that now he had to struggle to free his arms.

He wasn't a caterpillar emerging as a butterfly. After a night at the closest watering hole, his stomach roiled, a jackhammer pounded in his skull, and every joint throbbed, as if he had performed some athletic feat instead of merely getting drunk with the college roommate who should have been his best man and was now just a sidekick on Connor's personal road to perdition.

"Make...it...stop." He managed to sit up and rest his head in his hands. The hands shook; the head threatened to explode into a thousand pieces. The stomach gave him a thirty-second head start and made no additional promises.

He stumbled to his feet and made it to the bathroom just in time.

Afterward he managed a shower by leaning against the walls of the enclosure to let the water run over him until he had drained the hot water tank. Wrapped in a towel he lurched back to his bedroom and dug out a pair of cut-offs and a T-shirt that was so stretched out of shape, he could have fit his whole body through a sleeve and still had room for a friend.

A cough alerted him he wasn't alone. He looked up and saw his grandfather standing in the doorway, one grizzled brow lifted in question.

"Water or Gatorade?" Harry O'Keefe asked. "I've got Advil and crackers in the kitchen."

Connor waited for his stomach to make a decision. "Gatorade," he croaked when no help was forthcoming.

"Take your time."

Ten minutes later he found his way into the kitchen, fairly secure he and the toilet had no additional dates in the foreseeable future. He fell into one of two chairs at the metal table Harry had rescued from the roadside and rested his head in his hands once more.

"Start with the Gatorade," Harry said. "Just sip slow. When you've had a bit and it stays down, take the pills. You can try a cracker at the end."

"No cracker." The hands were still shaking, so Connor fell forward and rested his head on the table. His grandfather had spray-painted it a glossy emerald green, and he was forced to close his eyes in self-defense.

"Oh, how you make me miss my drinking days," Harry said. "The headaches, the shakes, the stomach bouncing up and down like a trampoline. Makes me want to run right out and buy a bottle of good Irish whiskey so I can join you."

"Not funny."

"Funny? Every time I stand up in a meeting, I remember how much fun I had as a drunk and all the places it took me. Jail. Hospitals. Homeless shelters."

Connor knew his grandfather hadn't picked "jail" out of thin air. Harry might have a reputation as a ne'er-do-well. He might have temporarily surrendered legal custody of his only grandson for a while when Connor was in middle school. He might have lost more jobs, women and money than ten men his age, but nobody thought Harry was stupid. Bull-headed. Rash. Mercurial, but brilliant.

He sat up and opened his eyes, reaching for the glass. Two small sips stayed down. He rested the glass back on the table and spun slowly in his chair to see Harry, who was chopping something at the counter.

"We had a designated...driver."

"How smart you are."

"Not...like last time."

"Yes, last time. And what a time *not* to have a designated driver. The night of your bachelor party."

Connor winced.

"We can assume that when you got drunk out of your mind for the first time this week, Grandson, you were making some statement or other about your upcoming wedding. Can we also assume that *this* time you were making a statement about cancelling it?"

"Vince was leaving...town." Connor reached for the glass and managed two more sips. Then he swept the pills his grandfather had left out for him into the palm of his hand and dropped them into his mouth, finishing with another sip.

"He seems like a good lad. Think he'll make his plane?"

Connor imagined that right now Vince–who had only nursed two beers all night–was on his way to distant Dulles International, smiling and laughing with Sandy, Reb's sister and maid-of-honor, or rather the sister who *should* have been her maid-of-honor. Vince and Sandy were on the same flight. Both had stayed to offer support to the distraught couple, but Connor suspected there might also be a romance brewing.

"Vince always lands on his feet." What could have been a compliment came into the world like an accusation.

"Finish that glass, and I'll make coffee if you want it."

Connor had no idea what time it was. Morning, afternoon, evening? Coffee might or might not be appropriate. He shrugged.

"On another subject? We got that commission you worked so hard for," Harry said.

Connor's brain was working just well enough to know that his grandfather was referring to a series of concrete benches to be cast on site and serve as retaining walls on a nearby mountain estate. He and Harry were partners in North Fork Concrete Creations, and with Harry's eye for design and Connor's engineering skills, business had doubled in the past year. There was almost enough income to support them both, although Harry didn't need the extra.

"Glad to hear it." The owners of the estate had as many friends as they had millions, and if they were happy with the benches, they were the kind of people who would share the good news.

"I told them we would start tomorrow," Harry said.

Connor groaned.

Harry busied himself with the single shot coffee maker, a new one Reb had bought him as a gift, after she'd been forced to drink from the one Harry had used for more than a decade. Now the old man loved turning out one designer cup at a time, and he never came home from a shopping trip without a box of pods promising a new flavor.

"I'm not getting any younger." Harry stood back, arms

folded, and watched the coffee spurt into a bright red mug. The room immediately smelled like hazelnut. "If you want to talk about what's happened, now would be the time. Tomorrow I might be a corpse."

"At least then I wouldn't have to go to work." Connor finished the Gatorade and got up to slide his glass into the dishwasher. Then he leaned against the counter, arms folded just like Harry's.

"I can't help but be curious, you know," Harry said. "One minute you're about to marry the sweetest, prettiest girl in Shenandoah County, and the next, you're sleeping on the floor because you can't find your bed. That's a transformation, wouldn't you say?"

"Better now than after I married her."

Harry cocked his head. "You mean it was inevitable? This change from a young man with a bright future to a scion of Satan?"

"That's overstating it a little."

Harry didn't answer, and listlessly, Connor examined him. There was a strong family resemblance. He had always known it, even without examining the framed photographs of a younger Harry. His grandfather's hair had once been dark brown like Connor's, although now it was white. They had the same green eyes under arching eyebrows. Same straight, narrow nose and rascal's grin—Harry's more rascally than his own. Both men were tall, and once Harry had been broad-shouldered with a back as straight as Connor's. Boozing and carousing had put a kink in the spine and a slump in the shoulders.

Of course, lately Harry's step had regained some of its youthful spring.

"Why don't you put the story in your own words then?"

Harry handed his grandson the steaming mug and turned to brew his own.

Connor wasn't cold, but he cupped the mug in his hands and savored the warmth, if not the hazelnut fumes.

"I was going to marry her," he said after his grandfather was facing him while his own mug brewed. "I asked her to marry me, after all. She said yes. I figured that was the whole story, except the wedding and honeymoon."

"But something changed your mind."

"I've never been good enough for Reb."

Harry didn't look surprised. "Is that right?"

"I can't talk to you about this."

"Let me try. You're an O'Keefe. A Blue Ridge mountains O'Keefe, not the best kind to be. At three, your father and mother abandoned you to a grandfather who barely stayed sober enough to keep you out of the foster care system—"

"Not entirely." Connor looked up. "I was in state custody at thirteen."

"The state sent you to camp that summer, Connor, while I was getting sober again, and you came back to me when summer was over."

"Camp was courtesy of some of your adoring fans who paid my tuition and went to bat to keep me out of a group home."

"It wasn't perfect. *I* wasn't, I know. And if I'd been a better father to your father, he might never have left you with me to raise."

Connor's father worked on oil rigs, gambled and drank between jobs and forgot to return home for visits. His mother . . . Connor didn't want to guess how his mother supported herself. He got postcards sometimes, always from some place new, always signed "love." To him she was nothing more than cramped, uneven handwriting and the vaguest memory of fists raised in anger.

"You always tried," Connor said. "You cared enough, even when it was hard."

"But you didn't have the easiest or most traditional upbringing, did you?"

"It's not about my upbringing..." Connor took a sip of coffee and found that it wasn't as bad as it smelled.

"Then what?"

Connor didn't want to talk about this. Humiliation was a deep well inside him, better left untapped until he built some defenses.

"You fell in love with another woman?" Harry guessed out loud.

"No." Connor couldn't imagine that.

"She fell in love with another man?"

"She ought to."

"Because the one she loves right now isn't..." Harry shrugged, clearly waiting for Connor to finish his sentence.

There was no point in delaying the answer, since Harry would continue until he was satisfied. Connor began. "Is Reb the kind of woman who deserves a man who slept off his bachelor party in jail? After he slugged a bartender?"

"Not slugged hard, if I heard the story correctly. Your aim was off. You grazed the man's cheek. He's not pressing charges."

"I'm you at your worst, Harry. I'm my father. Maybe even my mother. I'm a loser, a drunk in the making, a man destined to drag Reb down with me. I'm an O'Keefe waiting for destiny to step forward and work its evil magic."

Harry snorted. "And a bit of a silver-tongued devil, too."

Connor groaned. "I told you I couldn't talk to you about this."

"You didn't get drunk because of some errant gene you can't outrun. You got drunk because you've been sure from the beginning that you aren't good enough for pretty Miss Patterson. You were looking for an excuse the night of your party, and you found one, and lucky for you, it's one you can make yourself believe."

"Her mother believes it, too."

"Glenda Albritton is a snob who doesn't think anybody's good enough for her daughters."

"Well, this time she's right."

Harry turned off the coffee maker and removed his cup. He added half and half and sugar before he spoke. "So let's take a closer look. You put yourself through Virginia Tech with scholarships and loans, and you graduated near the top of your class. You've already set North Fork on the road to fiscal health, and you've won an award or two for your designs and execution. You found a woman who's perfect for you and convinced her to marry you. And at no time, in those years, was alcohol a problem. You don't do drugs. You don't gamble."

"I'm a time bomb waiting to go off."

"Is that right? The clock is ticking?"

"I pretty well proved it, didn't I? If the bartender hadn't knocked me out at my bachelor party, I would have gotten into my car and driven away. After all those drinks."

"You know that for a fact?"

"I don't know what I know. I just remember waking up in jail."

"You're not the first young man to misbehave at his bachelor party."

"Reb deserves better."

"Is that it? Or do you just need an excuse to sink to the level where you think you belong? To become the man everybody expected you to be?"

Connor shook his head and wished he hadn't. When the room stopped spinning, he set his cup on the counter. "I'm going back to bed."

"Take it from one who knows. Some things can't be slept off, Grandson. No matter how hard you try. And you can't drown them in alcohol, either."

"It took you a long time to figure that out."

"It did indeed," Harry said.

"Maybe it will take me just as long."

"Could be, but I'm betting not. You're smarter than I was. Try using that brain of yours."

As he made his way back to his room, Connor wished everything was that easy, but his brain wasn't the problem.

His heart held that honor.

CHAPTER

THREE

Rebecca listened as Dovey explained about an assortment of quilt blocks clinging to a portable design wall in the corner, each with a name beside it. Some were geometric, one had a flower stitched on top of a plain background. She knew enough to know that one was applique and time-consuming, to boot.

One group of four blocks at the left seemed to dance off the wall. Rebecca saw this sample had "Helen" written on the card beside it.

"So these are different ideas people have for our prison ministry raffle," Dovey said. "Each person had to make sample blocks, then as we leave today, each of us with an opinion—and there's no shortage of those around here—can cast a vote on which pattern we'll use."

"How do you decide?"

"It's a democratic process. We've already discussed it until we're blue in the face. Then Helen showed us what she came up with, and now everybody will vote for that one." The old woman winked, then she strode off to help a group who were learning to do something called English paper piecing. The room was buzzing with activity. Another group had set up machines and were working on blocks from a shared pile of fabrics.

Helen Henry came to stand beside Rebecca, tracing zigzag lines in the air with her index finger as she spoke, as if quilting. "My block's paper pieced, one of those new quilt ideas worth talking about, I guess."

Helen's four quilt blocks were all different but vibrant, jagged earth-toned peaks against backgrounds of oranges, pinks and golds. "The way I see it, no two blocks should be alike," she continued. "Each quilter can piece her portion from her own fabric stash, and when the final placement decision is made, I'll assemble it the way I see fit."

Rebecca had to smile at what would clearly be an abrupt end to democracy. "If it's chosen, it will be beautiful."

"Oh, it'll be chosen. Reverend Sam Kinkade already said the design will be perfect for us to raffle next spring because it looks like sunset over our mountains. He said we should call it Peaks and Valleys."

Rebecca saw how perfect the quilt would be for that purpose. She'd already learned that the money the bee would make from the raffle would help fund Sam's prison ministry for men who struggled to climb their own personal mountains for a wider view of a better world.

Helen took Rebecca's arm. "We're finishing a log cabin quilt for a family that badly needs one. You're going to help."

Before she could protest, Rebecca was sitting where she was told and taking up the needle, thread and thimble that Helen deposited in front of her with a few words of instruction. Two other women came to sit at the frame, one on each side, but while everybody nodded politely, nobody spoke. Rebecca had quilted for five minutes before anybody addressed her.

"You've quilted before, I take it," Helen said after leaning over to examine Rebecca's first neat row of stitches. "And you've been hiding your talents."

"My grandmother quilted. She taught me how."

"That would be the first Rebecca Patterson. Didn't know her all that well. She was a lot behind me in school. Didn't seem the quilting type, somehow."

"I knew Becky." Peony Greenway smiled at Rebecca. Rebecca guessed she was probably about the age her grandmother would be now, had she lived.

"She was Becky Stallard then, of course," Peony continued. "We studied home economics in those days, and Becky was good at everything. Cooking. Sewing. The second year we had to make skirts and blouses to pass the class. Picked out fabric and paid 35 cents a yard, if I remember correctly. Becky's was green polished cotton, not calico like mine, and every seam she sewed was exact and even. She top stitched the whole outfit in a darker green, a double line, just for effect, and she had to take out every bit of it, because our teacher, Old Mrs. Meanie—that's what we called her, but not to her face—hadn't approved it first."

"Wow, you remember that?" Rebecca was amazed.

"Small class. I remember most of the projects. Mine was pink and gray flowers. Pretty, too. But I wasn't as good a seamstress as your grandmother."

Rebecca looked up. "I miss her. It's nice to hear about Grammy from somebody who knew her as a girl."

"I could tell you a lot."

"Like what?"

Peony looked up from her own row of tiny, neat stitches. "I knew your grandfather, too. Watched them fall in love, as a matter of fact. John Patterson was some catch."

Rebecca had cried an ocean of tears when her paternal

grandparents and her father had died together in a private plane crash just three years ago. Now she swallowed before she spoke. "Gramps was a great guy."

"He and Harry O'Keefe were considered *the* catches in our school. Going out with anybody else? That was just settling."

"I should think talk of the O'Keefes would be off-limits today," Anna Mayhew said from the other side of the quilt. She was a woman in her forties, and Rebecca had noticed that she frowned as she sewed, as if no stitch could please her.

Peony stopped sewing and glared at Anna. "And why would that be?"

Anna just shook her head.

"Some folks think all the O'Keefe's are crazy," Helen said.

Anna gasped. "Helen!"

"What do you think?" Helen asked Rebecca.

Rebecca said the first thing that came into her head. "Not Connor."

"Is that so? Good to hear it."

Rebecca wondered why she had defended the man. When would she stop?

"Harry has certainly lived large," Peony said. "Hard drinking explains a lot of it. I suspect most of that was on account of the way he was brought up. He more or less raised himself, and nobody really tried to set him on the right path. I think a bottle kept him company at night when nobody else was around. Me, I think people were afraid of him. Even then he stood out. Smart? Oh my heavens, way beyond smart. And talented? Now we all know that's the case, even if we don't *all* appreciate his sculptures." She glanced at Helen as she said the last part.

Helen sniffed. "Me, I'm a country bumpkin. I want to see statues I can figure out. Them naked Greek gods? I can see what they're supposed to be, even if the statue maker ought to have covered up their private parts a little. But those thingam-abobs Harry O'Keefe does? Blobs with arms reaching out to grab you? Houses with walls collapsing and algae in the cracks and graffiti? That show of his in Winchester? My daughter marched me up there whether I wanted to go or not. Scared me so bad I couldn't sleep for a week."

Rebecca realized how much she was going to miss Harry O'Keefe. Connor's grandfather was mercurial, even erratic at times—or had been in the early days of her romance with Connor—but in the past months, sober and working to stay that way, he had been an added bonus to her upcoming marriage. Harry would never be conventional, or simple, but who needed either?

She would miss the trip to his crazy house, too, the winding road dotted with small buildings sporting flourishing gardens.

She hadn't really thought about losing Harry because she'd been busy mourning Connor. Now the realization that she had lost them both made her that much sadder.

"Your grandpa and Harry were good friends for a lot of years," Peony said. "I guess after your grandparents moved to Atlanta, Harry and John didn't see each other much."

"Harry was always in trouble," Helen said with a sniff. "Connor take after his grandfather?"

No one else said a word, but Peony and Anna both stared daggers at Helen.

Rebecca wasn't upset at the question. In fact she knew exactly what the old woman was doing. Rebecca had been raised in this church, something her father had insisted on, and everybody knew Helen Henry was a force to be reckoned with. She might seem tactless for no good reason, but looks could be deceiving.

"You want to know what happened, don't you?" Rebecca could get straight to the point, too.

"Will it help to talk about it?"

Rebecca considered. She couldn't give a quick answer, but not because she didn't want to. She really didn't understand everything that had happened.

"One minute we were happy," she said, feeling her way. "We had everything worked out. My sister Sandy and I own my grandparents' old house, and Connor and I were going to buy her out. After Gramps and Grammy moved away there was a steady stream of renters, so the house needs a lot of work, but Connor planned to fix it up, just a little at a time. He's so good at that kind of thing..."

She realized she was drifting into good memories, good feelings. She pulled herself back. "Connor's business is growing. I got a teaching job in Mt. Jackson starting in the fall. We talked about having children, about growing old together."

She looked up. "Then the night before the wedding, he said he wasn't ready, that he'd made a mistake. And that was that. He walked away and left me to clean up his mess."

"Well, that part would make me furious," Helen said. "A man who doesn't clean up after himself."

"He did offer to make all the phone calls." Again, Rebecca realized she was defending her former fiancé.

"You should have let him." Peony was no longer glaring at Helen, but she still looked uncomfortable. "He should have been the one to face everybody."

"I would have, but they were mostly my friends and family."

"And women are always the fixers," Anna said. "It's been that way since the beginning."

Rebecca finished quickly. "So now I'm going to move to

Philadelphia and live with Sandy until I can get a job and a place of my own."

"You want to leave the Valley?" Helen sounded the way she might if Rebecca wanted to chop off her hands and feet.

"I just can't ..." Rebecca shrugged. "I can't imagine living right here anymore. I could move to Mt. Jackson, I guess. Rent out Grammy and Gramps house again, find a little place near my school and try to make friends. But it would be hard, you know?"

All three women nodded their heads. They did know. A single woman. A stranger in a small Valley town. Yard sales and church bazaars on the weekends for entertainment.

Rebecca nodded, too. "Sandy's a social butterfly. I'll make friends quicker, have lots to do to keep myself busy."

"Kind of sudden though, don't you think? This move of yours?" Helen sounded doubtful. "Seems like something you and that boy have in common, at least. Making quick decisions that change your life forever?"

Rebecca was supposed to be on her honeymoon right now, not making plans for a completely different life. She should be lying on a beach in Cozumel, Connor lying beside her, his arm flung...

She still had the bikini, but the man had vanished.

"I guess I need distance. I thought we had a lot in common. I thought love made up for the things we didn't." She put down her needle. "Do you ever truly know a man?"

Peony held up her hands. "Never been married."

"Hardly married at all before my Fate was killed," Helen said.

"Divorced my husband after our second son was born. By that time I knew too much about him and none of it good," Anna said.

"At least I won't get to that point," Rebecca said. "Maybe Connor did me a favor."

She wondered, though, as she went back to quilting, jabbing the needle into the quilt with unnecessary force. No matter how hard she tried to tell herself she was lucky Connor had pulled the plug, she couldn't believe it.

She still loved the man. Until she found a way to make that stop, her own pep talks and the sympathetic wisdom of others weren't going to make the slightest bit of difference.

CHAPTER
FOUR

The house where Connor had been raised was a Harry O'Keefe original. It was a ramshackle country cottage, rooms–some with no purpose at all–led to more rooms. A space might be a bedroom one week and Harry's studio the next. The dining room had no furniture but had once sported a badminton net. Harry believed that the outdoors provided enough earth tones to keep a man happy, so the indoors should be a wild display of color. Connor had been astonished the first time he visited a classmate and learned that not everybody lived inside a rainbow.

The house was nestled on a three-acre plot not far from the Shenandoah River. Every dead tree had been turned into a totem pole, the pasture into a wildflower meadow. Paths wound through sprawling gardens and wildlife knew that if they could evade Harry's dogs, they were welcome to sup. The house was far enough from their nearest neighbor, a ramshackle log cabin, that Harry didn't worry his dogs would wander into trouble.

Most of Harry's dogs had arrived country-style, which

meant they'd been dropped off in the vicinity to fend for themselves. Harry found new homes for the semi-socialized mutts, but the suspicious, snappy ones settled in for the long haul. They served a purpose. The immediate yard was studded by sculptures that Harry had created, then rejected. Luckily his work was too heavy for thieves to haul away, but anyone foolish enough to try would be greeted by Harry's ever expanding and contracting pack.

Harry and the mutts had an understanding. He pointed out friends, and they pointed out enemies.

This evening when somebody knocked on the front door, Connor knew the visitor had to be a friend. He hadn't heard even a growl from the yard.

Right before he opened the door, he had a premonition about who was standing there. But by then his hand was on the knob, and the door was swinging outward.

Rebecca stood on the porch, an unsmiling blond vision. He didn't know what to say, so he just stared for a moment. Her long curly hair was pulled back from her face with barrettes, like a little girl's, but the rest of her was all woman. A turquoise T-shirt outlined generous curves, and white shorts emphasized her narrow waist and shapely legs. She wore little makeup, but she knew exactly how to use it to enhance lightly tanned skin, long-lashed blue eyes and Cupid bow lips.

"You've got new neighbors," she said in introduction. "A little girl was playing outside the old cabin. Remember that when you go speeding down this road."

Connor had seen the girl and her mother, a woman somewhere in her twenties, moving in a couple of weeks ago. No surprise, he'd been too preoccupied to introduce himself. "That's why you're here? To warn me to be careful?"

"No, I brought you something." She reached down and lifted a shopping bag off the porch floor and held it out to him.

"What is it?"

"The quilt the church ladies made for us. I tried to give it back to them, but they wouldn't take it. I love their generosity, but I don't want a constant reminder of you and what you did to us. So I think you should have that honor."

He knew better than to take the bag. He thrust his hands in the pockets of his not-quite-clean jeans. "I can't take that, Reb. It's your church, not mine, and those women are your friends."

Her arm didn't waver, and neither did her gaze. "The pattern is called Steps to the Altar, and you're the one who backtracked. Now the quilt belongs to you."

"Please don't do this."

"How interesting to hear those words come out of *your* mouth."

"What will I do with a quilt?"

"You can try giving it back to the women who made it. You might have better luck than I did today, and pretty soon I won't be around to try, so it has to be up to you. You'll probably make your home in the Valley forever."

"You're leaving?"

"Yes, I am." She smiled, but it was as genuine as canned laughter on a television sitcom. "Did you think I would enjoy staying in Shenandoah County watching you have a life without me?"

"Where are you going?"

"Does it matter?"

He started to say, "hell yes," then he thought better of it. "That's a beautiful quilt. If the women didn't want it back, that means they want you to keep and enjoy it. Put it away for a while, and when you take it out again, things will seem different."

"It's just a matter of time, huh? A week or two, maybe a month, and I won't even remember where I got it and why. I'll just slap it on my bed and decorate my new apartment around it?"

He cringed inside. Sarcasm and Rebecca were usually strangers.

"I didn't mean it would be quick or easy," he said.

"Do you have a timeline for me? That might help."

"If you're trying to punish me, you're too late. I'm at the head of that line."

"Poor Connor."

"I don't want the quilt."

She set the bag down at his feet and turned to take the steps back to her car, which was parked in front of the house. He saw that Harry's dogs were snuggled in a heap on the other side of a large maple hung with three dozen gourd birdhouses.

He lunged forward and grabbed her arm before she could take another step. "Reb, you know how sorry I am. I know that doesn't fix anything, but I'm sick about everything that happened. I really am."

"Sick? Really? I hear you've been out whooping it up."

He wasn't surprised that tidbit had already reached her. "Drowning my sorrows."

She didn't face him. "You look like hell."

"I'm sure." He dropped his hand to let her go. Instead she turned.

"Have you come up with a good excuse yet? Something better than cold feet? Something I can tell people that doesn't make me look like such a bad bargain?"

"Nobody thinks that. Anybody who thinks about it knows I'm the bad bargain."

"You certainly seem bent on proving it, but I'll be blamed anyway. I'm not pretty enough, or smart enough, or good enough in bed. You found somebody else, or you wish you had, or you were just so freaking bored you couldn't imagine a life together."

Her eyes were narrowed in anger, but he saw the tears glistening in them. He swallowed and stepped forward to wrap his arms around her. He pulled her close, even though she struggled to get free, and he kissed her. Not that it was easy. She turned her head from side to side and finally freed her arms to push him away.

Hard.

"That is not an answer, Connor! Why did you fall out of love with me? Or were you never in love with me in the first place? We were so happy together. What went wrong?"

"I went wrong! I was born wrong, Reb. You don't get that? You don't see what your mother and everybody else already knows? I'm an O'Keefe. I'm the tail end of that train, and a chip off the old block."

"Stop mixing your metaphors!"

"I am not good for you!"

She tilted her head and stared at him as if she was seeing him for the first time. "What?"

He let it all pour out. "I'm saving you from me. For whatever crazy reason you fell in love with me, but you can't see the truth. I'm no good and most of all I'm no good for you. You've seen my grandfather? Well, he's the best of the lot. At least Harry tries. But *his* father? Died in prison. Mine? A roustabout with a gambling problem made worse by drinking himself half-blind, and then there's my mother. The best thing she ever did was desert me. I might look okay on the surface, but underneath I'm more O'Keefe than you want to believe. I know who I am. When the stress gets too much for me, when you need me? Who knows if I'll be there?"

"Until this, you were always there."

"Until this, what stress did we have? I fell apart. I got drunk at my bachelor party. I ended up in jail."

She shook her head. "So did your groomsmen. It was stupid, sure, but it's happened before. It's a tradition, not a good one, but better than lap dances in some strip club in Vegas, Connor. And I thought..."

Her voice drifted off.

"What? What did you think?"

She didn't speak for a moment. She was clearly thinking. She wrinkled her forehead whenever she was puzzling out a problem, and now hers looked like a washboard.

He hated himself for it, but he wanted to kiss away every wrinkle.

She finally spoke. "I thought the whole sleeping off too much to drink in jail was because you had already decided not to marry me and didn't know how to tell me. But that wasn't it, was it? That night in the drunk tank is what made you decide."

"I've known since the beginning that you deserved better."

"Better than you getting drunk and combative, which you're sure is inevitable?"

There was nothing to say to that.

When he didn't answer she shrugged. "And you never thought to yourself, hey, if I'm worried about having a problem with alcohol, I could just stop drinking. Forever."

"I know how alcoholics get their start. They make a vow they won't drink, and the next night they're back in the gutter."

"Even the ones who never really cared about drinking? The ones, like you, who never had more than a beer or two with Monday Night Football or a glass of wine with dinner?"

"It has to start somewhere."

"You were with your best friends having fun. You were understandably nervous about making a big commitment. You drank too much. It happens. That doesn't mean it will happen again."

He was growing more and more frustrated because she just didn't get it. "What part of my needing to protect you don't you understand?"

"Really?" Her smile chilled him. "The part where you think I'm so stupid, so incapable of picking the right man to marry, that I need protecting. Oh, and the part where you pretend you're the good guy, when we both know you're just scared that you're not a *real* man."

This time he didn't try to stop her when she turned and took the steps two at a time. The dogs didn't even open their eyes. They slept on as he watched Rebecca get into her car and drive away.

CHAPTER
FIVE

Really, the ladies at the church quilting bee couldn't have been nicer. Considering the way he had expected to be treated, Connor was astounded. Nobody lectured him; nobody glared at him. After the thin woman with the white bun read the minutes from the previous week in a quavering voice, another woman, heavier and younger, had come right over to him—Cathy Adams, he thought, but he wasn't sure—and put her arm around his shoulders to guide him to one side of the room.

"It's a gorgeous quilt, isn't it?" she'd asked in the friendliest of tones. "We are always delighted to have another look."

Connor had tried to explain that another look wasn't his reason for bringing the quilt back, but she had continued to smile as she shook her head.

"We made that quilt for your wedding, yours and Rebecca's, and the two of you need to sort out who keeps it. But it's yours now. You have to decide where it belongs."

Cathy was probably in her sixties, not grandmotherly, exactly. The kind who seemed to know exactly how to move things along and when to do it. He wondered what she had done before she'd taken up quilting. High school principal? Labor and delivery nurse? Car sales?

He had explained a little more, or tried to, and she had smiled more. A few other women had arrived to coo over the quilt and help him find the door out into the hall.

And now, here he stood on the stairs, quilt folded against his chest, with no place to go except home.

He was pondering his situation when a familiar figure descended toward him and stopped midway.

"Connor," Reverend Sam Kinkade said. "This is great. You're saving me a trip to your grandfather's house to see you. His dogs like me well enough, but it's never relaxing to pass by all those bared teeth."

Sam was the Shenandoah Community Church's minister, as well as the man who would have performed his wedding to Rebecca. Sam was somewhere in his thirties, handsome, innovative and charismatic—and usually just a few steps in front of his detractors, who were certain church should be a less controversial place. Luckily the detractors' number was smaller than those who loved the energy and commitment he had brought to their dwindling congregation.

"Why were you..." Connor shrugged. "I mean, the wedding is off. I mailed a check."

"Very thoughtful, considering everything. I put it in our La Casa fund. We're saving for more computers for the kids."

Connor knew about the after-school program the church sponsored for the children of Latin American immigrants in the area. He had even considered offering his own services.

Back when he thought he had something to offer.

"Good." He waited for Sam to explain why he had planned to visit.

"Do you have time to talk?" Sam didn't wait for a reply, as if he knew he wouldn't like the one he got. "I'll meet you in my office after I say hi to the quilters."

Connor considered giving Sam the quilt to take in with him, to see if he could find a way to return it, but even Sam, who seemed able to accomplish miracles, would fail. Feeling doomed he climbed the stairs and wound his way through the hall to Sam's study. The older woman sitting at the desk in the next office told him to make himself comfortable inside.

Connor settled on a leather sofa in front of two windows that looked over a garden bordered by blooming spring bulbs and flanked by flowering cherries. His wedding had been planned for the outdoors, in that very garden if the weather cooperated. As it had turned out, that Saturday had been rainy, and the wedding would have gone forward in the sanctuary.

He didn't really want to think about that, but he supposed he wasn't going to have a choice. The subject of his wedding was going to come up when Sam joined him.

Connor set the quilt beside him. It was a beautiful piece of handiwork, and he remembered how touched Rebecca had been to receive it. Even though he had moved into her house two months before their wedding was to take place, she had insisted that the quilt could only grace their bed after their marriage. She was a puzzling mixture, traditional and unconventional at the same time. Unconventional enough to invite him to live with her, to share herself in every way once she was certain they were headed for a long-term relationship, but traditional enough that she had wanted a fairytale wedding to seal their commitment.

And he had been so besotted that he would have done almost anything she wanted.

Right up until the very end.

Sam came in and closed the door behind him. "If I don't go down there every week to see the quilters, I worry about what they're plotting. This way at least I know, although that's a group that can't be brought to heel. Not that I'd ever really want to try."

He joined Connor on the sofa. "Can I get you water? A cup of coffee?"

The offer of beverages didn't bode well. Connor had hoped their conversation was going to be short. He gestured to the quilt folded between them. "I just came to give this quilt back to the ladies downstairs, only they refused to let me."

Sam smiled. "Then I can guarantee it's hopeless. They won't change their minds. The quilters call their room the Beehive, and it's a hive mentality down there, so don't try to single out one of the worker bees and ask her to intercede. Seems to me the quilt is yours now, no matter what."

"False pretenses. It's a wedding quilt, and I didn't go through with the wedding. Steps to the Altar seems like a bad joke, doesn't it?"

"How are you feeling these days?"

Connor almost said hung over, but it wasn't really true. He hadn't been back to the bar where he had tried to drown his sorrows with Vince, and he certainly hadn't been back to the site of his bachelor party. He had been stone cold sober this week because there was no liquor in the house. Harry wasn't drinking, and Connor wasn't going to be the one to tempt him. Drinking alone had never held any appeal.

"Confused," he said, surprising himself.

"I should imagine. You've made two big decisions in the past year. One to marry Rebecca, and the other not to marry her. The decisions are at war. And it must have been so hard to find a way to tell her you didn't love her anymore and wouldn't be happy married to her."

"That would have been a lie."

Sam didn't even try to look surprised.

"I do love her, and being married to her would be incredible," Connor said.

"And yet you're not."

"Being married to me would *not* be incredible."

"Because?"

"You've been in the Valley long enough to know about my family."

"I know your grandfather. I'm a great admirer of his work and spirit."

"He raised me, and sometimes I raised him. Who was raising whom depended on how much Harry drank the night before."

"Clearly it wasn't always easy growing up in your house."

"He did his best. He struggled, still does. He loved me when nobody else did, and I love him for that."

"But he had obstacles to overcome."

"He didn't ask for them either. They come with being an O'Keefe."

Sam sat back. "So you watched Harry do his best and still fail, sometimes with spectacular results."

"I don't want anybody else to go through that."

"You think maybe you were setting Rebecca up for the same thing?"

"I'm an O'Keefe, too."

"And, of course, you're doomed to be like your grandfather, or your parents who, I take it, didn't stay around to struggle with their own shortcomings the way Harry did."

Connor was glad that Sam had understood so quickly. The minister was a surprising ally. "Yes." He sat forward, hoping they were finished.

"And so you've decided to be like your parents, not Harry," Sam said, in the same thoughtful tone of voice.

Connor sat back. "No. That's crazy!"

43

"Really? Harry stayed and struggled to be the person you needed, and your parents abandoned you, even though, let's face it, they were the ones who had the responsibility to raise you. Harry was more or less an onlooker at the start."

"I thought you understood. That's why I got out of this marriage when I did. I took a good look at myself and realized I couldn't put Reb through any of what I went through. She deserves better."

"When you took that good look, what did you see?"

"A man capable of acting like an O'Keefe."

"If I looked in the mirror right now, I'd see a man capable of acting like an O'Keefe," Sam said. "Any man would."

Connor held a fist to his chest. "But I never saw that man before."

"Connor, I'm down at the jail a lot. I know about your visit to the drunk tank. Any man under stress does things he wishes he hadn't. He sees parts of himself he wished he hadn't glimpsed. The good men take that information and work with it. The others? They just assume that someday the deficits they saw will overwhelm them, and they'll be nothing but. They can't face the reality that we all have to work to be the people we want to be. Constantly. Forever. It never comes easy."

Connor could feel his anger rising. "Why doesn't anybody get this? Rebecca wants a family, a happy home, roots here in Toms Brook. And I'm not the man to give them to her."

"Oh, I do get it. I would agree. Feeling the way you do, convinced that because you aren't perfect you're out of the running, you definitely aren't that man. But I would disagree that biology and the way you were raised are destiny. Either you tried to blow off all your fears the night of your bachelor's party, or you just went overboard having a good time. Only you can figure that out. But your reaction afterwards?" Sam shook his head.

Connor couldn't form a sentence because he couldn't figure out where to start. And suddenly the anger dissolved, and he was ashamed of himself. More than he'd been, and that said a lot.

Sam picked up the quilt and unfolded it. "I watched the women downstairs making this for months. They told me that this pattern, Steps to the Altar..."

Sam glanced up and waited until Connor nodded. "They said it's often used for a wedding quilt. They made Elisa and me a Double Wedding Ring quilt after we were married. It's our most prized possession because for a long time we didn't believe we would ever be blessed to share wedding rings."

Connor knew enough about Sam and his wife to remember that the road to their wedding had twisted and turned more than once.

Sam fingered the quilt. "I like the symbolism in this pattern, though. There are so many steps to the altar. Finding the person you want to spend your life with. Growing closer. Overcoming the obstacles that separate you. But I like to think the most basic steps have to be taken a certain way."

When he didn't go on, Connor knew he had a choice. He could ask what those steps were, or he could thank Sam and leave. His head chose the second, but his heart? His heart spoke the question.

"What do you think they are? The steps, I mean."

"Faith in yourself and your ability to be a good partner. Faith in the person you've loved and chosen—and that includes faith that she or he can forgive you for not being perfect. And finally faith in your strength as a couple to move forward, hand in hand, despite imperfections, despite adversity. Because it's easier to move mountains together."

The words sent chills through Connor. Sam made it sound so simple, yet it was anything but. It was a life's work.

Faith in himself, the first step.

"I lost my faith in myself," Connor said, when the silence had extended too long, his voice surprisingly hoarse. "I don't know where to find it, Reverend Sam."

"Not at the bottom of a bottle, that's for sure."

"I know."

"I'm a big believer in prayer."

"Makes sense you would be."

Sam smiled. "I'm also a believer in asking the right people for help. I suspect you already know who they are."

Connor *did* know, but that took commitment and a belief he could make a difference. "At this point I'm not sure any changes I make will make a difference to Rebecca," he said, rising to his feet. "She'll never forgive me for humiliating her the way I did. *I'll* never forgive me."

"One step at a time." Sam clapped him on the back as he rose to stand beside him. "Just take one step and then worry about the next one. That's the way we all move forward."

CHAPTER
SIX

North Fork Concrete Creations was housed at the front of Harry's property in a series of sheds, each unique and in some ways, puzzling, since the exteriors seemed to have little to do with the interiors. The prettiest little Victorian conservatory held sacks of concrete and tools hanging from vintage iron hooks. A plain metal shed from the lumber yard had been painted darkest eggplant, with scalloped turquoise trim on eaves and around windows. The shed was Harry's artistic retreat and held a long wooden table and everything else he needed to sketch plans and draft blueprints.

Connor found Harry in a "shack" farthest from the road, constructed from salvaged lumber. Of course, since Harry had designed and built it with his own hands, the shack was a work of art. The front, complete with a porch and matching windows Harry had reclaimed from a century home, was faced with black walnut. One long side was walled-in by sliding barn doors which allowed Harry to move his creations in and out without fuss. The doors were the backdrop for a mural of a sea of faces, people Harry had known and loved in his long life.

The interior was paneled with a variety of woods placed in circular patterns without so much as a half inch gap to be seen.

Connor was late, but he knew Harry wouldn't chide him. Once his grandfather began work on a project, he lost all sense of time and place.

Harry usually worked on large projects—furniture, counter-tops, benches, and best of all, sculpture. Today Connor was surprised to find him working on what looked like a series of pots. Three to be exact, large enough for trees, but still not quite what Harry usually created.

"I thought you were designing the housing for that outdoor kitchen in Fairfax," Connor said, moving closer to examine his grandfather's work. The pots were a mixture of concrete and other elements, Harry's signature. He knew exactly how much of what to add to reinforce the mixture, how to color, layer, and sculpt the finished product. The pot he was working on now looked like it had been carved from a cliff with layers representing eras long since lived and left behind.

"A friend has a small patio and loves to garden. I promised her a pot large enough for a tree and a couple of smaller ones for all the flowers she wants to tend."

Connor wondered if there was more to this than met the eye. "Discount stores carry patio pots, large and small."

"Not like these."

"Of course not. Does she realize once they're set in place she won't be able to move them?"

"If she needs to move them, I'll have somebody do it for her."

"Mighty kind of you."

Harry looked up and lifted a brow. "Something you want to say?"

"Only that when she retires, she'll have a nest egg right

there." Connor motioned toward the pots. "Harry O'Keefe originals."

"She *is* retired and you're out of line. She's not some floozy I woke up next to after one of my binges."

Connor held up his hands in defeat. "Just checking."

"I'm an alcoholic. I'll always be one. But you don't have to take care of me anymore. I'm just sorry you ever had to."

"It wasn't all bad. There were good times, too."

Harry sent him a wry smile. "I'm glad you remember that."

"How old were you when drinking became a problem?"

Harry straightened slowly. "Younger than you. I had a lot to escape, and I didn't waste time looking for ways to do it."

"You were programmed to drink."

"That's what they call an excuse, grandson. Mighty handy when you're reaching for the bottle."

Connor didn't want to think about that anymore. Sam's words were still echoing through his head.

Harry changed the subject. "I stopped by to meet our new neighbors yesterday, but they weren't home. Maybe they already moved on. People move into that old wreck because they think living in a cabin is romantic. Then the truth hits them."

"Well, I just saw the mom hanging laundry."

"You stop?"

"Maybe next time."

Harry straightened. "I'm about done here. We can get started on the benches when I get back. You're still working out the reinforcements anyway, right?"

Connor nodded. "Where are you headed?"

"A meeting. In Strasburg. You could come with me. And don't tell me you're not an alcoholic, because you just changed your whole life on the chance you might become one someday."

And there it was. All neatly laid out for him. Connor could just continue to moan about his genes, make excuses for his lapses, or he could take a step toward finding out who he really was and what he was made of.

Take a step.

Faith in yourself and your ability to be a good partner.

He wished he could brush away Sam's words. "Steps to the altar," he said under his breath.

"What's that?"

"Reverend Sam's advice."

"He's pretty wise for such a young man."

"No. He's tricky. He likes to play head games."

"You coming or not?"

Connor opened his mouth to say no. "I guess."

"We can take my pickup and stop at the lumberyard on the way back. I'll let you drive. The meeting hall cranks up the air-conditioning whether we need it or not. Bring something warm."

Connor's shoulders slumped, but he nodded. He couldn't believe he'd agreed to go to an AA meeting, and he knew for sure attending wasn't going to help. But he had said yes. He was still paralyzed from the weight of one broken promise and didn't need another one.

Rain was expected, and the temperature was dropping. He went inside to zip a hoodie over his shirt and smooth his cropped hair before he went out to start the pickup.

Harry liked jazz, and Connor had surprised him on his birthday by exchanging the pickup's radio for a stereo system with bluetooth, so Harry could play his favorites while he drove. As they turned on to the road, Harry was lecturing about this jazz great and that one, and Connor was silently asking himself how he'd gotten into this situation. He was so immersed in his own humiliation that Harry was the first to see the smoke.

"Stop!"

Connor slammed on the brakes. Only then did he note they were in front of the old cabin, and smoke was billowing out the two front windows.

He threw the pickup into reverse and backed up so he could turn into the weed-studded driveway that ran up to the porch.

Both he and Harry jumped out the moment he slammed the brakes a second time.

"Call 911," he shouted, without looking at his grandfather. "I'm going to see if anybody's inside."

Connor sprinted to the front of the house, leapt on to the porch without bothering with the steps on the side and flung open the front door. Smoke was so thick he couldn't see as far as a foot ahead of him. He pulled his zipped hoodie over his mouth, wiggling out of the sleeves as he did so he could tie them around his chin to keep it in place.

"Anybody in here?" he shouted.

He heard a cough from somewhere inside. He didn't know the state of the fire or how long the old dry logs and roof would last before collapsing. He plowed inside anyway. "Where are you?"

Something fell against him. Without thinking he wrapped his arms around a woman's slender body and dragged her backwards toward what he hoped was the open doorway.

"Here," his grandfather shouted. "To your left."

Harry helped him haul the woman to the ground below the porch. They sat her upright, and Harry began pounding her back, while Connor wriggled back into his hoodie. "The fire department's on its way," Harry said.

"Bet...ty." She was coughing between syllables and weeping. "Went... back...for Betty."

"Where is she?" Connor asked.

"In...loft...sleeping."

"The little girl," Harry said softly, aiming the words for Connor. "How bad is it in there?"

Connor had seen flames spreading from the direction of the fireplace. He knew it wouldn't be long before they devoured the structure entirely.

"I'm going back in." He stood up, leaving the young woman to his grandfather.

Harry jumped to his feet. "Connor, wait for help! That roof's going to collapse. Fire and rescue will get here as fast as they can. Don't make them go inside to search for you, too."

But Connor was already on his way back to the cabin.

If possible, the smoke inside was thicker now. He'd been here as a boy during months when the cabin was between renters. He still remembered a set of stairs leading up to a loft, directly across from the fireplace. He and a friend had found a way inside—he didn't remember how—and used it as a clubhouse until Harry had discovered what they were doing.

Hands extended, he felt his way across the room. The flames were leaping higher and spreading quickly. He was no expert, but he guessed that at most, he had only a minute, maybe two, before the fire was out of control.

He bumped into the steps and said a quick prayer of gratitude that he'd remembered correctly. Then he grabbed a railing to hang on to and began to climb.

He knew he'd reached the loft when his head bumped a rafter. The smoke was so thick here he wondered if he'd be able to find his way back down. He unzipped the hoodie and tied one sleeve to the end of the railing. Then he held on to the other as he ventured forward.

The hoodie didn't stretch far enough to take him more than a yard, but he hoped it would help him get down the ladder if he found it again. He stumbled forward, stooping as he went. "Betty? Betty?"

There was no answer. The child could already be overcome by smoke or too frightened to answer. He felt his way until his shins hit what felt like the edge of a low bed. He fell forward and spreading his hands wide, made swimming motions on the mattress, inching closer to the head of the bed as he felt for a small body.

Something moved under his hand. He grabbed for it and felt something dig into his shirt. He was coughing now, and beginning to choke. Whatever he had found was not a child. A loud screech confirmed his best guess. A cat. A small one.

He locked the cat under his arm and tried to ignore the claws digging into his flesh. A loud crack sounded from the direction of the fireplace. He heard Harry outside, shouting for him. Frantically he felt for the child, afraid he would dislodge the cat as he did, but by now, the animal was clinging so hard he wondered if it would ever let go.

Almost sobbing he felt along the floor with his feet. The child might have tried to escape and succumbed to the smoke between here and the steps. But there was nothing along the sides of the bed, and as he moved forward he felt nothing between himself and the stairs.

His time was up. Harry had been right. If he stayed inside, the rescue crew would be forced to search for him, too. Logic told him that he'd done everything he could. As he tried to find the head of the stairs, tears ran down his cheeks, and not just from the smoke. He had failed. Again.

Still.

He nearly stumbled, and he reached down to dislodge a lump under one foot. After an instant of hope that he'd found the little girl, he realized he'd only found the sleeve of his hoodie. He grabbed the cuff and followed the fabric to the head of the stairs. Then he took them as fast as he safely could, the cat still clamped under his arm, clinging to his shirt and worse, to the skin beneath.

He followed the direction of Harry's shouts. Fire had spread toward the doorway, flames moving quickly and licking at everything in their path, but he was able to skirt the worst and dive to the porch.

Harry guided him down the porch steps and far into the yard. "No girl?"

Connor was too emotional to speak. He shook his head and held up the wildly clawing cat. The young woman came up behind Harry, still coughing but upright. Connor didn't know what to say to her. He heard a siren, but as fast as the rescue squad had responded, he knew they were already too late. Another crack sounded behind him, and flames began to roar.

"I'm...so sorry." Tears continued to stream down his face.

The young woman wasn't looking at him. She stretched out her arms. "Betty..."

"I couldn't..."

She moved forward and grabbed the cat that was still clinging to Connor's shirt. The cat released its hold on Connor and sagged into her arms.

She held the little furry body in the air. "Betty! You found...her. You...saved her. Betty!"

The young woman snuggled the cat against her chest. She turned just enough to send Connor a watery smile. "You found her. She...was the only thing...in there I cared about. You're...you're a hero!"

CHAPTER
SEVEN

From an imitation leather love seat at Grant's Animal Clinic, Connor looked up to find his grandfather coming toward him, cradling a mewing Betty against his chest. The last of the day's appointments, a woman tugging a reluctant golden retriever, squeezed past Harry toward the veterinary hospital's examination rooms, and Betty hissed in warning.

Liza Smith shot to her feet, and Connor joined her, putting an arm around her shoulders to steady her. "Look like she's going to be fine."

"She's doing great," Harry said. "Here you go."

The young woman reached for the cat. "You're sure?"

"Best vet in the area," Harry said. "Watch her for a few days, and don't let her outside. Plenty of water and lots of air through open windows."

Connor noted that Liza wasn't quite steady, and now she blinked back tears. While Harry had tapped a neighbor to drive him here with Betty, Liza and Connor had submitted to cursory checkups by the rescue squad and refused more extensive precautionary trips to the nearest emergency room. Instead, as soon as the squad had allowed her to leave, they had raced here. Liza had scrubbed off soot and ashes in the vet's restroom while Betty was being examined by Dr. Grant himself, an old friend of Harry's.

This cleaner version of Liza was pretty, freckled, with pale lashes and brows and hair that wasn't quite brown or blond. She'd been evasive when Connor asked if she wanted him to call her family, only saying she wasn't from the area. He'd realized that was all she planned to say.

Now she clutched the cat hard enough to elicit an unhappy screech. "Oh, poor baby." She swallowed hard and looked up. "We haven't had her long. I found her by the roadside, and she was half-dead. I looked for her owners..."

"Most likely they dropped her off to fend for herself. You did the right thing when you rescued her," Harry said.

"The only thing I could do was fatten her up. I couldn't afford to bring her here or, you know, anywhere. I'll find a way to pay for this visit, though. I promise."

"Don't worry. Charlie says this one's on him. And he said he'll see her again in a week, just to check and get vaccinations started. That'll be free, too."

Connor suspected that Charlie Grant would soon be gifted with a sculpture for his waiting room.

"I don't want to pry," Harry said, "but Connor and I both saw you with a little girl. Lucky she wasn't with you today."

This time the tears escaped down Liza's cheeks. "Julie's spending the day with my friend Meredith and her daughter. I don't know what I would do if something..." She shook her head, unable to continue.

Connor reached for a tissue, thoughtfully provided on a side table for grieving pet owners. He handed it to her. "But nothing did. At least not to your little girl."

She winced, as if she had something to say but didn't know how to say it.

He stored that away after the silence stretched a moment. "Can you stay with this Meredith? Until you find another place?"

"She and *her* little girl live in a camper. There's hardly enough room for the two of them. They were going to move in with us at the end of the month." She wiped her eyes. "Merrie and I put everything we had into Delectable Mountain. We have to live cheap."

Harry inclined his head toward Connor. "That's the new bakery in Woodstock. I've been meaning to try it."

"Try it fast," Liza said. "I don't know how much longer we can keep going. Getting established was harder than we thought. And now this."

Connor didn't need more information to see the problem. Liza had no family whom she wanted to contact. Her friend and business partner wasn't able to help her, and she was a stranger in the area. Harry had outbuildings but no real guest quarters, certainly nothing where a child would be comfortable or safe. Connor had no idea who stepped forward in emergencies like this one, but before he could speak, the office door swung open. Three women stepped inside.

Bringing up the rear at a distance, was a fourth he knew all too well.

The woman leading the brigade spoke first. "We heard."

Connor wondered how Helen Henry always seemed to know what was going on everywhere in the county, even though she lived in a farmhouse on a rural road and didn't look like someone who checked social media on an hourly basis.

Liza looked at Connor, as if she needed an explanation.

Helen didn't let him speak. "That old cabin was bound to burn down one of these days. Owner never did a bit of upkeep.

Course, I've been saying the place was a problem for years and years."

Another woman stepped forward, one whose name Connor couldn't remember. She wasn't as old as Helen, and she was carrying one of the quilts. "We brought comfort quilts. One for you, and one for your little girl."

"You are so kind." Liza sniffed back tears. "I know we'll use them wherever we—"

Rebecca moved around the other women as she spoke. "Unless you already have a place to go, I thought you might like to come and stay in my house until you can find something more permanent. I have plenty of room and I love children." She nodded toward Betty. "I like cats, too. I'd be happy to have you there. You won't be an imposition."

Liza shook her head. "Oh, I can't. You don't even know me."

Rebecca smiled warmly. "But I know your muffins. I'm a big fan of Delectable Mountain. Maybe you'll make a batch just for us now and then? My kitchen's practically brand-new." Her gaze flicked to Connor. "Recently remodeled by an expert, even if he has a habit of not finishing what he starts."

She sniffed and turned back to Liza. "Anyway...you and I are about the same size, so I have clothes that will fit you. The house is for sale, but even if it sells tomorrow, it will be weeks before everything closes. Enough time for you to figure out what you want to do next."

The woman Connor remembered as Cathy stepped forward. "Did you have insurance, honey? I used to work in the field, so I can help you with whatever paperwork you'll need."

Liza shook her head. "Not a bit."

"Then we'll find out what the landlord had. In fact, I'm thinking we're going to find out all kinds of things about this so-called landlord. You can leave that up to me."

Connor watched as the women gathered around Liza, making suggestions as they edged her toward the door.

Harry moved to stand beside him as the door closed. "They move fast, don't they?"

"How did they even know? How'd they find their way *here*?"

"That was me. I called Rebecca the minute we arrived. I knew she had room at her place, and I figured she'd have a few friends who might help."

"*You* called Rebecca? Why not Red Cross or one of the churches?"

"I'm sure they'll all get involved, but I figured that young woman could use a little mothering right now. Rebecca could pull something together fast."

Connor was still staring at the door. "Yeah she's the kind of person who always wants to help."

"That's right. The kind who can be counted on."

"I know what you're trying to do, Harry. Everybody knows they can count on Rebecca. That was never our problem."

"Right. And I know you think you're destined to be an alcoholic someday in the future. It's just too bad, isn't it, that you couldn't count on her to help *you* if you ever started in that direction."

CHAPTER
EIGHT

Connor hadn't been back to Rebecca's house since the day he'd arrived to tell her they couldn't go through with the wedding. He hadn't had the courage to explain why. He'd just told her he had too many doubts, and he was releasing her from her promise to marry him. Then he'd taken off before he succumbed to his fierce hangover and overwhelming distress.

What if he hadn't left so quickly? What if he'd just told her the truth and begged for reassurance and help? He knew that the self-doubt that had finally gnawed its way out into the open on the night of his bachelor party wasn't something that would have succumbed to a pat on the back, but surely there would have been some kind of help available. Why hadn't he apologized and then asked her to help him find the right places to get it? At the very least, Reb should have had control over what happened next.

The house looked much the same except for a realty sign featuring a woman with a grin large enough to swallow everything within fifty feet. The grass had been cut but not with precision. He liked cutting grass, setting the mower to exactly the right height, moving first in one direction, then the other. He liked mulching and edging, too, and using the weed whacker around trees. He'd already planned how much grass seed and fertilizer he would need to fill in bald spots in the lawn.

Rebecca was keeping up with everything, probably with the help of a local crew. New plants were sprouting in the flower beds along with bindweed that was already maliciously twining around drooping winter pansies. If she left the bindweed there, if she didn't root it out now, all the perennials they'd so carefully planted would grow taller, strangle and die.

Of course, whoever bought the house might just extend the sidewalk or cover all the flowerbeds with gravel or concrete. Or maybe they would think the bindweed was morning glory and smile every time they passed it.

He knew he was procrastinating. He squared his shoulders and shifted the box he'd taken from the trunk to his left hip. He walked up the sidewalk to tap on the front door, then he stood back.

Rebecca opened the door, wearing denim shorts and a blouse tied under her breasts to reveal her flat midriff. He heard a young child's voice somewhere deep inside the house and the hum of a radio. Adele, he thought. Most likely one of her break-up songs. That would be appropriate.

As she examined him, she dried her hands on a dishtowel. At first she didn't say anything. Finally her gaze drifted to the box on his hip before she lifted an eyebrow. "Good planning. I found an old stack of your Concrete Decor magazines. You can carry them home in that."

He lifted the box off his hip. "Harry and I stopped at a garage sale this afternoon. They had great kids' toys. They look like they've hardly been played with. We bought the best, although I never did ask Liza how old Julie is."

"Four. What did you get for her?"

"A doll with lots of clothes, some still in the package. The woman holding the sale says her granddaughter would rather climb trees. A little blackboard and colored chalk, picture books..." He shrugged. "She's bound to find something she'll want to play with."

Rebecca stepped outside to the stoop and closed the door behind her. "Did Liza tell you how the fire started?"

He thought of their very first date, and how he had kissed her as she stood right there. They'd both laughed about how old-fashioned that was, and then they'd done it again for good measure.

He realized he hadn't answered. "She said it started in the fireplace."

"She told me she was burning mail, just a little pile toward the back. She thought everything was safe, so she turned away. When she came out of the kitchen, she saw sparks had drifted to a stack of kindling in front of the fireplace, and the fire was already spreading."

"I'm guessing there was no fire extinguisher. The landlord should have provided one."

"She tried to put the fire out, beat it with a blanket from the sofa, filled a pot in the sink to douse it, but by then, everything was out of control. She said if you hadn't shown up when you did, she's not sure she'd have found her way out. And Betty—" She narrowed her eyes and slapped her hands on her hips. "Connor, what on earth were you thinking? Going in after a cat! You could have died."

He set the box at his feet, because clearly this exchange was going to take more than a few seconds. "I thought the little girl was inside. I'd never met them, but I'd seen Liza outside with a little girl, so when she said Betty was inside, I just thought..."

She clamped her lips together, as if she wanted to say more but knew better.

When she didn't speak, he continued. "I was lucky to find the cat, but for a little while, I thought I'd failed completely. Finding that little girl was so important, and I just..." He cleared his throat. "I kept thinking that I could finally do something right, something important, and what do I do instead? I rescue a cat and leave a child inside!"

"Connor, nobody cares if you're a hero!"

"I wasn't trying to be a hero! I was trying to do something right. You can't see the difference?"

"What do I see? A man who does almost everything right and still thinks he's a failure. A man who thinks he's supposed to be perfect and falls apart when he isn't."

He felt a surge of anger. "Then you're better off without me, aren't you? Who needs that kind of stress in their life?"

"Apparently you decided that answer for both of us." She bent over to pick up the box. She started to turn, and then, she whirled to face him again. "You know, if you'd died in that fire, it wouldn't have made things right between us. I'd have spent the rest of my life asking myself what I did wrong because, you know, right now we should already be married, and who knows where you'd have been today when that fire broke out."

"That's not very sound logic."

She ignored him. "If you'd died, I'd be asking myself if I'd just done this or that, would things have turned out differently? If I'd told you more often how great you are, or maybe less often, would you have started to believe it? I'd never have gotten any peace. So thanks for surviving. I couldn't be happier you're still alive."

"And you're not a bit happy for any other reason? Like maybe because you love me or at least you used to?"

"How can I love a man who doesn't know how to love himself? How can I love a man who doesn't trust *me* enough to believe I can see him for who he really is and love him despite any flaws?"

"Maybe you can't love him then."

She threw open the door. "Don't put this on me, Connor. This is all about you, and you're going to have to figure it out by yourself. I'm out of the picture, and I wish you luck."

They were finished. She couldn't have said it more clearly. Then, when she was halfway through the doorway, she turned once again.

"But while you're being lucky? Do me a big favor, okay? Don't throw yourself into any more burning buildings. The next time you might not get out alive."

The door closed behind her. Not quite a slam, but close enough to substitute.

As he turned to walk back to his car, he saw a crescent moon glowing near the horizon. He thought of all the years of his childhood when he'd imagined himself reclining in the crook of similar moons, lulled and rocked and protected, the way he had never been in real life. Harry had taken him in when his parents could no longer provide even the barest essentials, but Harry, as much as Connor loved him, hadn't always been able to cope. Harry's love was unwavering, but his own life was topsy-turvy.

Until AA. Until Harry faced his demons and began to root them out, one at a time.

Connor recognized a crossroads when he came to one. He could be that little boy wishing for something he didn't have, or he could step forward and make that something happen.

He thought about the Steps to the Altar quilt. Sam had said

the first step was the belief in his ability to be a good partner. This was the step that was going to be hardest. And until he restored his faith in himself, he would be immobile, unable to reach out, unable to accept the love freely given him. Unable to ask Rebecca to try once more.

He didn't need to be a hero. He didn't even need to do the right thing every moment of every day. He just had to believe in himself. And to do so? He had to understand why he didn't, why he hadn't.

Harry was waiting in the car. Waiting patiently. He started the engine when Connor stepped inside. "Looks like she took the toys in. I'm glad they could use them."

"We missed that meeting this afternoon."

Harry nodded, as if that was a perfectly logical answer. "We did."

"I'm assuming there's another one soon."

"There's one tonight. We'll have to drive a ways, but we can grab some dinner, too. You want to go?"

"I'm not sure it's the right answer, but it's a start."

"You can start there, but I think there's a better place for you, Grandson, a more appropriate group. We'll talk about it. Shall I drive?"

Connor leaned back and closed his eyes as Harry pulled out to the road.

CHAPTER
NINE

After her first experience quilting at the church, Rebecca held off entering the Beehive for three weeks, but on the fourth Wednesday, she found herself walking down the steps to the basement room again. The real estate agent she had hired to sell her grandparents' house was showing it twice that morning, and Rebecca had been told to disappear. Liza and Julie were at Delectable Mountain, and Betty was napping in a cat carrier in their bedroom.

Rebecca hadn't needed the warning. The last thing she wanted was to watch other people examine the home that she had begun to make with Connor. She didn't want to see them walk across the heart pine floors he had so carefully refinished or make plans to tear down the wall between the largest and smallest bedrooms. She and Connor had debated that, too, but in the end they had decided the smallest bedroom would make a perfect nursery.

For the children they would never have.

She really didn't want to sell the house, but since neither she nor Sandy ever intended to live in Shenandoah County again, they had reluctantly decided that a buyer who would truly love it should have it.

Selling the house was the first big step toward her new life. The second—one she should have taken weeks ago—was to submit her resignation and give the Mt. Jackson school board time to find a teacher to take her place in the fall. She knew they had lists of qualified candidates, but her replacement deserved to spend the summer preparing for the school year the way she would have done.

She had been hired to teach fourth grade. In many ways it had been her dream job. So far she hadn't been able to force herself to make a phone call and bow out.

With luck, quilting would be a respite from decision making and disappointments.

By the time she stepped into the Beehive, Dovey Lanning had just finished reading the minutes, and the group was beginning show and tell. Smiles greeted her, and a young woman she didn't recognize gestured to the empty seat beside her.

"I'm Kate Brogan," the woman whispered as Rebecca took the seat. She was dark-haired and pretty, and she sported a blouse with what looked like cracker crumbs caught in the hem. "The kids making noise on the playground are mine."

Which explained the crumbs, Rebecca thought. She had never envied crumbs on clothing, but now she was starved for them.

A woman Rebecca didn't recognize held up a gorgeous quilt top with a giant star in multiple colors. As she explained what she had tried to do, her English was halting and occasionally laced with Spanish, but Rebecca thought the enthusiastic applause was as much for the explanation as for the fabulous quilt.

"She's one of the La Casa moms," Kate whispered again.

"And she learned to quilt with us. She's such a natural, and I feel like I have ten thumbs."

When it was Kate's turn to show her handiwork, she reached down into a bag and drew out four place mats with simple rooster appliques in very non-roostery colors. "Rory and Bridget picked out the fabrics. I had to let them, or they would never let me quilt."

"I have always been fond of green roosters," Peony Greenway said. "Second only to purple."

Kate smiled her thanks.

Rebecca liked the way the women teased each other almost as much as the way they offered support. She knew the group had grown in the past few years, but the newcomers seemed welcome. She certainly felt welcome.

Considering everything.

When show and tell ended, Helen came forward and asked her to take a place at the quilt frame, since Rebecca's stitches had actually survived the old woman's critical assessment. Kate took the seat across from her, although she acknowledged that Helen wasn't quite as happy with *her* stitches.

Helen threaded her needle as quickly as a teenager and began to quilt. "You'll catch on," she told Kate. "And besides, those children of yours will come in and drag you away before long."

"And you'll pull out my stitches and get somebody else to sit here and try again."

"Maybe not. You've improved a mite."

Kate looked thunderstruck. Rebecca tried not to smile.

The fourth seat was taken by the group's beleaguered president. Cathy Adams had been president quite a while, she told Rebecca, but like Dovey, the permanent secretary, she couldn't find anybody else to take the job. Rebecca guessed that neither of them really minded.

The women chatted about this and that. Rebecca was delighted not to have her personal life as the center of attention today.

The rocking of the needle in the quilt "sandwich" was relaxing. She hadn't slept well since the wedding-that-wasn't, and it wasn't because she had house guests. The bed she and Connor had all-too-briefly shared seemed huge now, although it was only queen-size. She missed his deep breathing, the way he pulled her against him as he slept, the just-showered fragrance of his skin. She missed their lovemaking, too. Connor was that perfect combination of passionate and considerate that women dreamed about, and from the moment she had surrendered herself to him, she had basked in her good fortune. Cocooned in her belief that they would be together until death, she had fallen asleep each night dreaming of their future.

These days warm milk, soothing music and meditation were poor substitutes. She hoped moving away and starting a new life would keep her so busy that she would fall into bed each night in Philadelphia exhausted.

She wasn't thinking about anything in particular when conversation at the quilt frame came to a halt, and a shadow fell over the quilt. She glanced up, expecting to find one of the other women admiring their handiwork, and found Connor gazing back at her instead.

"I had no idea you knew how to quilt." He leaned over so he could see her work more closely, his shoulder brushing hers, his hand propped on the edge, just an inch from her arm.

Rebecca was dumbstruck. Had she been able to form words, she was sure they wouldn't have been in any sort of order.

"Is this where you quilted the Steps to the Altar quilt?" Connor, dressed in dark jeans and a soft sage green Henley she had bought him for his last birthday, addressed his question to Helen. "Or do you send quilts out to be quilted by machine?"

"You can't tell the difference between a hand-quilted quilt and one of them machine quilted ones?" Helen grimaced at his ignorance.

"I'm pretty sure the Steps to the Altar quilt was hand-quilted," he said. "And probably right here. I bet you had something to do with it, Mrs. Henry." He touched Rebecca's hand. "Reb's stitches look as tiny and neat as the ones in that quilt. I don't know much about it, but I know that's hard to do."

He addressed Rebecca. "Why didn't I ever see you quilting?"

She glared at him as she jerked her hand away, taking her needle with her, but not the thread which snaked across the quilt top. "Probably because I was busy back then, wasting my time making plans."

He didn't flinch. "Harry says all of us spend too much time making plans and not enough time making art."

She twisted to look at him. "Well, Harry should know. But he's proved *his* art is good enough to excuse almost anything." She didn't add, "What's yours?" but she was fairly certain her meaning was clear.

"I'm not the artist he is, that's for sure. Or that you are, it seems. I love what you're doing here."

She was still staring at him. She couldn't be overtly rude. These women didn't deserve a scene, and she hadn't failed to note that the room had fallen silent. Everyone was listening. Maybe they thought she and Connor had negotiated detente, or maybe they were waiting for an explosion.

"I'm glad you approve," she said sweetly. "I'll take such comfort knowing you do." She smiled even more sweetly.

"You always surprise me, Reb. You're good at so many things." He glanced away, smiling warmly at the others—and

Connor had a powerfully persuasive smile. "She's a gourmet cook. I bet you didn't know that."

"Don't let us keep you from whatever you came here to do." Rebecca spaced the words as if each one stung her tongue.

He ignored her. "I'm not a big fan of vegetables, but Reb's taste like something from a five-star restaurant."

"I boil them, same as everybody else does." She narrowed her eyes. "Are you working on a project here at the church?"

"You could say that." He smiled down at her. She steeled herself against the magic and narrowed her eyes even more. If this kept up, her world would shrink to a pinpoint of light.

"She's also quite an athlete," he said. "Did you know she got a tennis scholarship to UVA?"

"One year," Rebecca said. "And as you well know, three months into it I twisted my ankle and had to drop off the team."

"But now she runs. Almost every day, right Reb?"

"Even more often these days, Connor, since I only have myself to take care of, and I can do whatever I want."

He seized on that. "And that's another thing she's good at. She's a natural caretaker. She loves making people feel comfortable, and kids? Kids think she's Mary Poppins and Cinderella's Fairy Godmother rolled into one. She's going to be a wonderful teacher."

She slapped the quilt frame and stood. "Connor, we need to have a little talk."

He smiled at her again, then he turned to the others at the quilt frame. She couldn't see, but from Helen and Kate's expressions, she was afraid he had just winked at them.

∾

"A<small>RE</small> you freaking trying to ruin my life?" she asked outside in the hall. "I won't be here much longer, but it would be nice to have one place left in this county that's not completely spoiled for me, Connor. These women have made me feel at home. I'm not a spectacle here, just another quilter."

Connor looked as if he wanted to put his arms around her and haul her close. He didn't because he probably realized she would hit him if he tried. She was that mad.

An angry Rebecca was something he'd rarely seen. She prided herself on her even temper and level head, and she gave everybody the benefit of the doubt, unless it was as clear as a newly washed window that they didn't deserve it. Now she was sure her blue eyes were blazing.

His words were measured and friendly. "I'm not trying to ruin anything."

"You don't try, yet you do. What's that about? A complete lack of common sense, or a refusal to see yourself for what you are. Which is it?"

"I just think those women ought to know how special you are."

She spaced her words so they would be clear. "You have lost your mind."

"You never blow your own horn, so I thought I would blow it for you."

"And, of course, they'll believe every good thing you say about me since you've shown so much respect for my talents, not to mention love."

"Reb, none of what happened was about abilities or talents you lack. And it wasn't about love. I love you now as much or more than I did when I proposed."

She felt the way she might if she'd looked up to see a mighty oak falling right toward her. She spread her hands, as if she hoped to catch it as it toppled.

"I can't believe you said that!" She cleared her throat. "I want you to leave."

"You're everything a man could ever want. You're everything I said in there and so much more."

"Oh, goody. Now I can sleep better knowing I was quite the catch, even if you threw me overboard just before we got to the dock!"

"I've been going to Al-Anon."

The change of subject threw her. "What?"

"You were right about me. I needed help, help understanding why I fell apart, why I was so sure I couldn't be the man you need. And now I'm finding real clues, along with people like me, people who've lived in the shadow of alcohol or still do. I've got a ways to go and always will have, but you were right about something else. If part of my problem is a conviction I'm an alcoholic-in-training, then the cure is just to stop drinking. Forever. Especially now, when it's not much of a wrench, although Monday Night Football will be a test in the fall. Think I'm up to it?"

She just stared at him.

"I do," he said when she didn't speak. "I *know* I'm up to it. And I know something else. I can be the man you need in your life. I *am* the man, even if I have moments of doubt that I'm good enough. I want to share your life forever. I'm sorry I panicked. You'll never know how sorry. But I hope you can forgive me and give me another chance. Because you're the only woman I'll ever want and need. And I'll do whatever it takes to start fresh. Marry me?"

She didn't take time to consider. "You're repeating yourself. You asked me to do that once before, and then you practically left me at the altar. Repeating *myself* is not a mistake I'll be making."

As if he had expected that answer, he seemed to stifle a

sigh. "I believe we should be together. I know we're good together. I have faith in you, Reb, not just because you're such a wonderful woman, but because you love me, too. You haven't stopped. I know we're going to work this out."

Tears replaced anger, and she felt humiliated as they slid down her cheeks. "How could I ever believe you meant it? After everything you put me through?"

He tried to rest his hand on her shoulder, but she took a step backwards. "We have to have faith in each other," he said.

"I *had* faith in you. Then my mother and I had to call a hundred people and tell them that you called off the wedding. I had to send back dozens of gifts. I had to nod and try not to cry every time people told me how sorry they were about everything that had happened. I can hardly hold my head up in this county. When my friends call, I don't answer. I cancelled my social media accounts so nobody could sympathize online. I doubt you understand what that kind of humiliation is like. And now you want me to go through it all over again, with the excellent chance it will end the very same way?"

"It won't."

"So you say!"

"We might need to skip step two and move on to step three," he said softly.

"What nonsense are you talking now?"

"Steps to the altar."

She stared at him, then she spun on one heel and stalked back to the Beehive door. She slammed it behind her leaving him alone in the hallway.

TEN

Rebecca hadn't been to a church service since before the wedding was cancelled, but almost two weeks after the Connor sighting at the Beehive she reluctantly rose, showered, and got ready to leave. Elisa, Sam's Guatemalan-born wife, had dropped by late last evening and asked if Rebecca could possibly substitute for the young man who usually taught the first grade Sunday School children. The class was studying the Old Testament, and today they were planning to construct an ark. Elisa had promised a closet full of art supplies, a colorful video of animals marching two by two, and a classroom of semi-unruly children.

Rebecca, who already missed the children in Mt. Jackson she would never teach, had agreed.

As she drove to church, she told herself that at least the classroom would be downstairs. She wouldn't run into too many people anxious to offer sympathy. Her determination to avoid it was, even by her own standards, a bit overblown. She had turned off her cell phone and cancelled her land line in preparation for the move. When she turned on her cell to call her mother or sister, she ignored the list of calls waiting to be returned. Someday soon she would have to rejoin the world, but it would be easier once she was on her way to Pennsylvania.

The house wasn't quite sold. A young couple had made an offer, but it was low, and their list of requirements silly and expensive. Negotiations were underway, but even if those didn't pan out, there had been enough interest that Rebecca knew getting the price she and Sandy wanted was only a matter of time.

She had finally forced herself to call the principal of the school in Mt. Jackson, too, only to find he was out of town for two weeks. So even though she hadn't quite resigned, at least she was on her way toward doing that, as well.

A wave of sadness swept over her. Soon all her ties in Shenandoah County would be broken. Especially the big one. After his stunning attempt to jump-start their wedding plans again, Connor had vanished. She supposed the man's disappearing act said everything about his intentions. Make an attempt to get back together, then run when the first foray is unsuccessful. If nothing else, the fact that he hadn't tried again showed how strong his commitment to her *wasn't*.

Okay, so she had cried herself to sleep too many nights since. So she had turned on her phone a time or two just to see if his was one of the calls she was missing. Better to feel deserted again in the here and now than down the road when children were involved and starting a new life twice as difficult.

The church parking lot was crowded, crowded enough to surprise her. She had stayed up until midnight going over the lesson plan and slept later than planned, so she parked at the far edge of the lot and gathered her supplies. She had a small cooler with healthy snacks, along with a funny quiz about which animals might have eaten the same things. She also had a CD of Raffi singing "Who Built the Ark?" so the children could learn to sing it, too. She was ready.

Elisa was standing just inside the door when she opened it, almost as if she had been waiting for her. Rebecca was touched. Elisa had probably sensed her embarrassment and wanted to buffer Rebecca from good wishes on the way to her classroom.

She was a lovely young woman, long black hair, cream-and-coffee skin, dark eyes that had seen too much sorrow but sparkled whenever she looked at Sam.

"The children are in the sanctuary," she said, taking Rebecca by the arm. "They're starting there this morning, then they'll move downstairs. Why don't you leave your things on the table and pick them back up on the way down?"

Rebecca swallowed disappointment as she set her supplies just to the right of the entrance into the sanctuary. Now she would be on display after all. "Can we sit in the back?"

"I think that might be the only place to sit. It's very crowded today."

"Why?"

"Because of what happened last week, I'd guess." Elisa stopped talking as she tugged Rebecca into the sanctuary, accepting a program from one of the ushers, whose eyes widened when he saw who had come in with her.

Silently Rebecca groaned, but it was too late now to do anything but find a seat. With luck she could escape unnoticed when the children left for their morning classes.

There were two places at the end of a rear aisle, which was surprising. Aisle seats always filled first, no matter how many times Sam asked people to move into the middle. Elisa led her to the seats and took the one farthest in, gesturing for Rebecca to take the one with the clearest view of the front.

And that's when she saw him.

Connor, dressed in the black tuxedo with the royal blue waistcoat that he should have worn at their wedding ceremony, stood at the front. Connor, who was gazing directly at her. She gasped, and her hands clenched the pew as she leaned forward.

"What's going on?" she whispered.

Elisa shrugged. "You'll have to tell me. He was here last week, too, standing right there. He stayed until the choir processed in with Sam, then he left. I'm guessing the same thing will happen today unless..." She turned to Rebecca and smiled a little.

"Unless what!" It was not a question.

"Unless somebody goes up there and talks to him. He seems to be waiting for somebody, don't you think?"

Connor wasn't smiling. His head was cocked a little, as if in question. He looked as amazing in the black tux as Rebecca had imagined he would. He looked delicious.

She wanted to run away. Under the circumstances she was sure that was the right thing to do.

Only, Connor had done that already, and now, to ask for her forgiveness, he had publicly humiliated himself in front of their entire church family.

He hadn't abandoned her. He had simply found a better way to let her know he wanted a second chance. He wanted a lifetime together.

She got to her feet. People began to turn around, and in moments everyone was looking at her, not the man standing in the front. She debated which direction to go, then she found herself walking up the aisle, taking the steps to the altar, the way she would have weeks before if things had been different.

She stopped in front of him. The proverbial pin dropping would have resonated like a shotgun in the silent sanctuary.

"You look pretty silly," she said softly.

"Which is nothing compared to the way I feel."

"You did this last week, too?"

"Nobody told you?"

"I'm not talking to many people these days." In addition, she suspected a conspiracy of silence.

"I knew you were still home last week, and I hoped you would come to church. I drive by every night to make sure you're there and safe, so I knew you hadn't left this week, either. I thought I would try again today."

"And if I had left before I knew what you were doing?"

"Then I was going to find your new church in Philadelphia."

She realized she had tears running down her cheeks, but she didn't care. What better time to cry? "Why?" she asked. "Why are you doing this?"

"Reverend Sam told me there are three important steps to the altar, Reb. Faith in myself. Faith in you as my life partner. Faith in us together. And we need to be together, Reb. I don't know if I'm good enough for you. I really don't. That's not just an excuse for what happened before, it's true. But I do know I plan to spend the rest of my life trying to be. I will never let you down again. If you marry me."

She saw tears in his eyes, too. She stepped toward him, he gathered her close, and to wild applause from the pews, he kissed her.

CHAPTER

ELEVEN

S ummer would soon pass its reins to autumn. In the last
week Rebecca had been at orientation meetings and
busy setting up her new classroom. Time had flown by.
She still came home in daylight, but before too long, after-
noons would fade faster into evening.

To celebrate the approaching change of seasons, at the end
of September Harry had cast half a dozen concrete jack-o'-
lanterns to add to Rebecca's front flower bed. The jack-o'-
lanterns were lined up behind the house in anticipation, and
the front bed was already overflowing with chrysanthemums,
pansies, and snapdragons. The jack-o'-lanterns' expressions
were so frightening that the beagle puppy she had claimed and
taken as her own from Harry's newest assortment bayed at
them every time they let the little guy outside.

The house itself was now a deep purple-blue with white
trim and a bright coral door. On weekends Connor had carefully painted the exterior while she made curtains and worked
on landscaping. At the end of each day, Connor had gone back
to Harry's house. He would move into Rebecca's house after

the wedding, when the Steps to the Altar quilt would grace their marriage bed at last.

The wedding that was supposed to begin in five minutes, in the very same church.

"You're absolutely certain you want to go through with this, dear?" Glenda Albritton straightened the waistband of her beaded mesh dress. The pale blue skirt skimmed her leg halfway up her calf, and she looked nearly as young as her daughter. Her eyes glistened suspiciously.

Sandy, who had flown back for another try at becoming Rebecca's maid of honor–and to re-encounter best man Vince–took their mother's hand and led her to the door leading out of the bride's room. "It's time for you to find Herb and make your own entrance," Sandy said, kissing her mother on the cheek as she opened the door to usher her into the hall.

"You both look so beautiful." Glenda looked as if she wanted to add something, probably a version of "that young man doesn't deserve you," aimed at Rebecca, but to her credit, she didn't. She sighed and moved away as Sandy closed the door behind her.

"You do look beautiful," Sandy said. "I'm going to have to elope."

"And so do you, even more than always." Sandy resembled their father, with the same curly brown hair and freckled complexion. Her dress, the royal blue of Connor's waistcoat, made her look like a princess. Rebecca's two bridesmaids and Julie, the flower girl, already in the foyer to begin the procession, wore cranberry red, which matched the waistcoats of Connor's groomsmen. Liza and her business partner and friend Merrie–who were now sharing a rental house that was much nicer than the log cabin and not nearly as flammable– were catering the reception.

All her original wedding party had returned. All of them were hoping that this time, things would be different.

"Connor will be blown away," Sandy said, adjusting Rebecca's veil. Glenda had folded and fluffed it to suit herself, and now Sandy put it back the way Rebecca liked it, to save her the trouble. The dress itself was simple, tulle falling to the floor and gracefully puddling at her feet, a strapless beaded lace bodice. The veil, which didn't hide her face, was even simpler, a mantilla held in place by combs, again tulle edged with the same lace and falling nearly to the floor. Her hair was softly parted and gathered in loops and knots at the back of her head. Her bouquet was pastel roses, callas and hydrangeas.

Rebecca hoped Connor really would be blown away, because she thought she looked as pretty as she ever would.

But that wasn't her biggest worry.

She told herself she wouldn't ask Sandy the obvious. Then, despite the self-administered lecture, she blurted out the question of the hour.

"He's here, right? When you looked, Connor was still here?"

"I told you before, I saw him in the hall a few minutes ago."

"But shouldn't he be waiting by the side door with Sam? Maybe even at the altar?"

When she paused for Sandy's answer, she realized she could now hear music because the organist had just increased the volume. This new piece wasn't meant to soothe and entertain as people settled into the pews for the ceremony. This was the signal for the wedding party to take their places. The next selection would be Pachelbel's Canon, and Julie would sprinkle rose petals, followed by the two bridesmaids. Then Sandy would walk down the aisle as the Canon finished and finally Rebecca, who had chosen to process to Beethoven's Ode to Joy.

Suddenly it all seemed silly. The pomp, the circumstance,

the terror. She wished Connor had taken her suggestion and booked two tickets to Las Vegas, but he had flatly refused. Rebecca deserved the wedding she had missed, and he was determined to give it to her.

This time around he had been the one to ask Liza to cater, the one to call the DJ, the church office staff, their guest list and finalize the arrangements. Connor himself had even reserved two full rows on his own side of the church for the ladies of the church quilting bee and issued a group invitation to all of them in person. He said they were now part of his extended family, meddlers and well-wishers all, and he wanted them there.

"Connor's right here at the church," Sandy said, in answer. "You don't have to worry."

Rebecca was worried anyway, although she forced a smile. "Let's go, then. Just, when you get there, make sure Harry is ready to walk me down the aisle?" Harry O'Keefe had been beyond flattered to be asked when her father's brother hadn't been able to return.

As it turned out Harry looked particularly fabulous in a tux.

Sandy opened the door, then she lifted Rebecca's skirt so they could make their way to the door of the sanctuary. They didn't speak. Rebecca tried to compose herself. She told herself she wasn't worried. Connor would be standing beside Sam at the front.

Only she was wrong. He *wasn't* there. As she watched her bridesmaids walk slowly up the aisle from the sanctuary doors, she realized that Sam was standing at the front with Vince beside him, but Connor was nowhere in sight.

Then someone stepped out of the shadows on her right as Harry stepped out on her left. She couldn't help it. She gasped.

"I know we didn't rehearse this," Connor said softly, as she whirled to face him. He reached for her hand and squeezed it tightly, "but Harry and I decided that you and I should walk up together today."

He looked worried she would be upset. He also looked, well, absolutely gorgeous. Suddenly, she knew everything was going to be all right.

They were going to be all right. Even better.

Harry held out his arm, and Sandy, a wide smile on her face, rested her hand there to begin their trip up the aisle.

Finally, Beethoven's *Ode to Joy* began and everybody stood.

"You are beyond beautiful," Connor said, still gazing at her. "No man anywhere in the world is luckier today. You're ready?"

"You're sure you don't want to reschedule? They say three's a charm."

He laughed, then he squeezed her hand hard. "As many times as it takes, Reb. But let's give this one a try, okay?"

They smiled at each other, then she leaned over and kissed him. Hard. After all, if Connor could start a new tradition, so could she.

Proudly, happily, they took the final steps to the altar together.

STEPS TO THE ALTAR QUILT

The Steps to the Altar quilt is an historical pattern often included in a prospective bride's hope chest. The pattern is a variation of Jacob's Ladder, which is still enjoyed by both beginning and advanced quilters. The blocks seem to create a ladder, or "steps" to a special destination. If the blocks are set off with sashing between them, cornerstones at the end of each sashing strip continue the impression of steps.

Are you interested in making your own quilt? You'll find patterns for all the traditional quilts in this story online. Just type the quilt pattern into your search engine and see what comes up. Or you might want to start with these two sites: allpeoplequilt.com and quilterscache.com, where lots of patterns are available.

Enjoy!

WOVEN PATHS

BY EMILIE RICHARDS

From the Shenandoah Album Collection
Peaks and Valleys, Book 2

CHAPTER I

"Mama won't like this. Too many people talking about her."

Kate Brogan glanced at her sister, who was sitting to her right, and tried to reassure her with a smile, even though their mother's sudden death and Kate's hastily arranged flight to Florida for the funeral had smothered all the smiles inside her.

Bejoy Clayton, Kate's fraternal twin, understood, at least a little, that their mother had died, died just like the robin with a broken wing that Bejoy and Kate had tried to nurse back to health when they were little girls. But for years afterwards, every time a robin hopped across their lawn or flew into the meadow beside their house, Bejoy had been certain it was *her* robin, come back from the dead.

It was no surprise that she expected her mother to reappear, as well.

"It's time for a prayer," Kate whispered, taking her sister's hand. "Close your eyes, and then this will be over."

Bejoy frowned, as if considering whether this was a

requirement, like brushing her teeth or changing her under-wear, but she finally forced her eyelids closed. Kate hoped the prayer was a short one.

She listened as the minister, a young man who had never known their mother, promised everyone in the Tampa funeral parlor that Nora Clayton had been the best of women and would rise from the dead with the faithful and greet her beloved daughters, Katherine Grace and Beatrice Joy, thus relieving them of their sorrows on their journey to heaven.

"I don't want to go," Bejoy said too loudly.

"Shh..." Kate opened her eyes and shook her head.

Bejoy glared at her. "I'm not going anywhere."

Her obstinate expression was so familiar, so, well, *Bejoy*, that despite her heavy heart, Kate was almost tempted to laugh.

"Please be quiet," she whispered. "Just another minute."

"Not leaving my house..." Bejoy shut her eyes again.

Kate was stabbed by her sister's words. As if he knew, Mickey, Kate's husband, who was sitting to her left, wove his fingers through hers and squeezed. Mickey always seemed to know when she needed him most. She squeezed back in gratitude.

Bejoy was less concerned about going to heaven than she was about going to Virginia tomorrow, and sadly, there was absolutely nothing Kate could do about it. Only fifty-six when she died, their mother had been energetic and physically active. Nora Clayton had always taken excellent care of her health, eaten well, dieted, exercised, even meditated each morning before Bejoy woke up. She'd been determined to outlive her intellectually disabled daughter, sure that if she tried hard enough, she could survive to a hundred so that Bejoy would always have a home.

Life was never a sure thing.

In the middle of a morning walk one week ago, Nora had collapsed to the sidewalk and died before a concerned passerby reached her side, the victim of a brain aneurysm that no one had suspected. The only comfort was that death had come so swiftly she probably hadn't had time to worry about anything.

Now Bejoy was Kate's worry. Nora had made that official when she'd demanded that a teenaged Kate promise she would always take care of Bejoy if Nora no longer could.

The minister finished quickly, and the small gathering stood to sing "Nearer My God to Thee." Bejoy stayed in her seat, arms folded over her chest and bottom lip drooping to her chin.

Cormick, the oldest of Kate and Mickey's three children, slipped between his parents and put his arm around his mother's waist. Cormick was a level-headed boy, with his father's good looks and gray eyes. At eleven, he was the only one of their children mature enough to make the trip. Rory, the Brogan's nine-year-old, was a rogue, and at seven Bridget was still shy with strangers and clingy. But Cormick had grasped the reality of his grandmother's death and done everything he could to comfort his mother.

Kate dropped an arm over his shoulder and kissed his auburn hair. "Thank you for being here. You were so well-behaved. Do you think you could sit with Aunt Bejoy while I say goodbye to everybody?"

Cormick looked worried, but he nodded.

"You can get me or your daddy if you need us. I brought paper and colored pencils. Maybe you can get her to draw with you?"

"I'll try." He sounded both willing and doubtful, which was an example of his good nature *and* his intelligence.

Kate got out the pad and pencils. Then she left her sister in Cormick's care, and with her husband went to say thank you to the handful of her mother's acquaintances and offer them punch, coffee and cookies in the next room.

Kate was an active member of the Shenandoah Community Church in Toms Brook, Virginia, and she knew that if anything happened to her, that church would be filled with mourners. Her mother hadn't belonged to a church, club or professional organization where she might have made friends to attend today or cater a reception. Nora's immediate neighbors were here, along with two people from the small business that had provided clerical work for her to do at home. Another woman introduced herself as a clerk at Nora's favorite grocery store. A young man with his mother by his side said he had mowed Nora's lawn and trimmed her shrubs. Kate found his presence most touching of all. She wondered if the gangly teen had worried that few people would show up, and he'd come for that reason.

"You have a good son," Kate told his mother, when the boy went to talk to Bejoy.

The mourners left quickly, along with the minister, and Mickey went into the office to settle business with the funeral director while Kate gathered up the framed photos of her mother's life that she had placed on the table beside the punch bowl. There was no casket in the room and no burial in the future. The funeral home had arranged a cremation yesterday, and Kate had attended alone to say her final goodbyes. Her mother's ashes would be sent to Virginia, and Kate would scatter them in the mountains her mother had so loved.

For now, there was nothing left to do except tie up the many loose ends and head back home.

Bejoy and Cormick were still drawing when she went back

into the chapel with cookies in a napkin for each of them. For the most part Kate's sister had ignored the well-wishers, who hadn't seemed surprised. If they knew Bejoy, they knew that while she was most often sweet-natured, she also had a stubborn streak as wide as a six-lane interstate.

With a familiar heavy heart Kate watched her twin sort through the cookies now. Thirty-two years ago they had emerged too early from the same womb. Kate had been first, a healthy five-pound girl with an Apgar score of 7, despite her low birth weight. Bejoy, just three pounds, with her umbilical cord twisted around her neck, had been blue at birth and survival had been unlikely. The small hospital where her mother had given birth had been ill-equipped to handle an impaired infant, and by the time she had been moved to a hospital with better facilities, Bejoy had already been called back from the brink of death twice.

Somehow, though, Bejoy had survived, a tiny miracle of medical science. Nora had never given up on her youngest daughter, staying by her side at the hospital as a sympathetic friend cared for baby Kate, once she was discharged.

Unfortunately, their father had given up immediately and disappeared. Over the years, from different sources, Kate had learned that her parents' marriage had been in trouble from the beginning, and that the pregnancy had been unplanned and unwelcome for him. He had stayed just long enough to see the babies' arrival, but when it became clear that one of them was going to require extraordinary care, he had walked away.

Over the years Kate had heard infrequently from Frank Clayton. Right after her mother's death she had left him a voice mail message with the news, but as yet, he hadn't returned the call. She wasn't surprised.

Mickey came out of the office, and the funeral director,

who had guided them through this experience with respect and consideration, came to say his goodbyes. As they approached, Kate smiled at her husband, whose answering smile was both warm and concerned. Tonight they would have to talk about Bejoy. For now, though, she was content to remind herself, as she often did, how lucky she was to have Mickey's broad shoulders to lean on and Mickey's strong arms around her to look forward to at the day's end.

"Ready?" he asked, after the director said his farewell.

She spoke softly. "I'm not sure Bejoy understands what happened today. She does on one level, I know, but I'm afraid she'll think we're kidnapping her tomorrow. She'll want to wait here in Florida for our mother to come back."

"I think the flight home will be the worst of it."

Kate didn't have to say how much she dreaded dragging Bejoy on a plane and keeping her quiet enough that they weren't asked to get right back off. "My mother was a saint, but their life was so calm, so uneventful..."

She didn't have to finish. Kate's mother had maintained an orderly, predictable life because Bejoy reacted so badly to change. Kate's twin had never been on a plane. A trip, in Bejoy's world, was an afternoon at the beach and an ice cream cone on the way home. Even those excursions had been rare, since Nora had claimed that the roar of the waves and the two-hour trip gave Bejoy nightmares afterward.

Nora had protected Bejoy in a way that neither Kate nor Mickey thought was healthy or helpful, but she had never been open to suggestions.

Now Mickey was watching Cormick and Bejoy, as if considering their options. "I think we ought to drive by the airport on the way home. Park, get out, take her inside and let her see whatever we can so it won't be so scary for her tomorrow."

Kate hated to add that experience to a difficult day, but Mickey was right. They needed to do it, although she doubted it would make much of a difference. She nodded reluctantly, and they went to persuade Bejoy to get back in the car.

Before Kate could speak, Bejoy got to her feet. As she stood her black pants bagged at the knee, and her flowered T-shirt flopped half in, half out from the waistband. Her dark hair, not a bit wavy like her sister's, was cut in an unfortunate Dutch-Boy bob, but even with the bad haircut, she might have been a pretty young woman except for the random expressions that floated across her face in waves, as well as something vital lacking in her blue eyes, a spark or a connection with the people around her.

"I'm going home now," Bejoy said. "Everybody else got to go home."

"You're right," Kate said. "But we're going somewhere special, first."

Bejoy frowned. "What does that mean?"

"We're going to visit the airport. Mickey thought you would like to visit it today, before we take the plane to Virginia tomorrow."

"Not going to Virginia."

Cormick interceded. "Don't you want to fly on a plane with me, Aunt Bejoy? It's so much fun, and I'll hold your hand the whole time."

"Not going with anybody."

"Let's just check out the airport today," Mickey said. "So you can see it."

"I don't want to see it!"

Kate looked at Mickey. He cleared his throat. "Let's get in the car, and then we'll worry about it."

Kate put her arm around her sister. "I love you, Bejoy. You're going to be fine. Mama wanted me to take care of you when she couldn't be here to do it herself. So we're both doing what Mama wanted."

Bejoy looked rebellious, but she let Kate lead her to the car.

The wailing didn't begin until they were looping around the airport, and it didn't stop until an exhausted Bejoy was safely tucked into her very own bed that night.

CHAPTER 2

"We're in luck. They sell red wine at the local drugstore." Mickey came out to the porch with a bottle of cheap wine in one hand and two plastic cups in the other. "Screw top. I suggest we drink the whole thing."

Kate sent him an exhausted smile. While Mickey made the trip to find wine, she had sat without moving and stared at straggly palm trees and patches of St. Augustine grass in her mother's front yard.

Nora had moved her little family to this house when Kate and Bejoy were eight, so she could take a job at a school for special needs children and keep an eagle eye on Bejoy's education. Kate had hated leaving Virginia, where she'd spent the first years of her life, and she had vowed to move back to the Blue Ridge mountains as soon as she could. At seventeen she'd won a scholarship to James Madison University in Harrisonburg, and she had never lived in this house again.

"An ocean of red wine can't drown memories of today. I couldn't imagine anything worse than my mother's memorial service..." She swallowed hard. "And then Bejoy taught me there are worse things after all."

"We have three kids. We're used to tantrums." But he smiled ruefully because both of them knew Bejoy hadn't thrown a simple tantrum. She hadn't screamed and screamed because she wasn't getting her way. The airport had terrified her. The interstate traffic getting there, the planes flying overhead, the crowds, even the skycaps in their dark uniforms with their stacks of suitcases.

"Then there was my father..." Gratefully Kate took the first full glass from Mickey's hand and raised it in toast when he joined her on the love seat. The love seat was the only piece of furniture on the narrow screened porch. The entire two-bedroom house in a downwardly-spiraling neighborhood was stripped down and sparsely furnished. The consignment shop that would sell or dispose of everything Kate hadn't packed to ship had asked for a hefty deposit, because they guessed they wouldn't make their expenses otherwise.

"Do you want to tell me what..." He cleared his throat. "...he said?"

She heard what Mickey had wanted to say, the name he'd wanted to call her father just then and had, more than once in the past. Tonight, though, he was making pains not to upset her.

She didn't want to upset him, either, but she needed to share her father's words more than she needed to protect her husband.

"Let's see." She sipped her wine first, gathering herself. "He gave me his condolences and said my mother was a kind and beautiful woman."

"Pardon me while I try not to choke." Mickey took a sip of his wine, too.

"That was the good part. The only good part." Kate stared

into space, the wine in her hand forgotten. "He told me Mom wasted her life taking care of Bejoy. He said she could have found a place to put Bejoy and gone on to marry again and have another normal child to replace her."

"He said *replace* her?"

"He did."

"The bastard."

"So much for your good intentions."

"I'm sorry, but Katy, it's hard for me to hear this. I can't imagine how *you* feel."

Mickey's family was large, brash, and charming—even when the brothers were taking a swing at each other, which had happened more than once at high-spirited wedding receptions. They loved to argue, to tussle, to gang up on each other, but most of all, they loved. No Brogan would ever be left on his or her own. They were generous, loyal, effusive, and so different from anyone Kate had been used to, that the night Mickey introduced her to his family as the woman he intended to marry, she had temporarily lost the ability to carry on a conversation.

Rory was Brogan through and through. Bridget was more like Kate, quiet and contemplative. Cormick was a combination. Kate loved all her children and loved that they were unique. Apparently that gift had not been a legacy from Frank Clayton.

Kate swiveled to see her husband's profile. "That wasn't even the low point. The conversation went straight downhill after that. He said I shouldn't waste my life the way Mom did, that whether I promised Mom I would take care of Bejoy or not, I still need to stick her somewhere and walk away."

Mickey's eyes closed for a moment, but his nostrils flared. "Somewhere. Anywhere?"

"Pretty much." She remembered her wine and finished half

before she spoke again. "He ended by telling me he couldn't help and wouldn't help, even if he could. I'm supposed to turn my sister over to the state and save myself, the way he did. He as much as said I should use him as my role model."

"That was it?"

"Except for the part where I told him not to bother calling me again. Ever. So I guess I said goodbye to both my parents today."

His arm came around her, and he pulled her to rest more closely against him. "I'm so sorry, Katydid."

"We both knew that's how the call would go. He wasn't suddenly going to appear, knight-in-shining-armor, and sweep Princess Bejoy away to a better life."

"Right, but I guess I'm surprised when people *don't* surprise me."

"Yeah, we share that."

She looked up at him; he looked down. She had never been sure what gorgeous Mickey Brogan saw in her. She was petite with large dark eyes that saved her face from being completely ordinary, but three children and a tiny budget kept her from doing much to enhance the attributes she had. She shopped for clothes at discount stores and rummage sales and wore every item until it fell apart. To save time and money, she kept her wavy hair shorter than Mickey liked it. And still the man looked at her as if she'd just stepped off the red carpet.

Now he leaned over and kissed her. He tasted like red wine and desire. This time, as so many others, the desire would fizzle. She would sleep in Bejoy's room on the second twin bed, and Mickey would sleep with Cormick in her mother's room. There were no other choices and no privacy.

The situation at home wasn't much different, although there, at least, they had their own room with a door that locked. Once all the children were safely asleep, if she and

Mickey were still awake and functioning, desire could finally have its way.

"We have to talk about your sister," he said, when he sat back.

"I know."

"Of course, she has to go back with us. That's written in the stars."

"Thank you."

"From that point on?" He shook his head. "Katy, she can't live with us for long. I know you see that. Our house is almost as small as this one. Two bedrooms, one bath. If one of us takes a step, everybody else has to move to make room. Bejoy will have no place to get away. Rory alone will drive her bonkers."

"Well, she'll be in good company."

He lifted her chin to see her eyes. "What are your thoughts?"

None of her thoughts were coherent. She had been agonizing over this decision since learning of her mother's death. "I *promised*," she said. "I told Mom I would take care of Bejoy if something happened to her."

"She *made* you promise," Mickey said. "And as much as I liked your mother, that wasn't a bit fair. You were a teenager. She was playing on guilt."

"I was the lucky one. Somehow I thrived in the womb while Bejoy didn't. I was in the right position to be born. Nothing wrapped itself around my neck."

He didn't tell her how silly that was, because, of course, both knew she'd had no power to direct her birth. She *had* been the lucky one, but it was luck she hadn't asked for, luck that had turned to guilt as she matured and understood the differences between herself and her twin, as well as the cause. She had been blessed and her twin sister? Bejoy had been left to suffer the consequences of oxygen deprivation and prematurity for the rest of her life.

"I've made a mental list of possibilities," he said. "We can find a larger house, but it means our rent will increase dramatically. I don't see how I'll be able to start school in the fall if we do."

For years they had saved every possible penny so that Mickey could do a three-year doctorate program in physical therapy at nearby Shenandoah University. He was a physical therapy assistant at a nearby hospital now, and for the past three years, he had spent evenings taking classes to finish a bachelor's degree. A stint in the Army right out of high school guaranteed financial help for graduate school, a benefit he had deferred for that purpose. They could manage with that, financial aid from the university and their savings. But their budget was already tight. A larger house would sink their carefully laid plans.

"I want you to get your degree. I could go back to work," she said, although her chosen field, preschool education, probably wouldn't pay enough to make much of a difference.

"If you could find a full-time job in the area, maybe, but what would you do with your own children in the summer? What would you do with Bejoy?"

Now that all their children were in school, Kate had searched unsuccessfully for a likely job, so she knew the chance of finding one that paid enough and had flexible hours was slim.

"Maybe I can get some other kind of job and work nights when you won't be in school."

"We would have to move to Winchester for you to find a job like that. There's certainly nothing in Toms Brook. And I guess we could try it, but we would never see each other until I graduate."

She couldn't imagine not having time with Mickey. Besides he would need time to study at night when he got home. Right now, as long as their little family was awake, there really was no time for anything but them. Even quilting, the one thing she did for herself, had to be pursued late in the evenings or at dawn, before anyone else was up.

"Maybe there are bigger houses at the same rent. If they aren't in good shape I could play Mrs. Fix-it."

"There *are* no houses like that." He paused, as if he regretted having to relay more bad news. "I've had a friend looking this week while we were away, a rental agent. It seems we have the bargain of the century. Anything large enough for all of us, even in dreadful shape, will cost at least another five-hundred dollars a month. We could camp, but it gets cold in the winters."

"I won't put her in an institution. I can't."

"Katy, it's a different world than it was when you and Bejoy were born. Those kinds of places are few and far between. The alternatives are much better."

She could almost hear her father's voice, although she knew Mickey was nothing like him. "First we have to get her home."

"About that..."

The awful truth was right there in front of them, and she grimaced. "She won't be able to fly tomorrow, will she? I know. You don't have to tell me."

"I took your mother's car for a test drive early this morning. I knew it was old, but not how old. It's a wreck, and it sure won't make it to Virginia. In fact, you'll need to have it towed away before you sell the house."

One more thing to do. Kate sighed and Mickey took that as a sign to continue.

"I called the rental car company and asked about extending

our rental for another week. They said no problem. You can take care of the paperwork tomorrow when you drop Cormick and me at the airport."

She knew the answer to her own question but asked it anyway. "It has to be me?"

"One of us has to fly home and rescue my mother. She loves Rory and Bridget, but she sounds completely done in. And she has things to do back home."

Home was Massachusetts, where Mickey had grown up. His mother had taken leave from her job as a sales rep to fly in and assist.

Kate knew he was right. He could drive Bejoy instead, and she could fly home, but Bejoy would be more comfortable with her sister at the wheel. Even then, Bejoy was going to pitch a fit most of the way.

She was Kate's responsibility. From now on she always would be.

"Me and Bejoy. In a car. Driving from Florida to Virginia."

"The trip will give you time to assess the situation, Katydid. It's only, what, maybe fifteen to twenty hours of solid driving? You should be able to do it in three days max. Maybe you'll come up with a way to work this out that doesn't include Bejoy living elsewhere. And maybe you won't."

She rested her head against his shoulder and let him stroke her hair.

"We'll get through this," he promised.

She hoped he was right, but part of her wondered if Mickey was glad things had turned out this way. Because three days on the road with Bejoy might give her answers she really didn't want.

CHAPTER 3

As they disappeared into the airport's secure area the next morning, both Mickey and Cormick looked so relieved that in any other circumstance Kate might have laughed. Unfortunately Bejoy, hands over her ears and moans increasing steadily in volume, took all humor out of the situation.

Kate waved her hand in front of Bejoy's eyes to get her attention. "We're leaving in a minute. I just have to stop by the car rental desk."

"I don't want to go on an airplane!"

"We are not going on an airplane. Mickey and Cormick are flying without us." She tugged her sister's arm. "Come on!"

When Bejoy stayed rooted to the spot, Kate weighed her options and started through the airport alone. As she hoped, Bejoy weighed her own options and followed, still moaning steadily.

Bejoy didn't like elevators, and coming up, she had caused a scene on this one. Unfortunately, Bejoy also refused to use an escalator, and Kate hadn't been able to find stairs. At the elevator again, Kate waited until the door opened before grabbing her sister's arm and then pulling her inside. As Bejoy tried to escape, Kate stood in front of her and held out her arms like a traffic cop.

"We have no choice," Kate said loudly, over Bejoy's shrieks. "And look, we're already there." She stepped aside as the door opened, and Bejoy jumped off. Luckily she didn't try to run.

Kate started toward the car rental counters. "Come on. We'll finish the paperwork and get out of here."

Maybe "get out of here" was a magical phrase, because Bejoy stopped moaning, and even though her hands were still clamped over her ears, she kept pace with her sister. Of course, when they were together, Kate's pace was always measured and slow. Bejoy lurched sideways as she walked, and while years of physical therapy had tamed the worst of it, she would never be completely steady on her feet.

Kate was delighted to see that the rental company Mickey had used—because it was the cheapest—had almost no line, although the others were crowded. She guided Bejoy to a seat not far away, but she refused to sit, so Kate took her arm and dragged her to the counter. Once they got into line, Bejoy slapped her hands over her ears again.

She realized immediately why this line was so short when she saw a sign announcing there were no cars available. She was glad Mickey had taken care of everything by phone. When it was her turn, she stepped forward with Bejoy in tow and told a middle-aged woman with a pleasant smile who she was.

"We were told I just need to put the car in my name instead of my husband's," Kate said after explaining why she was there.

"No problem. I see you called. And you'll be returning it to us on. . ." The woman checked her calendar. "The 17th?"

"We'll return it on the 17ᵗʰ, but not here. Do you have a location in Winchester, Virginia?"

The woman looked puzzled. "Winchester?"

"I'm sorry. Maybe Harrisonburg? Even Fairfax, if that's the best option."

"I'm sorry, but we don't do one-way rentals. We don't have offices out of state. Nobody told you?"

Kate's throat was closing, and she cleared it too loudly. When he'd made the phone call, Mickey hadn't asked the right questions. She suspected he hadn't even imagined this would be a possibility.

"No chance?" she said, clearing her throat again.

"No, I'm sorry." The woman glanced at Bejoy and immediately saw the problem. The professional smile turned sympathetic. "You'll have to try one of the other agencies. I hate to tell you this, but finding any car isn't going to be easy. There's a convention this week, in fact several conventions. As of this morning, almost everybody's booked solid." She pointed to the sign on the counter.

"Any suggestions who to try first?"

The woman chewed her lip. "Start at one end and just keep moving down. Be systematic, and give everybody your cell number in case there's a cancellation while you're standing here. Good luck."

Kate glanced at her sister, who was breathing hard. Any minute the moans would restart. "Thanks. We're going to need it."

TWO AND A HALF HOURS, one full-fledged screaming fit, a visit by the security guard, and no cars of any make, shape or size for rent, Kate finally got lucky at the last possible counter.

"We do have one that just came in. It's the only car we have available because it was just serviced." The agent looked sideways at Bejoy with every third word he spoke, as if he were afraid she might leap the counter and wrap her delicate little hands around his neck.

Kate was beyond weary, and apparently Bejoy was, too, because she had finally stopped moaning and was simply slumped against the counter.

"I don't care. Whatever it is, we'll take it," Kate said.

The young man readied the paperwork, asked the standard questions, took her license and credit card, and told her where to sign. She frowned at the amount, which seemed exorbitant, but she was in no position to haggle over price. Then he explained where to find the car.

"Keys are in the ignition," he said. "She's not going to be driving, is she?" he asked as an afterthought.

Kate just stared at him. He shrugged.

Kate took Bejoy's hand and tugged her around the roped off area and into the garage where the car was located. Bejoy slapped her hands over her ears again.

"Noise can't hurt you," Kate said, patience gone. "Car engines are noisier inside the garage. We'll be out of here in a minute."

"It hurts my ears!"

Kate was certain her sister could have learned to tolerate more stimulation of every kind if their mother had introduced it slowly. She immediately felt guilty that she was having critical thoughts about the woman to whom she had just said a permanent goodbye. Her mother had made certain Bejoy's life was peaceful and serene. Maybe Nora just hadn't realized her daughter's life couldn't stay that way forever.

Bejoy's life certainly wasn't going to be serene once she started sleeping on the sofa bed in the Brogans' living room.

The boys slept in one bedroom, and Mickey and Kate slept in the other. Bridget's bed was in the dining nook off their kitchen, which was screened from view by a tension rod and curtains, and the family had to eat at a table squeezed into one end of the living room. She could move her sons to the sofa and Bejoy into their room, but she knew that would only work temporarily.

Kate followed the agent's directions and found the correctly lettered row. Bejoy was trailing behind her, but closely enough that Kate could keep her safe. Cars were passing, but Bejoy stayed to the side.

She followed the numbers in each parking space until she was standing in front of the correct one. But the car? Had she made a mistake? She shuffled through the paperwork, until she read the description. The only mistake had been saying yes without asking for more information.

The car was perky, sporty and a bright cherry red. The wheels were shiny aluminum with as many spokes as a bicycle. But that wasn't the problem.

"A convertible," she said out loud. "Just exactly what we need." She considered what to do. Drive this car to the next city where the same agency had an office and exchange it for something smaller, simpler—and cheaper? Try to make the trip in her mother's old clunker after all?

She wished Mickey were here. Guys and cars. He would know what to do, while all she cared about were full tanks of gas and tires with tread. She was still debating her choices when Bejoy clapped her hands.

"I like this car!" She looked thrilled, and for the first time since Kate had arrived, her sister actually grinned. "I love it!"

Sometimes decisions could be just that simple.

∿

AN HOUR later they were almost back at her mother's house when Kate saw a sign in front of a hair salon on the corner. They had an afternoon and evening to kill before they left in the morning, and Kate knew leaving was going to be quite a scene. On a whim, she stopped and parked. Then she faced her sister, who had been humming tunelessly as she turned the knob to try every radio station within range.

"We have some time, and I need to get my hair cut. It's so out of shape, and they're having a cut-a-thon here for...charity," she said. The sign announced that all proceeds would go to a local agency for the developmentally disabled. She wasn't sure Bejoy would feel offended, or even understand if she explained, but she didn't want to take a chance.

"I need to get my hair cut, too," Bejoy said. "Mama said I did. She makes me."

Kate managed a smile. "Then let's go together. Will you promise not to yell?"

"I like getting haircuts. Sometimes."

Kate thought her sister must not have liked the last cut, because in addition to ugly, it was lopsided.

She disembarked and went around to help her sister get out. Bejoy seemed to understand how to fasten her seat belt, but she'd been having trouble getting out of the other car. This time, though, she managed on her own, swung her legs around and stepped to the curb. Kate smiled her praise and locked the car with the remote.

Inside she waited until the receptionist had finished with another woman before she stepped forward and explained what they wanted. The receptionist, red hair piled high and a fortune in glittery eyeshadow brushed up to her eyebrows, glanced at Bejoy, then back at Kate. "I'll make sure you get our best stylist."

Kate was warmed by her thoughtful response. Even better, they didn't have to wait long. A young man with a fohawk sporting a side design of stars, came to welcome them and took them to the back of the shop, which was crowded with chatting patrons.

"Which of you two lovely ladies should I take first?" he asked.

Bejoy giggled at the compliment, and Kate smiled thanks at him. "My sister will go first."

He motioned to the chair, and Bejoy quickly sat, as if she was looking forward to this. "What would you like done?" he asked. He glanced at Kate as if checking to be sure the question was appropriate.

"Do you know how you would like your hair to look?" Kate asked. "Do you want to look at some pictures first?"

Bejoy was already looking at the numerous photos on the wall. She scrunched up her face and pointed. "Mama chooses, but I want to look like that."

Kate was delighted. First, that Bejoy had understood so quickly, and second, that she had made her wishes known. Almost better, Kate thought the hairstyle Bejoy had chosen was not only possible but would probably look great with her bone-straight hair. The style wasn't too short or too long, and best of all, it would frame her pretty face and shape her hideous bangs. It would also be easy to keep up with.

"Can you do that one?" she asked the stylist.

"With pleasure," he said. Then he turned to Kate. "And I can't wait to get hold of *you*. We're going to shape that beautiful hair of yours a different way, so you can let it grow a bit. Longer will be more flattering. I'll show you what I mean when it's your turn."

She was delighted, and she knew Mickey would be delighted, too. But most of all right now, Bejoy was delighted.

Her sister clapped her hands in excitement, then she followed the young man to the shampoo area and didn't protest once when he asked her to lean back so he could wash her hair.

CHAPTER 4

The next afternoon Bejoy was no longer delighted about anything. "Not leaving until I find Squeaky." She glared at her twin and made a fist. Kate knew exactly what that meant.

Kate glanced at her watch. The morning had flown by, and they had no hope of putting significant miles behind them before evening. Now Kate's only goal was to get away from the house and on the road before dark.

So far, with no help from Bejoy, she had packed a small suitcase for her sister to bring on the trip, packed another bag with her sister's favorite snacks, as well as a few keepsakes to put beside Bejoy's bed at their motels to make the rooms seem homier. Then she had finished boxing and addressing everything else they were keeping to be shipped later.

Finally, while her sister had gone outside on her hunt to find and say goodbye to the neighbor's gray tomcat, Kate had sealed the household items no one would ever buy or use into black garbage bags. Then she had hauled them to the curb, because anything she could do herself was something the consignment shop didn't have to. And they charged by the hour.

"We have to get going," Kate said. "But let's go out together and take one more look for Squeaky."

Bejoy stuck out her bottom lip, but she followed Kate outside.

The cat's owner, a gray-haired woman named Martha, stood on her front porch in slippers and watched as Bejoy searched. She had agreed to let the shippers into the house tomorrow to get the boxes, and then to pass the key to the consignment crew next week. Kate had to wait for her mother's will to be finalized before putting the little house on the market, but Martha had agreed to watch out for the property in the meantime.

"McTavish doesn't really like Bejoy," Martha said in a conspiratorial whisper. "She likes to hug him to death. I don't know if she's going to be able to coax him out today. If I had thought about this, I would have kept him inside this morning."

"McTavish?"

"I know Bejoy calls him Squeaky. I didn't have the heart to correct her. She needed a pet of her own."

Kate understood why her mother hadn't wanted another burden, but Martha was right. Bejoy would have loved a pet, and with a few lessons, she would have taken good care of one, too.

"She looks real pretty with her hair cut that way," Martha said. "I'll miss her. She used to come over whenever I made sugar cookies and help me ice them."

Kate thanked Martha for everything, then followed her sister's voice until she found her yelling for the cat.

"Bejoy!" Kate waved her hands in front of her sister to get her attention. "You'll scare him if he's out here. Use your indoor voice." She demonstrated. "Here kitty, kitty, kitty. . ."

"His name is Squeaky."

"But he's a cat. A kitty. Most cats know the word."

Martha came around with a bag of cat treats. "I forgot I had these. Bejoy put one in your hand and call him real soft-like."

Bejoy looked rebellious, which faded to skeptical, then to compliant. She took a handful of treats and squatted on the ground. "Here kit-ty, kit-ty, kit-ty," she said woodenly.

"Make it sound like you want him to come, only not loud," Kate said.

"Here kitty, kitty, kitty." Bejoy sounded a little more enthused.

Kate heard a meow and saw the cat coming out from a clump of palmetto on the opposite side of the house. "Now, don't jump up and scare him. Just stay quiet and he'll come."

Bejoy glared at her, but she did as Kate asked. The cat padded slowly in their direction, stopped, looked at Bejoy as if he wanted to reconsider, then came closer, drawn by the smell of food. The moment he got close enough Bejoy lunged at him and clasped the struggling cat to her breasts.

"I'm going to take him with me," Bejoy said.

"No, you're not," Martha and Kate said together.

"I want to," Bejoy said, but it was clear she understood she couldn't really do it.

"Say goodbye, then we have to get on the road," Kate said.

"I'll never see him again!" Bejoy burst into tears, wailing uncontrollably.

"Would you like me to send you photos of...Squeaky?" Martha asked. When Bejoy continued to cry, Martha looked at Kate. "I have a photo of him in the house. She can take it now."

"Oh, thanks. That would be great."

Kate leaned forward and stroked her sister's hair. The cat,

though clearly not happy, had stopped struggling. Kate was surprised he hadn't scratched Bejoy.

She tried to comfort her. "Sissy, I know you don't want to leave Squeaky. I know you don't want to come with me..." Bejoy was quieting a little, and Kate took that as a good sign. "But we have to go. Mama's gone now, and I'll take care of you. But I have to do it in Virginia. You loved Virginia when you were a little girl, and you'll love it again. You just don't remember."

"I do remember." Bejoy was sniffing now, but the wailing had stopped.

"Do you?"

"I think...maybe."

"I can't wait for you to see it again and find out if you do."

"Can I have my own cat?"

Both Rory and Bridget were allergic to animal dander, and there was no hope of having a cat in their house. But Bejoy's future was such a question mark that Kate nodded. "Someday you might be able to have a cat all your own."

Bejoy looked torn, but finally she kissed McTavish on the head and released him.

Kate helped her to her feet. "I packed peanut butter sandwiches for dinner."

"Really?" If given the opportunity, Bejoy would live on peanut butter. Nora had been forced to ration.

"Really," Kate said. "I promise I did. And sliced apples."

Martha came around the house and presented Bejoy with a small framed photo of McTavish. "You need this more than I do," she said.

Bejoy grabbed it and held it to her chest, the way she'd held the cat. "I can keep this?"

"You can." Bejoy hugged the older woman, and Kate saw tears in Martha's eyes.

"You stay safe on the roads," she told Kate.

~

HALF AN HOUR after they finally got away, and thirty miles down the interstate, Bejoy turned to her sister. "Where's my pillow?"

Kate glanced over and saw that Bejoy had the photo of McTavish on her lap and was sitting quietly with her hands folded tightly over it.

"Your pillow?"

"*My* pillow. I want to go to sleep."

Kate didn't remember a special pillow. "Can you tell me which pillow you mean? Because I packed the pretty flowered one on your bed, and it will probably be waiting in Virginia when we get there."

"No, *my* pillow! The one I sleep with at night. Under my head!"

Kate kept her expression neutral. Now she knew which pillow Bejoy meant. Unfortunately, she had tossed that particular pillow in the trash while Bejoy was out hunting the cat. The pillow had been stained and squashed as flat as a tortilla, and never had Bejoy mentioned any attachment to it. Nora would have known, but Nora hadn't written instructions in her last seconds before exiting this world.

Now Kate kept her voice neutral. "I'm sorry, Bejoy, but that pillow's still at the house." It was most likely true. The trash service hadn't arrived before they left.

"My pillow! My pillow! I want my pillow!"

"We're too far away now. I'm sorry. We'll get a new pillow for you."

"My pillow! My pillow!"

Kate rolled her eyes and took the next exit so she could double back. She knew which bag the pillow was in, or she hoped she did. If not, she would sort through all of them. Some battles weren't worth fighting.

As it turned out, she didn't need to sort, because thirty minutes later, when they drove up to the house, all the bags were gone.

She didn't even stop, because she knew if she did, there would be no hope of getting Bejoy in the car again. She gunned the engine, did a wide turn that nearly took out a neighbor's mailbox, and took off back down the road.

"My pillow!" Bejoy wailed.

"I'm sorry, but your pillow is gone," Kate said. "Now we're going to get you a brand-new pillow. And a brand-new pillowcase to put on it."

An hour later Bejoy had reduced screams to sniffles. Kate knew her sister was exhausted, because *she* was exhausted from listening. She took the next exit and pulled up to a long strip mall. Never had she been so thankful to see a Dollar Store nestled next to a pharmacy at the end.

"We'll get that new pillow here," she said. "And you can choose a pretty new pillowcase."

"Two," Bejoy said, eyes narrowed.

"Two," Kate agreed. She parked outside the store and turned off the engine, but she wasn't quite ready to exit. It was time to establish who was in charge now, so they didn't have another scene inside.

She started with a deep breath. "Bejoy, I won't put up with you screaming any more. If you scream at me, I'm not going to give you what you want. You can tell me what you want, and you can listen when I answer. Then we can talk about it. But I will not listen to you if you scream."

Bejoy was silent, as if she was mulling that over. "Mama wouldn't let me scream."

Kate knew that wasn't strictly true, since sometimes Bejoy

was difficult to control, even for Nora, but she was mollified. "Mama is gone, and you and I need to show respect for her by following her rules."

"Does she know?"

The question was a good one, and Kate had no answer that didn't involve a complicated theological debate. She put her hand on Bejoy's shoulder. "Before she died Mama knew that I would take good care of you, and that means making sure you follow the rules. So back then she knew for sure. Okay?"

"I want her to know now."

"Me, too. Maybe she does."

"I want flowers on my pillowcase."

"If we have a choice, that's what we'll get."

Bejoy knew how to milk success. "I want a candy bar, too."

"Chocolate sounds like just the thing to me. For both of us."

"We're sisters," Bejoy said. "We like the same things. Sisters do."

CHAPTER 5

Bejoy wasn't fond of the clothes that Kate had packed for her, but the next morning she dressed after only a little grumbling because Kate promised to take her to McDonald's for breakfast.

"And I want an egg muffin," Bejoy said for the fourteenth time. "Don't forget."

"You'll be right there with me, so you can remind me."

"No, I have to sit in a chair by the window and be good, or I can't have anything to eat."

Kate wondered what beyond-the-pale behavior had precipitated that particular rule. She decided not to meddle with a good thing.

She hadn't brought much along in the car, but the convertible was still stuffed with this and that, including Bejoy's new pillow. After she'd repeatedly punched it into a shape that pleased her, Bejoy had tolerated her new possession well enough. Kate thought pillow punching was probably a form of therapy, too. Her sister had a lot to contend with and more was coming.

Unfortunately, they had only put fifty miles behind them yesterday, so Kate was anxious to get moving. The motel had been cheap and just clean enough to be acceptable, but the closet-sized bathroom had smelled strongly of mildew, and the air-conditioner had rattled like a freight train.

Swimming in the postage stamp pool had been the one highlight of their stay. Bejoy liked the water, and Kate had broken down and found a cheap suit for herself at the discount store. Luckily she had pictured the fuss if Bejoy wanted to swim at a motel and Kate hadn't been prepared to join her.

Despite the exercise, she had slept poorly, and she hoped that tonight, if they managed enough miles through the day, they could spend a little more on a motel. The budget she and Mickey had worked out for the trip had been largely depleted by the expensive convertible.

Bejoy insisted Kate take a photo of the motel before she would get in the car. Kate snapped one with her phone and showed it to her sister, who nodded approval. "I will want to remember," Bejoy said.

Kate was touched. "Let's keep a photo journal. I'll take photos along the way for you." An explanation of "journal" took them to the local McDonald's.

"I want a camera," Bejoy said, as they got out of the car and crossed the parking lot. "But Mama says I take too many pictures."

Kate had solved that problem with her own children by buying them disposable cameras with a set number of photos. Now they could take a dozen photos of the same thing, but they knew they couldn't take more once the camera was used up. She knew she could probably find one for her sister and teach her to use it.

No stranger to bribery, she hatched a plan. "If things go well today and we travel far enough, I'll buy you a camera all your own when we stop for the night. But you have to let me drive without a lot of interruptions, so we'll have time to shop after we get to our motel."

"I can try."

Bejoy sounded so skeptical, Kate had to struggle not to laugh. "I know you will."

Inside the restaurant Bejoy stopped in the doorway. "Not McDonald's. You said McDonald's."

"Of course it is, silly." Kate took her arm, but Bejoy shook her off.

"No!"

Kate went through a list of possibilities and chose the most likely. "Does it look different than the one you're used to?"

"Not McDonald's."

"Bejoy, you saw the sign outside. McDonald's looks different in different places. This is definitely McDonald's, so let's play a game. Help me find all the things that are just like the one you go to."

"Bathroom should be there!" Bejoy pointed her finger in a corner where three surprised patrons sat at a small table and were now staring at them.

Kate took Bejoy's arm more firmly this time and tugged, because people were coming in behind them, or trying to. "We'll walk around the room and you can show me all the things that are the same. Not different, Bejoy. The *same*."

After one prolonged turn around the room with a clock ticking loudly in Kate's head, Bejoy finally calmed. She had found enough similarities to reluctantly agree that Kate was correct.

Kate guided her to a row of tables, and Bejoy sat at the one they decided on. She settled herself slowly in the unfamiliar chair, as if to be sure there was nothing beneath it that might rise up and swallow her. Then one last time, she told Kate what she wanted to eat.

"And orange juice," she added.

"I'll be right back."

Kate ordered for both of them. The food came quickly, and she carried it with Bejoy's orange juice to the table, returning to the counter to get her own coffee after she'd dropped everything off. She was stirring cream into her cup when she heard her sister shriek.

Whirling, she saw Bejoy on her feet, jumping up and down, her arms flailing uncontrollably. Coffee forgotten, Kate rushed back to the table. "Bejoy, what happened?"

"Cheese!"

Kate stared at her. "Of course it has cheese. They come that way."

"Mama knows I don't like cheese. I hate it! I hate it!"

Kate grabbed her sister's arm and held it firmly, dodging the other one when Bejoy made a fist and tried to hit her. "Stop this right now. Right...now!"

She didn't have to glance around the room to be certain that everyone in the crowded McDonald's was staring at them.

In a final act of rage Bejoy swiped all their food to the floor with her free arm. Then she stuck out her lip and glared at her sister. "Mama knows!"

Kate wasn't certain what to do. She couldn't release Bejoy to clean up the mess. There was no telling what her sister might do next. But neither could she leave their food on the floor.

She was saved from a decision when a restaurant employee came over with a tray, gave Kate a brief wary smile, bent and began to clean up Bejoy's temper tantrum.

"I am so sorry," Kate said. "Thank you."

The woman, probably in her sixties, stood. "You have your hands full."

"We're leaving."

The woman nodded, as if she thought that was a good idea.

"I'm hungry," Bejoy said, still pouting.

Kate refrained from telling her she deserved to be. She waited a moment until she felt kinder. "I bet you are. I am, too, but our food's gone now, so I guess we'll just be hungry until lunch."

"Buy more now. No cheese," she said, narrowing her eyes. "Mama knows."

"Mama isn't here anymore. I am, and you have to tell me exactly what you want. This will happen again if you don't, so we'll practice how to do that in the car."

"I'm hungry."

Kate didn't say a word.

The fight went out of her, and Bejoy's shoulders slumped. "I'm hungry, Sissy."

Kate knew this was going to be a very long trip if she gave in. Bejoy's world had changed, but whatever world she inhabited, she needed to learn acceptable manners. Their mother had avoided this kind of behavior by making sure Bejoy's life was predictable and well-ordered. But those days were gone.

"We'll eat an early lunch," Kate said. "But we can't afford to buy two breakfasts, and you ruined ours."

Tears trickled down Bejoy's cheeks. "Can I still have a camera?"

"Not today." Kate turned and started for the door. She was opening it when Bejoy rushed up behind her.

"Don't leave me."

"Stay with me then," Kate said. "That way we'll always be together."

TEN MILES down the road Bejoy's keening stopped. When she had been quiet for another five, Kate pointed at the clock on the dashboard. Bejoy had learned to tell time when she was still a teenager, but a digital clock was a blessing.

"When it's eleven-thirty we'll start looking for a place to have lunch. Will you tell me when it's time?"

"Is that a long time?"

Bejoy could tell time, but the math involved in computing the hours and minutes between now and eleven-thirty was too difficult.

Kate computed Bejoy's frequent demands for restroom and rest stop breaks. "Two and a half hours. I know a way to make the time go faster."

"What?"

"We're going to practice ordering at a restaurant."

"No, you can do it."

"I don't think so. You need to be able to tell people what you want. You didn't tell me this morning, but the next time we go in to eat, you'll know how."

"I don't want to."

"I could do it wrong again. You could get awfully hungry that way."

"*I* could do it wrong."

Kate felt a tug of sympathy. Her sister was aware she was different from other people. How aware Kate didn't know.

"We all make mistakes," she said. "So we have to practice, and that way we make fewer. Let's do this together. I'll pretend to be your server—"

"What's that?"

"The person who comes to your table and takes your order at a restaurant."

"Waitress."

"There's more than one name for that job. Waitress is a woman. Server can be a man or a woman."

"Ser...ver." She said it as if she were committing the word to memory.

"Okay, pretend now, okay?" Kate said.

"I like to pretend."

Kate knew Bejoy didn't always understand the difference between reality and fantasy, but she seemed to understand they were playing a game.

"Hello," she said. "I'm your server, and I'm here to take your order. Did you have time to look over the menu?"

"We don't have a menu," Bejoy said.

"Pretend we do."

"What does it look like?"

"Forget the menu. Let's just pretend you've decided what you want to order and now you're going to tell me."

"I haven't decided." Bejoy smiled. "If it's pretend, I can have anything I want, right?"

Kate smiled, too. "Absolutely."

"I will have six hamburgers, five bags of French fries and a whole carton of orange juice." She looked very pleased with herself.

Kate punched her sister in the shoulder, and Bejoy giggled.

BY THE TIME eleven-thirty rolled around Kate was tired of driving and of coaching her sister, and wow, had she regretted leaving her coffee on the counter so she could shepherd Bejoy out to the car. But Bejoy had made significant strides. She could order five different meals, giving all the details to be sure everything was correct. Of course, one meal was her favorite

McDonald's breakfast sandwich, without the cheese. Now she knew how to be very specific. "No cheese" was her new mantra.

Kate wasn't sure what would happen if Bejoy was asked in any depth to clarify what she'd said, but she told herself she would be sitting beside her sister if help was needed.

She avoided a fast food establishment for lunch, so there would be fewer reminders of breakfast. Instead she chose what looked like a Mom and Pop café not far from the interstate. It sat alone, surrounded by a parking lot dotted with pick-ups and sedans, but it wasn't crowded. Someone else would wait on them. They could sit. Kate could relax a little, and Bejoy could probably have almost anything she wanted.

"I'll have an egg salad sandwich on white toast," Bejoy practiced, as they started inside. "I would like French fries, too, and a glass of milk."

"Excellent. And what if I say we ran out of egg salad and don't have anymore."

"Then I will be mad."

Kate stopped and pulled Bejoy to a stop beside her. "Wrong answer."

Bejoy grinned, as if she'd made a joke. "I will ask for a grilled chicken sandwich and French fries. But I might want iced tea without ice. I have to think."

"Great. Let's go."

When the woman overseeing the counter told them to choose their own seats, Kate turned to her sister. "Where do you want to sit?"

Bejoy looked happy to be asked. "By the window."

They took a seat looking over the parking lot. The scenery had already begun to change. Fewer palm trees, more live oaks and pines. Another car pulled in as they waited, and finally the sallow young woman who had been staring at them from the other side of the room sauntered over with two glasses of iced water.

"I don't like ice. It hurts my teeth," Bejoy said carefully, as if she had been practicing that sentence, too.

"Well, we can't have that," the woman said, rolling her eyes.

Kate knew sarcasm when she heard it, but Bejoy didn't.

"You didn't know," Bejoy said sweetly. "I will let it melt."

"Or you could get her a glass without ice, if it's not too much trouble," Kate said, her gaze connecting with the woman's. "And would you mind taking our order now? We know what we want."

"Imagine that. And you haven't even opened your menus. Can't *wait* to hear." The young woman put both hands on the edge of the table and leaned forward, staring snidely at Bejoy. Four men in caps sitting in the booth beside theirs turned to watch, as if they felt the tension.

Kate debated whether to stay or go, but after missing breakfast, dragging Bejoy out of the restaurant would be a disaster. "Bejoy, why don't you tell our server what you would like?"

Bejoy proudly announced her choice, just as she'd repeated it in the parking lot.

"You want sweet potato fries, curly fries, steak fries, cheese fries or regular fries?" The young woman smirked. "We have them all—which you would know if you had *read* the menu at the end of the table."

Kate refused to jump in. At least not yet.

Bejoy frowned, then she brightened. "I don't like cheese. I will have steak fries. I like steak."

One of the men behind them laughed. Kate wanted to turn around and hit him over the head with the menu she hadn't taken from the stand.

The waitress made a disparaging noise. "That just means they're big fries, like you would eat if you had steak. That's all."

"But I want egg salad."

The woman rolled her eyes. She mouthed something to the men beside them, something that to Kate looked like it might well be "retard." Then she turned back to Bejoy. "You can have steak fries with egg salad. Or you can have regular fries or curly fries. Which is it?"

Bejoy looked confused, and Kate suddenly sympathized with their mother's attempts to isolate and protect her from moments like these.

"My sister will have regular fries," she said, growing angrier by the moment, "and I'll have a grilled cheese sandwich and your house salad. I'd also like to see the manager."

"He's in the kitchen and busy."

Kate got to her feet. "Good. I'll talk to him there. In front of the rest of your staff."

Alarm began to spread across the young woman's features. Kate noted that the men had turned back around now and were talking among themselves. Kate stepped close to the woman; the woman stepped back. Kate continued stalking her until they were far enough from the table that Bejoy, who was playing with her knife and fork, wouldn't hear them.

"Bejoy is intellectually disabled," Kate said, "but I'm not. I'm sure you weren't hired to insult your patrons. How small is your ego that you want her to suffer for *your* inadequacies? Do you feel better about yourself now? Proud you could insult somebody who's unable to return the favor? Do you feel bigger?"

"Jeez, lady, get a grip."

"Go tell my sister you're sorry you were rude, and do it loudly enough that the guys in the next booth hear you. Then bring us lunch."

"Or?" The server sneered, but her narrow lips wobbled.

"Or, after I'd told your manager to his face what I plan to do and *why*, I will plaster this encounter over every relevant social media site on the internet. Especially the restaurant review sites."

It must have been clear she wasn't kidding. Kate could see that the young woman had realized what that kind of publicity could mean for her job.

She whirled, stomped back to the table and stood at the end, this time without touching or leaning. "Miss, I'm sorry if I was rude. I'll get your food as quickly as I can. And some water without ice."

One of the men in the next booth began to applaud. Bejoy looked baffled. "That will be nice," she said. "I am really hungry."

CHAPTER 6

Every thirty miles Bejoy needed a bathroom break. Kate pulled off the interstate each time, sometimes traveling for miles before they found a convenience store or service station. Then came the drama of getting her back into the car, the protests of exhaustion and demands for snacks or drinks, the pleas to stop at every rest stop and do exactly what the name suggested.

By five o'clock Kate gave up hope she could put more miles behind them today and pulled into a fried chicken chain for a bathroom break and dinner. They were still in Florida, and there were three states between them and Virginia.

"We'll get food and take it to our motel for a picnic," she said. "Let's see what they have."

Half an hour later she managed to get both food and sister back into the car and start the search for reasonably priced lodgings. She was delighted to find that one of the cheaper national chains had just built a new motel off the next exit, and she was able to book a room with two double beds. The interstate was audible, but as soon as she turned on the air conditioner, outside noise was negligible. The carpet was a pretty turquoise, clean and fresh, and while the bathroom was tiny, it was sparkling and more than adequate.

Kate wanted to move in and be done with this trip forever.

She asked Bejoy for help getting their suitcases inside, and while she grumbled, Bejoy managed to get hers to her bed, open it, unpack pajamas and toiletries and head to the bathroom for a shower before dinner. The shower was her own idea, too, which delighted the weary Kate. They investigated the dials and knobs together and Kate made sure that Bejoy knew how to operate everything before she left the room.

Kate wanted to rest for the few minutes she was alone, but she had to call home. The sound of Mickey's voice would be an antidote to the day, and it was time to let him know that there was no telling when they would finally get to Virginia. So far this part of the trip had taken more than twice as long as Kate had expected. She didn't think it was going to get better. The longer Bejoy was in the car, the more restless she became.

The answering machine picked up, which didn't really surprise her. Friends knew Mickey was alone with the kids and had probably invited them for a cookout. Or quite possibly Mickey was breaking their mutual rule and taking the whole gang out for fast food. She wouldn't blame him. She hoped he remembered that Bridget got sick if she ate too many fries, that Rory always wanted his burger and bun served separately, and Cormick hated mayonnaise.

She missed her family. Arms under her head she lay down on the fresh sheets and closed her eyes.

When she heard the shower stop, she pulled herself out of bed to open her own suitcase and take out what she needed once Bejoy was in bed for the night. She made a neat pile on the sink counter, which sat along one wall in the sleeping area, and went back to close her suitcase. She had unpacked at her mother's house and until now hadn't noticed the bulge in the compartment in the top. She unzipped it to see what she'd missed.

She was still looking at the little bag of treasure when Bejoy emerged, drying her hair with a towel. In blue pajamas and barefoot she looked younger than her thirty-two years, her cheeks rosy, her eyes focused and shining. For a moment Kate saw the woman she might have been had Bejoy been born full term and somehow escaped the strictures of her own umbilical cord.

They were not identical. Bejoy would probably always have been a little shorter and built a little sturdier. Her eyes were blue, and Kate's brown. Their features showed a family resemblance but even without Bejoy's disabilities, nobody ever would have mistaken one for the other. They were each attractive in their own way. Bejoy was, in Kate's opinion, a pretty woman.

"Did you have a good shower?" Kate asked.

"It got hot. Then it got hotter when I tried to fix it."

Kate had told her to leave the water as it was or call her for help. She was lucky this hadn't been worse.

"You could burn yourself, Sissy. This is all new to you. Next time let me help."

"I fixed it myself." Bejoy narrowed her eyes. "I am not dumb."

"New things can be confusing. I get confused, too."

Bejoy stopped drying her hair and looked squarely into Kate's eyes. "Next time let me help."

Kate burst out laughing, and Bejoy smiled. She loved to make people laugh. She always had.

For a moment Kate was flooded with memories. Helping her mother teach Bejoy to walk when they were three. Teaching her the alphabet when they were six. Crying together when they had to leave Virginia for the unknown wilds of Florida. They had been eight, and Nora hadn't been pleased enough with the local school's plans for Bejoy's education. She had wanted total control, and the school—in their wisdom, Kate thought—felt that Bejoy needed to learn independence from her mother.

She also remembered how much she had resented the attention that Nora had focused on Bejoy and how little she had focused on Kate. The school plays with starring roles that Nora never saw. The soccer games, the Girl Scout campouts Nora couldn't attend. Kate had been Nora's right-hand when it had come to helping her twin. She had been expected to fetch and carry, to frequently clean and cook, to give up things she needed so that Bejoy never went without. Nora had never apologized for or explained her choices. Now Kate realized that her mother had thought it was better that way, that the moment she did either, she would have made Kate's situation sound unusual or pitiable. And Nora didn't have time for Kate to rebel when she already had so much on her plate.

Through it all, though, Kate had always loved her sister. She had never wanted anything but the best for Bejoy. She had never forgiven herself for being the lucky twin. And now she was afraid she was going to fail her.

"What's that?" Bejoy asked, pointing to the bag in Kate's lap.

"It's part of a quilt I'm making. It's called Woven Paths, and it's my hand piecing project. I forgot I'd thrown it in my suitcase before we flew to Florida. I haven't had time to work on it."

Bejoy joined Kate on her bed, and Kate made more room for her. "See, I'll sew these strips together when they're all done and it will make one block, a big one. I haven't decided how large I want the quilt to be. I'll probably just make blocks until I get tired, then I'll put them together."

"You can make a quilt? Not buy it from a store?"

"When you get to my house, I'll show you the quilts I've made. I'm not very good, but it doesn't matter. I do it for fun."

"I would like sewing like that. I can thread a needle. I can cut."

"Have you ever sewn anything?"

"They taught me to sew a hem in school, but I pricked my finger too much. Mama didn't like that."

Kate reminded herself not to judge her mother. "Doing this is relaxing for me, but not for everybody. It keeps my hands busy and gives me time to think. This pattern is easy to make mistakes on, though. I've had to pull out rows on some of the other blocks because I didn't pay enough attention."

"It's okay to make mistakes?"

"You can always take them out."

"I like doing things where I can make mistakes."

"Do you like the colors I chose?" There were four fabrics in the quilt, a soft green with a slightly darker swirl, white, a pink polka dot, and a darker rose. The pattern formed squares that stepped up and down from each other diagonally, and the different colors were woven in and out of the blocks, coming back together and diverging again across the block and later the quilt.

Looking at the block now, Kate supposed her color choice meant that Bridget would get this one. She couldn't imagine Cormick or Rory with pink on their beds.

"I love green and I love pink." Bejoy tilted her head to look at the block from a different angle. I would love purple. Lav-en-der, too."

Kate looked at the block and realized that lavender would have been a good choice for one of the colors. "That would be pretty, too."

Bejoy loved to draw and color. It was no surprise she would enjoy picking out fabric, too. And that gave Kate an idea.

"Bejoy, would you like to do some sewing in the car while we drive?"

"I don't have thread."

"I noticed a fabric store in the shopping center we passed." Kate didn't add that quilters had a sixth sense about fabric and quilt stores and always seemed to find them when they traveled. "We could buy you some fabric and scissors, needles, thread, and you could sew. We could go over there after we eat."

Bejoy's eyes shone. "Mama says I prick my finger too much."

"You might, but you'll learn not to. You just have to practice. Besides I'll show you how to use a thimble. That might help."

"What would I make?"

Kate had already come up with an idea. "We bought two pillowcases, remember? Why don't you cut out things you like and sew them to the white pillowcase? You could put anything you liked on it. Flowers, shapes, squiggles–"

"Squiggles? Squiggles is a funny word." Bejoy was grinning.

"Squiggles." Kate drew a wavy line in the air with her finger. Bejoy laughed.

"What do you say? Would that be fun?" Kate hoped her sister said yes, because if she could keep Bejoy busy in the car, then she might be able to drive farther tomorrow before they stopped for the night.

"Mama says–" Bejoy put her hand over her mouth.

"Mama's gone," Kate agreed, nodding. "But Bejoy, she always wanted you to be happy. Will this make you happy?"

Bejoy looked as if Kate had just handed her the moon.

CHAPTER 7

The next morning after they pulled into the parking lot of a friendly looking chain restaurant for breakfast, Bejoy didn't want to leave her new sewing supplies in the car, but Kate convinced her that she might drop food on the fabric. She finally agreed, tucking everything carefully under the seat and out of sight, in case a quilt-burglar walked by.

Last night, after much thought, Bejoy had chosen six neatly folded fat quarters from a discount bin. A fat quarter was one-fourth of a yard, cut once horizontally, then again vertically to create larger chunks of fabric. She had debated her choices until the store was about to close, but in the end, she had chosen the brightest available options like sunshine yellow and sapphire blue.

To go along with them, Kate had purchased several new colors of thread, scissors with a slightly rounded point so Bejoy would be less likely to stab herself, a thimble, and straight pins with brightly colored glass heads. Bejoy had spent the rest of the evening turning the fabric this way and that, imagining,

Kate thought, what might spring to life when she finally began to cut it. Kate had been delighted with her twin's surprising ability to delay gratification.

"Okay, let's practice ordering breakfast just one more time," Kate said, putting her arm around her sister's shoulders. She had accessed the menu using her cell phone and discussed it with her sister before they left the room. She'd seen the restaurant last night on their way home from the fabric store.

"I would like blueberry pancakes, please, with two strips of bacon."

"How do you like your bacon, Bejoy?"

"Crisp."

"And do you want maple syrup or blueberry syrup?"

"I would like maple syrup."

"How about to drink?"

"I don't want to drink maple syrup."

"*What* would you like to drink?"

"I would like orange juice and a glass of water without ice, please."

Kate squeezed her sister's shoulder. "Perfect."

Inside they didn't have to wait long for a table. They were ushered to one along the wall, and their server, a young man with a ready smile, arrived almost immediately and asked for their drink order.

Bejoy sorted out her responses and gave the correct one, and Kate asked for coffee and cream. He returned and Bejoy performed the next round without a bit of difficulty. After yesterday, Kate had been wary Bejoy might have to face more bigotry, but the young man was respectful. He asked where they were from, and Bejoy proudly answered for both of them.

"He is very nice," Bejoy said after he left. "I like him."

Kate's cell phone rang, and she checked the number. She put the phone to her ear and spoke quietly, because this was a call she couldn't miss, and she wasn't about to leave Bejoy alone at the table.

"Mickey." Her voice reflected her smile.

"I'm so sorry we missed you last night. We went out for pizza."

He had successfully dodged the French fries, burger bun and mayonnaise hurdles. Everybody loved pizza, although that would change when cheese-hating Bejoy moved in.

He asked about the trip, and she told him they weren't making good time. As she had expected, he wasn't surprised. He had managed to round up child care for the hours he worked or was in class. Another stay-at-home mom on their street had agreed to help out. "But she won't be willing to do it for long," he warned.

Kate offered a few more childcare suggestions and no promises they would travel more miles each day. She knew that Mickey recognized the reality of her situation. She asked him about the children, and he regaled her with stories. He asked about Bejoy, and she told him her sister was sitting right across from her. "I'll put her on," she said.

She held out the phone. "Mickey wants to talk to you," she said.

"He does?" Bejoy looked thrilled. She took the phone and Kate watched her chatter away. A minute later she gave the phone back to Kate so she could finish the call, but Bejoy was beaming.

"Is Mickey my friend?" she asked Kate, after she hung up.

"Of course he is. And he's your brother-in-law because he's married to me. That makes him even more special."

"You love him," Bejoy said. It was not a question.

"I do."

"I would like to love somebody."

Kate felt the all-too-familiar pang she always experienced when she realized how much Bejoy had missed out on.

"I'm sure you do." She reached across the table, took her sister's hand and squeezed it. "I'm glad you love me and my family."

"I would like a boyfriend to love. I don't have friends. Sometimes it makes me sad."

To Kate's knowledge Bejoy hadn't had opportunities to make friends. Their mother hadn't liked any of the programs that Bejoy could have taken part in. They cost too much or provided too little. Bejoy's chances to bond with anyone except neighbors had been few and far between.

"I promise we'll find friends for you in Virginia," Kate said, and meant it.

"I am loud and silly."

"What?"

"Mama says when I have friends, I am too loud and too silly."

"Wait till you spend time with Rory. *He's* loud and silly."

"More than me?"

"Rory is the champion."

"Maybe Rory will be my friend."

"You can count on that."

Their food arrived, and they finished it quickly. Out on the road again Bejoy looked through a quilt magazine Kate had bought her at the fabric store. The issue featured applique, which meant that pieces of cloth in different shapes were sewn to a background fabric. Kate's Woven Paths quilt was pieced, which meant small pieces of fabric were sewed together to form a pattern. Kate had wanted her sister to see the difference.

"Look, ducks!" Bejoy held up the magazine so Kate could

see it. Kate risked one quick glance before she went back to staring at the road.

"Are you going to cut a duck out of your yellow fabric?"

"It will leave a hole."

Kate understood. "I know what you mean. I love fabric so much sometimes I hate to cut it up. But you can buy more after you use what you have."

"I can?"

"Of course. After you cut that up and sew it on the pillow-case if you need more we'll buy more. Just try to cut from the edges so you'll have more in the middle you can still use."

"Should I draw a duck on it?"

"You could, or you could just cut. Maybe drawing first is a good idea, though."

"I have a pencil." Bejoy rummaged around in the canvas bag with all her things inside.

"Why don't you draw on paper first until you're happy with what you've done."

Almost half an hour down the road Bejoy had drawn a duck that satisfied her. Kate was surprised to see how good it was, primitive yes, but folk art applique was popular with many quilters. She thought maybe Bejoy was going to be a star.

"I love it." She was completely sincere, and Bejoy beamed. "So now you're going to draw it on the fabric?"

"Trace," Bejoy said.

Kate figured she'd stumbled on a good idea when she managed another thirty minutes of driving before Bejoy demanded a bathroom break. They had gone a whole hour without stopping.

She had congratulated herself too soon. Once Kate had filled the tank at the closest gas station, and both she and her sister had used the restroom, Bejoy didn't want to get back in the car.

"My head feels funny." Bejoy clamped her hands on her head. "And my stomach."

Kate was afraid she knew why. Bejoy had often gotten carsick as a girl. Now Kate remembered those moments all too well. Drawing and leafing through the magazine had very likely kick-started it today.

She explained her theory to Bejoy.

Bejoy nodded. "Mama said no reading in the car."

"I guess Mama was right." Kate could almost see the extra miles she'd hoped to cover today waving goodbye.

They hung around the station, bought cold bottled water and crackers to help Bejoy's stomach settle, and chatted with the woman behind the counter. Kate was reluctant to purchase medication, since Bejoy often reacted badly to over-the-counter substances.

When Bejoy claimed her head was still "moving," they took a short walk down the road. The fresh air seemed to help, and Kate decided the right moment had arrived to put the top down on the car so Bejoy would get even more. So far they had traveled with top in place because the Florida sun had been bright and hot, and Kate had worried about sunburn.

She bought her sister sunglasses and a cap with the longest, widest bill she could find on a rack in the station. An alligator with a grin waved happily with the words "Later Gator" emblazoned on it. Bejoy thought it was sensational.

"Bejoy, there's something about our car that you don't know." Kate explained that the car was a convertible and she was going to put the top down. Bejoy should stand clear as she did.

She wasn't sure what her sister's reaction would be, but Bejoy started to clap the moment the top began to fold and she was still clapping by the time it was all stowed in place. For her own part Kate felt like clapping, too, because she'd dreaded putting the top down for the first time, in case something went wrong. Nothing had, and now Bejoy was gazing at it like a child who's just watched Santa deliver a Christmas pony.

"Can we ride in it without a top?" Bejoy looked doubtful, but that changed when Kate told her to hop in. Bejoy could hardly wait.

The first half hour was a time of wonder, and Bejoy's car sickness faded away. The second half she fell sound asleep, and Kate ignored the rumblings of hunger to put more miles behind them while she could.

When Bejoy woke up they ordered fast food from a drive-in window, but Kate knew there was no chance she could hurry off. Food had to be eaten slowly and settle, and Bejoy had to walk a bit to be sure she was ready to get back in the car. They found a picnic table at a nearby park and took a long break from the road. Kate hoped this meant Bejoy would be ready to get back in and cover more miles, once it ended, but only half an hour after they had crossed the Georgia border, Bejoy was ready to stop for the day.

First Kate put the top up again because Bejoy had begun to complain about the wind. Then they stopped at the Georgia welcome station for a bathroom break and fresh water from the vending machine. Five miles down the road Bejoy swore she was hungry. Five miles more she complained that the crackers Kate had told her to eat were making her sick. Kate had generously calculated two hours from the welcome station to Savannah, where she had hoped to stop for the night, but the trip took four. The ritual lowering and raising of the top several additional times, bathroom breaks and rest stops all took their toll.

The motel was just good enough to pass muster, and this time Bejoy brought in her own suitcase without being asked. Kate wanted to wait a little before they found a place for dinner, to be sure Bejoy was up to eating again. So she settled herself next to her sister on Bejoy's bed and suggested she pull out her sewing supplies. Bejoy had brought that bag in first and reverently laid it on her bed.

"How do I sew things on?" Bejoy held up the plain pillowcase.

"First you have to cut something out. Then I'll show you."

"Don't watch."

Kate laughed. "I know what you mean. I have friends I quilt with. You'll like them. But when they watch me do something, I feel like I can't do anything right."

"I will cut. Then you can see."

Kate got up and made a pretense of unpacking her nightgown and bathroom bag until Bejoy spoke again.

"I'm done. It's a duck."

Kate didn't need an explanation. The shape was clearly a duck. "I love it, Bejoy. It's a very pretty duck, too."

"I want to put it right in the middle." Bejoy smoothed the duck exactly where she wanted it.

Kate hoped the next part was going to be that easy. "Let's pin it first, then I'll show you how to sew it down."

Twenty minutes later they were both exhausted, but Bejoy had taken her first steps, threading the needle, knotting the thread, and sewing a running stitch around the edges of the duck. Her stitches were surprisingly good, if a bit large. The duck would ravel eventually since Bejoy wasn't turning the edges under to secure them, but Kate was optimistic that her sister would learn to do that, as well, after she had practiced this way for a while.

"Wow, I'm hungry now. How about you?" Kate asked.

Bejoy carefully put her sewing away and her shoes on again. From a discussion with the desk clerk, Kate knew there was a seafood restaurant not far from their motel. The restaurant was casual, paper place mats, iced tea in Mason jar mugs, and plastic menus that had been updated with magic markers as prices rose and fell. There was laughter from the surrounding tables, and two small children ran from one to another before they fell into the laps of people at both, clearly a family gathering of some kind.

Kate missed her own children and could hardly wait to be home with them again.

After a look at the menu they both ordered fried shrimp, which was the house specialty. While Kate ordered cole slaw and fries, Bejoy carefully ordered salad and a baked potato. "I have to have salad if I eat shrimp," Bejoy said, when their server departed. "Mama said. Nothing else fried."

Kate noted the difference between "Mama says," and "Mama said." She thought her sister was beginning to come to terms with what their mother's death really meant. "Mama wanted you to be healthy. You're eating more sensibly than I am tonight."

"Mama said that Florida has the best fried shrimp in the whole world."

Clearly both daughters had gotten their love of seafood from Nora. "Georgia shrimp is pretty good, too," Kate said. "You'll like it, I promise."

"Georgia?" Bejoy looked perplexed.

"We're in Georgia now. Remember the welcome station?" She was sorry she hadn't shown Bejoy the map at the entrance.

"Not Florida?"

Kate had a feeling she might be making her way through a minefield. "We're traveling to Virginia, remember, to see Mickey and the children? We go through several states to get there. It's just like the trip we made when we were little girls, only we're going the other direction. Do you remember how much fun we had? Mama bought us dolls and we dressed them—"

"I want to stay in Florida."

"When we were eight you wanted to stay in Virginia. You'll love it again, Bejoy. You haven't seen mountains in a long time, and you loved mountains when you were a little girl. And snow. Remember playing in the snow and making snowmen? Someday maybe we can go back to Florida and visit."

"I don't like Georgia."

"You liked it just fine a few minutes ago. Don't let a name spoil this, okay? We're still in the same country. It's all the United States."

"I like Florida."

Kate searched for the right response. "That's okay. You can like a lot of places, and when you go back you'll still like them and be glad you can visit again."

"I would like to go home." Bejoy said the words carefully and slowly, as if by doing so Kate would finally understand.

Kate reached across the table and covered her sister's hand. "I know this is scary, Bejoy. You haven't been very many places, so you don't know how you're going to like living somewhere else. But I'll make sure you're happy. I love you. I want you to be happy."

Their server arrived with Bejoy's salad. Kate was afraid her sister was going to cause a scene, but instead she began to eat. Kate was careful not to sigh in relief.

They skipped dessert and went back to the motel. Bejoy was quiet, but she seemed more tired than upset. When Kate asked if she wanted to take her shower first, Bejoy told her she would wait until Kate took hers. She picked up her pillowcase and began to work on the duck. Kate was ready for a hot shower and a good night's sleep. She took what she needed into the bathroom. There was plenty of hot water and a strong spray in the shower. By the time she got out, dried off and changed into her nightgown, she felt much better.

Until she stepped outside the bathroom into an empty room.

Bejoy was gone.

CHAPTER 8

Kate was dressed again in a minute. She slipped on her tennis shoes and tied them quickly, pocketed the room key and went outside to find her sister. She told herself she would call the police if she didn't find Bejoy right away, but she wanted to search alone first. Bejoy's social skills were poorly developed. She was as likely to go off with a stranger as she was to throw a tantrum because a passerby wouldn't let her pet his cocker spaniel. Out in the world, alone without somebody to keep a watchful eye, Bejoy was at risk.

She just hoped her sister realized she couldn't find her way back to Florida and their mother's house on her own.

The motel was laid out in units of eight rooms top and bottom, with eight more back to back behind them, clustered in half a dozen buildings. Kate systematically circled each one, beginning with the first floor rooms, then climbing the stairs to do the same on the second floor. A clock ticked loudly in her head as she did, ending each time back at her own room where she hoped to find Bejoy pounding on the door to get back in.

But no such luck.

After the last building, she ranged out to the edges of the parking lot. A few people were still out and about, coming back from dinner or visiting travelers in another room. No one had noticed Bejoy.

Kate debated what to do. She could get in her car and drive through the surrounding streets. Their motel was right off the interstate past the city, and the area was fairly rural, with stretches of land that hadn't been cleared and neighborhoods with houses set far apart. Even if Bejoy was finally ready to be found, Kate wasn't certain she would see her. The sky was dark, and the area away from the hotel wasn't well lighted.

She decided to do one quick turn, spend fifteen minutes in the car, then call the local police and ask for help. She knew the police would frighten Bejoy, who was afraid of anyone in uniform, but she certainly couldn't wait for her sister to return on her own.

At the entrance to the parking lot, she considered which way to turn and decided to go right, back toward the restaurant where they'd eaten dinner. She drove at a crawl, carefully looking both ways and ignoring the driver of the muscle car with the absurdly tall tires who screamed profanity as he roared around her.

She was about to try the other direction when she saw something white under a huge live oak in a field not far off the road. She slowed even more and realized the "something white" was Bejoy's T-shirt. Her sister was sitting on the ground under the tree, head resting in her hands.

Kate pulled over and parked on the roadside, then she got out and joined her sister, standing above her and gazing down.

"I was worried sick about you," she said. "Why did you disappear like that?"

"I wanted to take a walk." Bejoy looked up. Clearly she had been crying. "I can do what I want."

Kate tried to figure out what to say to that. Bejoy couldn't do what she wanted, and she was smart enough to know it.

"Did you want to end up here?" Kate asked, after moments had gone by and no better response occurred to her.

"I got lost."

Kate sighed and joined Bejoy on the ground, hoping she wasn't sitting in a nest of ants. She would know soon enough.

"I hate getting lost," Kate said. "So I try hard to make sure people know where I'm going, in case I do. That way they can find me if they need to."

"You wouldn't let me go alone."

"Probably not."

"I just wanted to walk and think about Florida."

"Were you trying to go home?"

"Too far, I guess."

Kate was glad she realized it.

"I wanted to walk on grass," Bejoy said.

"So you left the motel."

"I turned too many times."

"That happens."

"So I sat here. I knew you would find me."

Kate was touched, but she was also frightened at the responsibility that conveyed. She dove deeper. "Bejoy, you can't go back to Florida to live. You need to be with me, and that's the way it has to be. Mama wanted that, too. That's what she would tell you if she were here."

"I might not like it in Virginia. I don't like Georgia."

"There's nothing wrong with Georgia. You're just scared. I understand. I might be scared, too, if somebody made me move to a different place, and I wasn't sure what was there."

"I wish Mama hadn't died."

Kate put her arm around her sister's shoulders. "Me, too."

"Does she miss me?"

"Mama loved you very much. She always missed you when you weren't right there beside her."

The answer seemed to satisfy her. "Can we go back? I'm tired."

They walked back to the car, and Bejoy closed her eyes for the short trip to the motel.

Once they were in their room Bejoy said she just wanted to go to sleep, but Kate, with visions of chiggers and other creepy, crawly things on the ground under the live oak, promised that a shower would make her feel better. She was planning a second one herself, so she didn't change.

As if all the fight had gone out of her, Bejoy showered, and when she was ready, she fell into bed, obviously exhausted by her day.

"Mama told me stories before bedtime," Bejoy said.

Kate thought about that. Bejoy was still a little girl inside and would remain one until the day she died. Even though she could read on a 4th grade level, Kate's sister still liked to listen to a story, too.

"Once upon a time," Kate began, "there were two little girls who were born on the very same day. In fact they had the very same mother. They were twins."

"Like us."

"Exactly like us. In fact the story is *about* us."

"A real story."

"When they were little they liked to run in a meadow near their house. It was wide and green, and in the spring, flowers bloomed."

"I had braces on my legs."

For a moment Kate couldn't speak. She cleared her throat. "You remember that?"

"I had them a long time. So I could walk."

"You did. Then your legs got better. You walked faster and faster and one day I took your hand and you ran."

"I wish I remembered *that*."

"The flowers in our meadow were pink and gold. And you could see mountains in the distance. The man next door had cows, and we would stand at the fence and watch them graze. You were never afraid of them. You called one of them Bossy."

"Bossy." Bejoy smiled.

It had been one of Bejoy's first words. Kate remembered it well.

"What color are our mountains?"

"They're green right now because there are so many trees. In some places they're gray, because trees can't grow through the rocks. In some places there are waterfalls, streams that run down the mountain and spill over cliffs into pools below. You can walk up paths and see everything up close. Then, when you're high, you can look out and see faraway, Bejoy. We like to hike with Cormick and Rory and Bridget. You'll come with us, and I promise you'll love it."

"I think I remember a waterfall..." Bejoy closed her eyes. In a moment she was breathing slowly.

Kate hoped she was dreaming of the good things that waited for her in Virginia.

When she was certain Bejoy was sleeping soundly, she got up to plug in her cell phone to recharge before she showered again and realized, as she took it from her purse, that she had missed a call from Mickey. She took the phone outside and called him back, leaning against the trunk of the convertible, parked three doors down from their room.

"Kids asleep?" she asked after he answered.

"Mine are. How about yours?"

Kate told him quickly what had happened.

"She's okay?"

"She is now, but the change is hard on her. I just need to be extra careful, I guess, although I think getting lost scared her enough she won't try that again."

"There are a lot of things that can go wrong for Bejoy if she doesn't have constant supervision."

Kate could picture Mickey as he spoke. He was probably raking his fingers through his hair, exhausted from his busy professional schedule topped with three rambunctious children who needed his full attention at night when he got home. She hadn't really had time to consider how having Bejoy in their lives would affect Mickey. They had talked strategies. They had talked possibilities. They hadn't talked about feelings.

"You sound tired," she said.

"You know how it is. We chose the path to our future, and we knew it wasn't going to be an easy climb. Tiny house, little money, me working and going to school and leaving you with housework and kids and cooking. Now that I'm trying to do that, too, the path is pretty precarious."

He'd put it so succinctly. "One loose pebble underfoot and down we all go," she said, finishing the analogy for him.

He was quiet a moment, as if he was trying to figure out what to say next. She didn't fill the silence.

"Katydid, I've been looking at places where Bejoy can live. Because if she lives here with us, we're going to tumble back down that hill, and I don't know if we'll ever be able to climb it again."

Tears sprang to her eyes. Mickey wasn't selfish. Nothing he was doing was just for him. Everything was for them, for all of them. Every step he'd taken for years was meant to give them a better, more secure life. They weren't going to be rich, that was never the point. But if all worked out as they intended, they could send their children to college and give them the things they needed, like a home with enough bedrooms, and a father who could enjoy them while they were still young.

She wanted to tell him he had wasted his time, yet how could she? "What are they like? The places, I mean."

"Some are better than others, of course, even though I asked around at the university and at the hospital to find the best. But for the most part, I've been pleasantly surprised. There's an assortment of possibilities. Larger places that seem almost institutional but have a lot of programs, like crafts and life skills classes. Smaller places that are more like roommates sharing a house, with somebody on site making sure things run smoothly. Lots of the residents I saw have jobs, and they seem happy. I'm not just saying that. Really happy living their lives the way we all do."

Bejoy just living her life. Kate blinked back tears. "She needs friends, but she needs me, too."

"She'll have you, *us*, no matter what. You know that."

They moved on to her own children, to Rory, who might need to get a tooth pulled, and Bridget, who had started sucking her thumb again after nearly giving it up a month ago.

"She misses you," Mickey said. "We all do."

"I'm hoping I can make it in two more days."

"Just stay safe."

She hung up a minute later, missing him the moment she put the phone back in her pocket. The trip home seemed never-ending, but it was giving all of them, Bejoy most of all, a chance to adjust.

She just wished she knew what she should do about Bejoy's future.

CHAPTER 9

I f somebody had asked Kate to give a reasoned explanation why she veered off course near Columbia, South Carolina, and headed west–adding several hours to the trip home–she would have been at a loss to answer. One minute she and Bejoy were about to bypass Columbia to the east, and the next she'd made the decision to take a different route instead, one that would lead them through the mountains of western North Carolina. Bejoy had been talking about mountains all day, and Kate had decided that seeing them sooner was a good idea.

Of course, after she was on the road, and turning back was no longer a good option, she questioned her decision for the next forty miles.

"I'm tired," Bejoy said, and not for the first time.

Kate was tired, too. As usual there had been too many breaks, and it was getting late in the day.

"Let's get to the mountains, then we can stop for the night," Kate said. "Agreed? But you have to let me drive and not complain."

"I need to go to the bathroom first."

"Of course you do." Kate looked at her gas gauge and decided the time was right to fill the tank, too.

Back on the road, Bejoy closed her eyes and actually napped. Kate exceeded the speed limit and nearly got them to North Carolina before Bejoy opened her eyes.

"Mountains," Kate told her, when it was clear her sister was awake. "Look." She took the next exit off the interstate.

The Blue Ridge mountains had been a distant vision, but the quaint little red brick town where Kate hoped to find a room had a much closer view. Green foothills sat against towering mountains, and from the car it was clear they had entered horse country. Bejoy was delighted.

The town was too small for a traditional motel, but at their last stop, Kate had called her friend Gayle Fortman, who ran a bed and breakfast inn in Toms Brook and asked for help. Gayle had looked up Kate's route and recommended two bed and breakfasts at this exit. Kate hadn't made a reservation at either because she hadn't been sure how far they could go that day.

The first bed and breakfast was right in town, with a large yard and a church beside it. The owner answered the door but told them she was booked for the night. She recommended the second bed and breakfast Gayle had mentioned, and Kate drove there next. This location was off their route, but according to the map, there was a scenic two-lane road that would take them to the next entrance on the interstate if the bed and breakfast was full.

The modern Victorian-style house was surrounded by acres of rolling hills, and horses grazed in the pastures flanking it. This time the innkeeper had a room, and they had time to enjoy the countryside before they drove into town for dinner. The price was half again more than they had paid each night before, but Kate was too tired to care. Best of all, the owner promised she would make them an early breakfast to speed them on their way by nine.

The next morning Bejoy carefully recorded scenery with the disposable camera that Kate had bought her during their dinner trip into town. After a little tutoring and more than one warning to count the photos she took, she couldn't have been more thrilled.

Dragging Bejoy away after an elaborate breakfast was the only challenge of their stay. Kate had loved the extra pampering, and Bejoy had made solid friends with the owner's dog, a golden retriever who never tired of chasing the balls Bejoy tossed for him. Bejoy snapped enough photographs of King Midas that she would never forget him.

"It's a beautiful morning," Kate told her after they had finally said their goodbyes. "Today let's put the top down so you can see the mountains. It's going to be a beautiful drive."

It *was* beautiful. As they crossed the border into North Carolina the scenery became grander, and Bejoy couldn't stop pointing out everything and taking more pictures. Kate was glad she had anticipated her sister's enthusiasm and bought a second camera as a surprise.

As they neared Hendersonville, Kate noted clouds overhead, but she wasn't worried. The forecast hadn't called for rain. They were making such good time that she decided to push on and not veer into town to sightsee, although that would have been a joy, since it looked promising.

North of the city the clouds grew a little darker, and the temperature dropped, although Kate thought moving deeper into the mountains was responsible.

They had eaten so much for breakfast that they didn't start looking for a place to stop for lunch until after one. By then Bejoy was getting cranky, and even the scenery and the camera didn't hold much appeal.

The little roadside café that popped up just past the next bend seemed heaven sent. It was attached to a motor court with half a dozen units stretching away from the road, and the sign in the window read, "home cooking." Kate knew better than to believe that, but at the worst, they would be out of the car for a while, and their stomachs would be full.

"See any rain?" the middle-aged blonde at the counter asked, and Kate assured her they had not.

"Later today, I bet," she predicted as she showed them to one of only five tables in the café. "Maybe by evening."

The food was decent, and the woman who waited on them—who looked like a younger version of the hostess—was patient with Bejoy who ordered a hamburger then changed her mind twice before she settled on pulled pork—only to be disappointed when the sandwich arrived and there was nothing to pull.

Back at the car, Kate silently made plans to scoot through lovely Asheville, one of her favorite places, and see if they could make it as far as Virginia, to Roanoke or even Lexington tonight. Now that they'd been fed and still had majestic scenery ahead to occupy Bejoy, she was hopeful. Alone she might have made the whole trip home, but by now she knew there was no point in thinking that way.

She debated raising the top and decided against it. If the sky darkened more, she could close it at their next stop. Bejoy loved the open view, and anything that kept her busy was Kate's friend.

Ten minutes up the road thunder rumbled through the mountains and before Kate could take the next exit, the first raindrops fell. She got off a few miles down the road, but the exit was a rural one, with no businesses to shelter them.

"It's raining!" Bejoy lifted her arms over her head. She didn't sound upset.

"I have to close the top," Kate told her. She cruised to a stop on the shoulder and pushed the button to the left of the steering wheel that would raise the top. She hoped it would close quickly enough to spare the car's interior. By now rain was beginning to fall in earnest.

Nothing happened.

She wondered if in her haste she hadn't pressed it firmly enough. She tried again. Again, nothing happened.

The third time produced the same result. She knew better than to park under a tree when thunder was rumbling, but she cruised farther and stopped beside a fence with thick branches arching over it that immediately gave them some relief from the rain. She reached behind her for a small travel umbrella and gave it to Bejoy, who opened it with a flourish. Then she scrambled to find the rental papers and got out her phone.

"I'm still getting wet," Bejoy said, as if this might be a surprise to Kate.

"I'm going to find out what to do." Kate, dripping by now, dialed the number and instantly found herself on hold. She remembered that Mickey had made certain she had their auto club card, so she disconnected her call to the rental company and called the auto club's 800 number. To her relief that call was answered immediately.

She explained her predicament, and the woman promised to find somebody who might be able to help. Again she was put on hold. Minutes passed as the rain fell faster, and finally a man came on the line. She quickly explained what had happened, and he told her he was going to help her override the system. He explained the procedure. Five short punches of the button as quickly as she could initiate them. In thirty seconds the top should begin to go up.

"If that doesn't work?" she asked.

"Get out of the rain." He offered to stay on the line and

make arrangements to send a truck if necessary, but she thanked him and hung up. If it came to that, getting out of the rain sounded like a better option than waiting here in the open.

"Here goes." She punched the button five times and waited. And waited. She tried once more, but by then she knew their situation was hopeless. The top was down for good.

"We're going back to the place where we ate lunch," she told her sister. "Put the umbrella down and hang on."

"I want to leave it up."

"You want to fly away like Mary Poppins?"

Kate didn't wait to learn Bejoy's decision. In a moment they were on the road again, and in three they were on the interstate heading back the way they had just come.

CHAPTER 10

The tiny motor court was surprisingly comfortable and, even better, had vacancies and a choice of rooms. In the afternoon, after they had showered and changed into dry clothes, both Bejoy and Kate napped to the patter of raindrops on the roof of their cozy unit, and in the evening, after a chicken and dumplings dinner that actually *did* taste homemade, they watched old sitcom reruns and worked on their quilting. Bejoy added a parade of smaller ducks waddling after Mama Duck, and Kate finished a block of her Woven Paths quilt and started the next one.

The convertible was now under a carport that connected the last motor court unit and the owner's house. Kate had done what she could to dry it out with towels, but she imagined that in addition to fixing the top, at the least the car would have to be professionally detailed to counteract the soaking.

An agent at the rental car company had looked up Kate's paperwork, checked the details, and promised to have a new car delivered sometime the next afternoon since, even if their roadside assistance crew could get the top up, the car would probably still be wet inside.

"Looks like we've had the same problem with that particular car before," the woman on the other end of the line told Kate, although she probably wasn't supposed to. "Supposed to have been fixed, but you know how that goes. Nobody's going to question the fact you couldn't get the top up either. You won't be charged."

Kate hadn't expected to be charged, nor had she expected to rent a car that had already proved defective. Now she understood why this car, and this car alone, had been for rent at the airport.

She bit back a harsher reply and explained that the quicker the company could get them another car, the happier she would be. If they left tomorrow by noon and drove long and hard, they could reach Toms Brook just after dark. "And please give us a smaller, cheaper car," she finished.

The woman cheerfully offered to charge the minimum rate for the entire trip and hung up. Kate decided she would also ask to be reimbursed for their motel room when she turned in the second car.

The next morning breakfast was early, since they'd gone to bed early, too, and Bejoy was up with the birds and almost immediately cranky about being cooped up. While Kate and Bejoy waited for omelets, the rental agency called to inform her they would deliver a new car around noon. Kate saw a long morning ahead of them.

"Is there anything we can do within hiking distance?" she asked the younger of the two blond women, who had just arrived with freshly brewed coffee for Kate. Bejoy was drawing flowers on her place mat as patterns for her pillowcase.

"Hiking?" She shook her head. "There's a rock slide where locals like to go, but it's a couple of miles along the highway."

The young woman glanced at Bejoy, as if to signal that particular hike along a busy road wouldn't be a good experience for Kate's sister.

Kate considered taking the convertible the short distance, since it wasn't raining, but she was afraid yesterday's soaking might have damaged something. Plus she didn't want to explain to the rental company that the car was now sitting by the side of the road, instead of under cover.

"Thanks." Kate foresaw a boring morning ahead, as well as a restless sister. Bejoy restless was not a pretty sight.

"I can take you," the woman said. "It's just a few minutes away, and it's no trouble. You can tell me when to pick you back up or call me if you have a cell phone. I really don't mind."

"Are you sure?" Kate was desperate to get Bejoy out of their room for a while, and the offer sounded wonderful.

"I've done it before. It's no trouble."

They finished breakfast and back in the room, they changed into their bathing suits and topped them with shorts.

"I don't know what rock slide means," Bejoy said.

"Me either."

"There are things you don't know?"

Kate smiled. "A lot of things."

Bejoy looked sad. "Too many for me." She seemed to brighten. "But I can learn."

Kate thought about that on the short ride down the highway and into a forested area off the road along a dirt path. She was glad their hostess had four-wheel-drive.

Bejoy *was* learning things. She had stopped screaming when she didn't get her way. She was ordering her own meals now. She was quilting. In the short time they had been together on this trip, Kate's sister had made some important changes. They had been gradual enough that Kate hadn't thought about them until now. But Bejoy could learn and was. She just needed exposure to new situations.

The young woman slowed to a stop. "I'll drop you here. Walk along the path to the edge of the clearing. You can swim in the pool at the bottom of the waterfall, or you can climb up the side of the rock on the other side and let the water there wash you down into the pool. If you need it there's a rope to hang on to as you climb, but it's a gradual slope. We have bigger slides farther into the mountains, but this is a good place to begin."

Kate imagined how much her children would love this. She thanked their driver and told her that unless she called, they would be waiting in this same spot at eleven-thirty.

They got out and watched as the young woman backed up and turned around. Then they were alone.

"An adventure," Kate said, suddenly wondering what she'd done.

"Ad-ven-ture." Bejoy clearly liked the sound of the word, and Kate's stress level went down a notch.

They walked about fifty yards along a well-trampled path and finally entered the clearing. Water sluiced down a smooth rock into a shallow clear pool, and on the other side of the pool, a waterfall trickled over a high ledge and fell into the pool like Mother Nature's shower.

"Oh, wow!" Kate was delighted. It was perfect. For her. "What do you think?"

"Where is the slide?"

Kate watched Bejoy's expression for signs of rebellion as she explained. "It's not a slide like they have at a playground. You walk up the side of that rock slope by holding on to that rope," she pointed, "and then you sit and scoot over to where the water's going down and slide down the *rock* into the water."

Bejoy looked skeptical.

"Do you want to watch me do it first?"

Bejoy nodded.

"Remember, this is an adventure." Kate didn't test the water temperature, pretty sure that if she did, she might take a long time to gather her courage. She walked to the rope, which somebody had tied to a tree above the slide, and holding it for security, found her way up to the top. Then she moved out on the rock, sat, and scooted near where the water ran down into the pool. The distance down looked smooth and slick, and the water whooshed past her just fast enough.

She smiled bravely at her sister, scooted into the water and pushed away.

"Oh my–" She was underwater at the bottom before she could finish. She popped up quickly, and realized the water was only as high as her chest. She could stand there easily. If she wanted to stand there. Which she didn't. She floundered to the edge, walked over to Bejoy, rested her palms against her thighs and struggled to catch her breath.

"Was it fun?"

"It's cold," Kate said. "But we'll get used to it. Let's swim first. It's not deep. You'll be fine."

Bejoy looked doubtful, which was a perfectly normal reaction, Kate thought, in fact a very *smart* reaction.

She knew better than to hesitate. She held out her hand and Bejoy took it. "Let's run," Kate said. "Ready, set, go!" She tugged hard, and Bejoy came with her, which was the biggest surprise of the day.

Both women screamed when they hit the water. Then arms around each other, they screamed until they were dancing together to the music of their own happy shrieks.

~

THEIR NEW RENTAL car was a small sedan, and while Kate missed the snappier convertible, this one was dry inside and smelled brand new. After they said goodbye to the mom and daughter, who had taken such good care of them, she and Bejoy finished goodbyes with thanks to Grandma. Grandma, it seemed, was the cook in "home cooking." She promised to send Kate her recipe for chicken and dumplings.

As they pulled out to the highway Bejoy settled in for the rest of the trip without complaint.

"It's a long trip to my house from here," Kate said, taking advantage of the calm. "Let's try to make it tonight, okay?"

"I'm tired of the car." Bejoy brightened. "If we get there, I won't have to be in it tomorrow."

Kate was pleased with her logic. "You're right. We'll eat a good dinner on the road, then we'll cruise in after dark. You can nap if you're tired."

"Swimming makes me tired."

"Me, too. You should be tired, though. You must have gone down the slide two dozen times."

"I liked to slide. But my bottom hurts."

Kate laughed. She understood that too well. They had probably overdosed on rock sliding, but once they had both adjusted to the cold water, they had loved every minute of their time there.

She'd had fun with her sister. How many times had she and Bejoy really had fun together?

Growing up she had often been angry over their situation. There had been other twins in her schools. Identical twins, who had seemed inseparable. Fraternal twins, who might not look alike or even be the same sex, but who had shared a strong bond. Her life had been so different. *Her* sister had been in a special school, and many of Kate's own classmates hadn't even realized she was a twin. Nora hadn't wanted Kate's friends to agitate Bejoy, so most of the time they hadn't been welcome.

Even when the girls were at home together, they hadn't been treated like other twins. Nora had always been right there, standing between them. Kate had been expected to meet Bejoy's needs, but not to be her friend.

And she had never quite realized it before.

Which twin had Nora been trying to protect? Kate honestly didn't know.

She reached over and squeezed Bejoy's shoulder. "I loved being with you today. That was so much fun."

Bejoy smiled shyly. "We swim the same."

That was another thing she hadn't noticed, Kate thought, but Bejoy was right. Bejoy was as strong a swimmer as she was, much more coordinated in the water than out of it. They had done laps to stay warm, and their strokes had matched.

"I bet we'll find a lot of things we do the same way," Kate said. "We're twins."

"You are smart and I am not."

Tears sprang to Kate's eyes. She wasn't sure what to say. There were many things Bejoy didn't and never would understand, but she did understand that she wasn't like everybody else.

She glanced at her sister, then back at the road. She swallowed her tears. "Bejoy, I wish things had been different. I'm sorry my birth was easy and yours wasn't. It's never seemed fair to me. I wish I could change it."

"Change what?"

She soft-pedaled, because being completely honest would be too harsh. "In some ways, your life's been more difficult than mine."

Bejoy was silent. When Kate glanced at her again, she thought Bejoy was considering that. This, too, was something

Kate really hadn't given her credit for. Maybe they didn't think in exactly the same ways, but Bejoy did think about her life and what was happening to her. So far nobody had given her enough credit for that, and Bejoy had been given little opportunity to make her own choices, even when she was perfectly capable of doing so.

"I have been happy," Bejoy said. "I like being me."

Tears spilled down Kate's cheeks, because one thing Bejoy really couldn't do was lie. "I am so glad."

"Why are you crying?"

"Because you're happy."

"That's not a very good reason to cry."

"You're right." Kate swiped at her tears.

"Are you happy?"

"Very."

"I'm not crying, Kate. I'm smiling."

Kate punched her in the shoulder, and Bejoy laughed. She knew she'd made a good joke.

The time had come to talk about what was coming up. Kate realized that doing it in the car was probably a good thing. It was the most important conversation they had ever had, but driving as they talked might make it less intense.

"Bejoy. . ."

"That's my name."

Kate smiled, sniffed, smiled again. "We have a tiny little house. You won't have your own room. There isn't a room we can give you, and we can't afford a different house right now. I think you need privacy and a place all your own."

"By myself?"

"Absolutely not. No. That wouldn't be a good thing because you would be too lonely. But there are places..." She cleared her throat. The words didn't want to emerge. She had promised her mother. She had promised...

"What places?" Bejoy asked.

"Houses with other people who want to be together. There's always someone to help if you need them, but you would be more independent. You would make lots of decisions for yourself. You would take care of yourself, too. Help with cooking, cleaning." Finishing was too much. She couldn't.

"Other people? People like me?"

"I think there will be different kinds of people, but everybody there will need a little help and lots of friendship."

"Friends?"

Kate looked at her sister. Her face shone. Absolutely shone, like she was radiating her own sunshine.

"Friends," Kate said.

"I would have *friends*?"

"I think you will have plenty of friends, Sissy, probably all different ages and kinds of friends. And you'll have me, and Mickey and Cormick—"

"You won't be living there?"

Kate analyzed the question and realized what her twin was really asking. Bejoy wasn't afraid she might be abandoned. Bejoy was hoping Kate would answer no, that her sister wouldn't be living right there taking care of her the way their mother had. Because Bejoy wanted to be free, really free, to be herself. To grow. To change.

To make friends without intervention.

For a moment again, Kate couldn't speak. The entire conversation was overwhelming. Slowly she pulled herself together and realized that what was best for her own family was also a gift she could give her sister. The best gift in the world.

She was giving Bejoy a life of her own.

She cleared her throat. "No, I *promise*, I won't be living with you, or hovering over you, or making your decisions. I know you don't want that, and I don't think you need it, either. But we–Mickey, me and the kids–we'll always be nearby. You can visit and spend holidays with us any time you want. And we'll always be there if you need us."

"I will need you," Bejoy said. "Only, not all the time. Not like Mama."

"I know. I promise. Not like Mama."

"I will miss Mama."

"Me, too."

"But I will have you, and I will have friends." Bejoy settled back against the seat, closed her eyes, and promptly went to sleep.

Kate choked back tears until she no longer could. She was glad her sister wasn't awake to see them. Because it would be difficult to explain her feelings.

One person might have understood, though.

She took a deep breath. "I'm keeping my promise, Mama," she said softly. "I'm taking care of Bejoy. Maybe not the way you expected, but wherever you are, I really hope you're happy, too."

CHAPTER 11

K ate was fully aware of today's date. Exactly two months had passed since the trip back to Virginia with her sister. Each day since had been eventful, and this day, when she was about to see Bejoy for the first time in two weeks, promised to be eventful, too.

Two months ago she and Bejoy had come home to a hero's welcome. When they had finally parked the rental car in front of the Brogan home, Mickey had been waiting with a hot meal and a hug for each of them. That night Kate's sons had given up their room so that Bejoy would have a little privacy, and they had spent the next six weeks on the pull-out sofa bed.

To make the move an adventure, the boys had claimed they were camping out, and even though they were a little old for "let's pretend," Kate had furthered the illusion by draping a blanket over the dining table that took up nearly half of their living room. She set up the "tent" every night after dinner and removed it every morning, and it wasn't unusual to find one boy sleeping there while the other took up all the space on the pull-out. A time or two Kate had found Bejoy under the blanket instead. By the end she had half wanted to crawl under the table, herself.

The confines of the Brogan's tiny house had made those weeks difficult, but Bejoy had been surprisingly resilient. They had cooked together and done a thorough cleaning after Bejoy announced that she liked to clean and was very good at it. With Bridget for company, they had hiked together, visited local shops, taken a day to drive a section of the Blue Ridge Parkway, and worked on their quilts.

On the first Wednesday after the trip, Kate took Bejoy to the church quilting bee and introduced her. The women made her right at home, and Grace Cashel, well-known for her art quilts, was excited about Bejoy's pillowcase quilt. After the bee Grace invited the sisters to her house for lunch, and she turned Bejoy loose in her extensive fabric stash to choose a dozen pieces of fabric to add to her own. Then Bejoy and Grace discussed each one and the shapes Bejoy might create from it.

Kate would never forget that day. Bejoy was warmly welcomed by her quilting friends, and Grace's enthusiasm for Bejoy's work was genuine. She was even learning to hand quilt. Her stitches were already better than her sister's.

Kate had been so proud of her twin. After they had attended more of the bees, Bejoy had enjoyed giving her opinion on the blocks for the raffle quilt, which were just beginning to arrive. The bee had chosen Helen's idea, of course, and named the quilt in progress Peaks and Valleys.

Most important, Kate had completed the paperwork to make sure that Bejoy received all the assistance she was eligible for, including a program that would help train and find work for her. Then both Bejoy and Kate completed a series of interviews with the case manager of an organization that worked with intellectually disabled adults who immediately began to search for appropriate housing for Bejoy.

As Mickey had reported, there were a variety of options. Some situations were close to Toms Brook, some farther away, and Bejoy and Kate were encouraged to visit and meet the people who staffed and ran them.

After four trips, and with Kate's approval, Bejoy had chosen a group home near Luray, Virginia, with seven other residents and enthusiastic full-time and support staff. Best of all, the comfortable Colonial was nestled against a hill that was surrounded by acreage on a quiet rural road.

Bejoy, who would never be fond of city noise, had immediately loved the house and the countryside, but more important, she'd been enchanted that she would be living with people who had experienced life much the way she had. Ages varied, diagnoses varied, abilities varied, but a common thread ran through all their lives and bound them together.

Bejoy said it best. She was ready for friends.

Now Bejoy had been living in her new home for two weeks. Kate had been strongly counseled to let her settle in on her own. There would be difficulties, and the staff had assured her that Bejoy would feel at home faster if Kate weren't there to referee or even a phone call away whenever she got upset.

On the day she'd helped Bejoy move into a breezy, medium-sized room that was painted an unfortunate Easter egg purple, Kate had explained the situation to her sister. In two weeks she would come back, take Bejoy into town to buy paint, and they could paint her new room any color she chose. Until then, Bejoy needed to get used to her new home without Kate's interference. She hadn't been entirely sure Bejoy could project herself into the future and understand exactly what that meant, but her sister hadn't argued.

They had hugged goodbye, and the house mother had come out to see Kate off, too. In her rear view mirror she had watched the gray-haired woman drape her arm over Bejoy's shoulders as Bejoy watched her sister vanish from her life.

Since that day they had talked only once on the phone. Yesterday she had called to tell Bejoy she was coming for a visit, but the call had lasted less than a minute. Her twin had been in a hurry.

Mickey had offered to come with her today, but Kate had decided to come alone. She needed to see Bejoy by herself to determine whether her sister was happy or had a chance of being happy soon. Kate didn't want reassurance, and she didn't want Mickey to influence her.

The trip to Bejoy's new home was a lovely one, less than an hour on either the interstate or the meandering US-11, which Kate chose today. When she drove up to the house, no one was outside, which was surprising. A gazebo sat on the lawn, surrounded by flower beds and billowing shrubs. There were rocking chairs and a swing where residents had been enjoying a late summer afternoon on the day Bejoy moved in, but today it was empty.

She parked and walked to the front door and listened. From inside she could hear laughter and music. She knocked and nobody answered. She tried again, louder, and this time a young man came to the door to let her in.

The man, probably in his twenties, was dressed in a striped T-shirt and jeans, and from his features, Kate knew he had been born with Down Syndrome. He smiled, and she smiled back and told him why she was there.

"Bejoy!" he bellowed.

The music stopped, but only momentarily as one song ended and another began. "Bejoy!" he shouted again.

Bejoy, dressed in a blue summer dress that Kate didn't remember packing, came skidding around a corner. Kate barely had time to open her arms before her sister fell into them.

"You came!" Bejoy stepped back. "You said you would."

"How are you?" Kate rested her hands on her sister's shoulders and looked her up and down. Bejoy looked great, tanned and rosy-cheeked with her dark hair swinging around her face every time she moved.

"I am very fine." She grabbed Kate's hand and drew her into the great room that opened into the kitchen. Clearly there was a party going on. The room was filled with people, not just the residents and on-duty staff, but at least a dozen more. Crepe paper streamers were strung across the ceiling, and balloons were tied in clusters everywhere. The table was loaded with food, plates of cheese and crackers, sliced fruit, crudites with dip, and at the end, a three-layer cake with chocolate icing and candles.

"It's Marlene's birthday," Bejoy told her. Then she addressed the crowd, shouting loudly over "All You Need Is Love," from a tape player on the floor. "Hey everybody, this is my sister, Kate. We're twins."

People smiled in her direction, and Bejoy took Kate by the hand and introduced her to several individually, including the birthday girl, who sat in a wheelchair and looked a little overwhelmed at the attention.

"Marlene has a job," Bejoy said. "These are friends from her work. I am going to get a job, too." She looked as if somebody had handed her the whole world tied with silk ribbons.

The house mother, Mrs. Gervais, came up to greet Kate and tell her they would be cutting the cake in thirty minutes if she and Bejoy wanted to spend some time alone first.

Bejoy, still holding her hand, pulled Kate toward the front door.

"I want to show you everything!" she shouted over the music. "Come on."

Kate had already seen the house and grounds on their first

visit, but she had never seen it through Bejoy's eyes. Bejoy described everything for her, the swing hanging from an old willow, and the way one of the residents, a girl named Lucy, hadn't known how to kick her legs, so Bejoy had demonstrated until Lucy could do it.

"She swings a lot now," Bejoy said.

Bejoy showed her the flourishing vegetable garden, particularly the pumpkin patch in one corner. "We will carve jack-lanterns," she said. "And make pumpkin pies. But we can't do it now."

"Do you help in the garden?"

"Not yet. I clean the kitchen. I like to clean, and I am very good."

"They're lucky to have you. My house isn't nearly as clean now as it was when you were there."

Bejoy showed her the chicken house with its five rowdy hens, then she took her to the equipment shed. "Watch this." She squatted and called softly, "Kitty, kitty, kitty."

A big yellow-striped cat came out of the shed where it had likely been sleeping, and rubbed against Bejoy's leg. She picked him up, and he began to purr.

"This is Mittens." She held Mittens close. "He likes me best of all."

He certainly seemed to like her, and Kate saw why when Bejoy reached in her pocket and gave him a treat. "I am allowed," she said. "I get three treats a day to give Mitten. Now they are all gone."

She put the cat down. "He is not allowed inside because Mrs. Gervais is allergic to him, but he is warm enough, and there are mice to play with."

"You seem so happy here."

"I get happier every day."

Kate wondered how many people could say that. She

wondered how many people would even notice? This ability to monitor her own feelings and see them positively was one of Bejoy's talents, and Kate gave her a spontaneous hug in appreciation.

They went back to the house after Kate stopped by her car for a bag she'd brought with her. Bejoy, arm through hers, pulled her up the stairs toward her room. "This probably isn't the best day to get paint and start moving furniture, is it?" Kate asked.

"Wait till you see."

Bejoy pushed her door open and stood back. Kate stepped in first. Bejoy's room was now a lovely soft green with shiny white trim. Gauzy white curtains hung at the windows and a rug that had clashed with the Easter egg purple walls had been removed. The wood floor was lovely.

"It's beautiful," Kate said. "I love this color."

"Like your quilt."

"The Woven Paths quilt?"

Bejoy nodded. "The green squares."

"You have such a good memory for color."

"I remembered that green. I like it."

"Did somebody help you paint?"

"Mrs. Gervais took me to town, and we bought this color. Mr. Gervais made sure I did everything right, and he painted, too. Bob. . ." She smiled a little more widely. "Bob likes me. He helped, too."

Kate was intrigued. "Bob?"

"Bob is my friend." Bejoy looked delighted.

"Bob lives here?"

"Downstairs. He can play the ukelele. I want him to teach me."

"Will I meet Bob?"

"He is with his parents today. Maybe he will come back in time."

Kate noticed pictures on the walls, some they had brought from Bejoy's room in Florida and new ones, too. There was a bulletin board with notes pinned on it, including a work schedule for the house. In the middle was a funny picture drawn with colored pencils of a woman who looked like Bejoy. It was signed Bob.

"I love your room, Bejoy." Kate turned and gathered her sister close for a hug. "It's a wonderful room, and you've made it a home already. But there's one thing it needs." She held out the bag she had carried in. "This is for you."

"Good. I have something for you, too. We can trade." Bejoy took the bag, removed the brightly wrapped box and her eyes shone. "It's a real present!"

"Open it."

Bejoy tore through the wrappings quickly and shook out the Woven Paths quilt. She looked up at Kate. "I can keep it?"

"I worked on it until it was big enough for this bed. Then I machine quilted it. I had to quilt by machine so you would have it in time. It's the biggest quilt I've ever done, so it's not perfect. I finished it at the bee and some of the women helped, but it's sturdier and—"

Bejoy was holding the quilt to her chest. Kate felt tears prick her eyes. "You like it?"

"It's the most beautiful quilt in the whole world," Bejoy said.

"Our paths were woven together from the moment we were born," Kate said. She hoped Bejoy would understand that sentiment. "No matter where you live, we will always be together here." She touched her heart.

"I want to put it on my bed."

The two women draped the quilt over Bejoy's bed. Then

they stood back and examined it. The quilt added a joyful note to the serene green of the walls. Bejoy was clearly delighted.

"I have a present for you, too." She went to her closet, but Kate already knew what the present was.

"Are you sure?"

"You will love it most of all." Bejoy took down the pillow-case quilt from the top of her closet and held it out to Kate. Over the weeks in Virginia, the ducks had been joined by all manner of flowers and trees, by a sun and a moon, and by a rainbow-striped cat who was clearly smiling.

"That's Mittens," Bejoy said, pointing to the cat.

"I'll treasure this forever, Bejoy. I'm going to hang it on my wall."

"Bob wants one, too."

Kate was fairly certain her sister had a boyfriend. Kate was *more* than certain her sister had found the life she deserved.

The music stopped downstairs, and Bejoy took her hand. "There is cake. We have to sing. Come on."

"I love you," Kate said, holding her sister back a moment to kiss her cheek.

Bejoy smiled, but she didn't look surprised. "I know. We are both lucky."

For the first time in her life, Kate fully realized just how true that was and always had been. Bejoy had helped make Kate the woman she was. She had taught her compassion, patience, and tolerance. But along the way Kate had encouraged, nurtured, even challenged her sister, so that now, Bejoy could finally blossom into the woman she was meant to be.

Their paths had always been woven and always would be. They were sisters, twins, but best of all, friends.

She let Bejoy pull her out of the room. "So very, very lucky," she said softly, as she followed her sister downstairs for cake.

THE WOVEN PATHS QUILT

Woven Paths is another traditional quilt pattern. The Woven Paths blocks look difficult at first glance, but while there are a lot of pieces, each block is large, so you won't need to make too many, depending on what you plan to do with the finished quilt. Four twenty-four inch blocks would make a pretty wall hanging or baby quilt.

Are you interested in making your own quilt? You'll find patterns for all the traditional quilts in this story online. Just type the quilt pattern into your search engine and see what comes up. Or you might want to start with these two sites: allpeoplequilt.com and quilterscache.com, where lots of patterns are available.

Happy quilting!

CONTRARY WIFE

BY EMILIE RICHARDS

From the Shenandoah Album collection
Peaks and Valleys, Book 3

CHAPTER 1

Most of the time Cathy Adams enjoyed being president of the Shenandoah Community Church Bee. She had the job for as long as she was willing to show up, and she knew she was appreciated for doing it. Today, however, she was sorry she couldn't sit quietly at the frame in the corner, stabbing the simple charity quilt in progress with her trademark meandering stitches instead of making sure everything else was running smoothly. A few quilters were occupied at the frame now, waiting for the meeting to start. She envied them, and she was looking forward to relaxing once the business meeting was completed.

Peony Greenway looked up from the list of agenda items she was discussing with Cathy. She was older than Cathy's sixty-four, but probably by fewer than ten years. She was slender and petite with fine features and bright blue eyes behind rimless glasses. Cathy outweighed her by at least forty pounds, but they were a match for energy and determination.

"And in the bad news category," Peony said, "Helen took

the Peaks and Valleys quilt blocks to her house last week. You know she's making the top."

The Peaks and Valleys quilt was to be a fundraiser for the Shenandoah Community Church's prison ministry, and Helen was arguably their most experienced quilter, as well as the designer of the block that the quilt was based on. Members of the bee had created more than enough blocks from their best scraps for a queen size quilt to auction in the spring. The quilters had wrangled good-naturedly about whose blocks went where, but in the end, they had voted on their favorite design. Helen would make sure all blocks were perfectly square and sew them together exactly as specified. Soon they could stretch the top on to their frame. Dovey, another of their prize-winning quilters, was already working on a quilting design.

Cathy's own block had been relegated to an edge, which had not been a surprise. In fact she was delighted hers had been included. She knew she would never be a better than average quilt maker, and she didn't need to be more. She could play at quilting, as she hadn't been able to play at many things in her life. She could make mistakes, waste time, have fun.

Quilting was one of the many joys she'd found after she and her husband moved from their complicated life in Washington D.C. to the more relaxed pace of the Shenandoah Valley.

"I think Helen told me she'd have the top here for show-and-tell next week," Cathy said.

"Well, there might be a teensy problem..."

Cathy wasn't sure whether to ask for more information or to hope Peony didn't elaborate. She managed not to sigh. Peony was a fixer, the bee member most likely to step in and smooth troubled waters without making a fuss. She knew when to speak and when to stay silent.

This time she spoke. "Seems the box that the blocks were in fell when Helen was getting out of the car."

Cathy slapped her hand over her heart. "Fell?"

"Flipped and dropped, unfortunately. Anna took Helen home, and you know her car's low to the ground. I'm surprised Helen was able to get in and out at all. Helen swung her feet over the side, but she stumbled and the box fell. We should have fastened it with tape."

"I bet we won't make that mistake again." Cathy was trying not to imagine the scene. Helen lived out in the country on the farm where she had been raised, and if Cathy remembered correctly, the quilters had all left the church during a downpour last week. She tried not to think about mud, about carefully created quilt blocks being soaked and wrinkled and stained.

Peony continued. "Of course she and Anna scooped them up as fast as they could. But apparently they didn't go back into the box in quite the same order."

"Or quite the same condition?"

"Afraid not. Anna tells me she tried to help Helen figure out what went where, but Helen said washing them was more important and shooed her away."

"Was she able to salvage them?"

"I don't know. Anna tried calling, but Helen never answered."

A reliable young couple, the Claibornes, lived in the house with Helen, so Cathy knew the old woman was fine, but, as usual, she was probably being ornery. "Well, I guess we'll know when we see her today."

"If she'll tell us."

Cathy couldn't help but smile. Helen Henry was a hard woman to corral. If she didn't want to discuss what had happened, no one would be able to pry it out of her. "I'm sure Helen will make certain this turns out fine. She'll remake the blocks if she has to. She was probably going to remake half of them anyway because they were a fraction too small or not properly squared. And whatever placement she comes up with will be wonderful."

Peony smiled, too. "That kind of optimism is the reason you'll be president of the bee for life."

They finished their list and Cathy greeted members as they came in, although Helen was not among them.

She started the meeting with the usual officers' reports, then old and new business. Ten quilters showed off their latest projects to appropriate oohs and aahs. She was just starting a discussion about a new quilt they were planning when Cathy looked up and saw someone she had never expected to see in the Beehive.

Her husband.

She stared as Alford Adams III quietly took a seat in the back of the room. For a moment she wondered what emergency had brought him here, but he gave a brief wave, as if to encourage her to keep going. If someone had died or their house had collapsed, Alf would have come right up front and taken her by the arm. Alf wasn't shy, and he always knew exactly what to do—or thought he did.

Someone made a new suggestion, and Cathy used the ensuing discussion to ask Peony to moderate. She walked to the back, nodded toward the hallway, and Alf rose to follow.

Cathy had been married to Alf for thirty-five years. Years ago, on one of the many nights he'd been in another state on a business trip, she had done a rough calculation of all the nights he'd been away from home since they said, "I do." She had decided they should subtract at least seven years from their next anniversary. Still, no matter how she looked at it, she'd been married to this man for a long time. And as ridiculous as it sounded at her age, she always felt happier when he walked into a room.

"The house is still standing?" she asked. Two weeks ago, as their ongoing renovation was winding down, a contractor's assistant had mistakenly removed a load bearing wall without sufficiently bracing it. She and Alf had come home to a sagging ceiling. Now they had a better brace in place until a steel beam arrived, but she remained skeptical.

"The house is fine," he assured her. "Nobody's working today because the new beam goes in tomorrow."

Alf was tall, and if he no longer stood as straight as a Marine drill sergeant, he certainly didn't slump. He had gained weight over the years, especially now that they were eating every meal together, but he carried the extra pounds well. His brown hair was more than half gray, but he still had lots of it. His skin had been darkened by hours in the sun tending to the acreage he could only fantasize about when they'd lived in the city. His smile seemed even brighter against it.

Today he wore a tweed sport coat, a dress shirt fresh from the local dry cleaner, and neatly pressed khaki pants. No overalls for Alf. He was a gentleman farmer with an MBA from Wharton.

"So what on earth are you doing here?" she asked, after she closed the door to the Beehive behind her. "Have you decided to take up quilting?"

"I took the pickup to the garage for an oil change, and they found some problems. Remember I told you that's where I'd be? One of the mechanics dropped me here."

He probably had told her. She'd probably nodded without hearing a word. "What kind of problems?"

"The kind that take a couple of days and a lot of money."

"That's too bad. Unexpected, right?"

"The engine's been cutting off on me. Not that I go much of anywhere."

She pondered that. He wasn't complaining exactly, more

like stating the obvious. After racing through life at top speed, these days Alf meandered. Some mornings he seemed reluctant to get out of bed.

"How do you plan to get home?" she asked. "You can take the car. I'm sure someone here will give me a ride."

"I'm in no hurry. I'll wait until your meeting is over."

She tried to imagine Alf sitting through upcoming discussions of what items to make for the church Christmas bazaar, how many lap quilts were needed at a local nursing facility, and which instructors they wanted to bring in for workshops the following spring.

"I don't think so," she said.

"Why? How much longer will you be?"

"There's more to our meetings than business. After that's complete, everyone brings out their own projects or works on a quilt we're finishing together. We have lunch. Today some of the mothers with children at La Casa Amarilla made tamales for us. I'm usually here until sometime in the afternoon." La Casa Amarilla was an after-school program the church sponsored to assist and tutor Spanish speaking children in the community. Some of the moms were quilting with them now.

"I was hoping to take you to lunch."

Cathy had been about to repeat the suggestion that he take the car, but she fell silent, trying to remember the last time she and Alf had gone anywhere together, other than the grocery store.

"It's a pretty day. We could eat outside," he said, as if he sensed her reluctance.

She considered offering to go out for dinner instead. She considered being honest about how much she'd been looking forward to quilting with her friends. She was looking for ideas for a new quilt to make for their master bedroom, a project she now felt she could handle, and her friends would have advice.

As they'd settled into retirement, she had begun to stand up for herself–not that she'd ever really kowtowed to Alf. It was just that he'd been away so much that when he came home, she'd valued his advice.

But something was going on here. No matter how she counted the years of their marriage, there were many. She knew when this man had something on his mind.

"Can you amuse yourself until about noon?" she asked. "Weren't you planning to go to the hardware store?"

"I can do that."

She suggested a good place to pick up sandwiches and drinks, and he suggested they take them to the county park nearby. She told him where the car was and watched him disappear up the stairs to the parking lot.

Was Alf bored? Was he ill? Or was he simply using this opportunity to cross an obligation to Cathy off his list. He'd been a top-level executive for so many years that he always looked for ways to combine the things he needed to do. He was stuck in town, so why not take his wife to lunch, hit the hardware store and probably the lumberyard, all at the same time.

She didn't know what was going on, but she would find out that afternoon. If there was a problem, he would not waste time burying it. Alf never hesitated to say what must be said, and she never failed to listen. Together they always found a compromise both could live with. Today would be no different.

CHAPTER 2

Alf was at the curb by the time Cathy came out of the church lugging the canvas bag filled with supplies for the quilt squares she had planned to work on after the meeting. She hoped that whatever he had found for a picnic was at least as good as the green chili tamales and refried beans her friends were about to enjoy.

One deep breath of the crisp, fresh air and she let go of resentment. The day was perfect for enjoying the outdoors, low seventies, sun shining brightly on leaves that were such brilliant autumn colors she had to blink. She slid into the passenger seat and fastened her seat belt as Alf started away from the church.

"I had lots of choices for lunch, along with lots of time to make them," he said.

Since he was the one whose schedule had changed, she hoped he wasn't complaining that she'd stayed at the church too long. "Did you find cedar for the closets?"

He shook his head. "I didn't look."

That surprised her. Lining the closets was her husband's

latest project. "Are you thinking you'll need to pick it up in Northern Virginia somewhere?"

"I haven't decided."

Alf had learned woodworking at his father's knee, and he was both creative and skilled. His father, Alford Adams II–long on name but short on income–had been a cabinet maker by day and, unfortunately, a gambler by night. He'd taught Alf everything he knew, hoping, she suspected, that Alf would join him in the family business. But Alf had known better than to be tied to a man whose financial shenanigans had made his mother's life hell until she finally divorced him, taking her son with her. Alf's life had headed in a different direction, and he had never looked back.

When they'd decided to add space and charm to their valley home, which they had purchased for its setting and acreage, Alf had taken charge. He'd hired a contractor for the heavy work, but he had done all the finishing himself. They'd never been interested in creating a showplace, but now, near the end of the renovation, she suspected they had managed one anyway. The outside was attractive and welcoming, the inside open and spacious, and the kitchen, with cabinets and an island Alf had built from recycled barn wood, was a decorator's dream. Cooking with everything right at her fingertips was pure pleasure and part of the reason both she and Alf had gained too many pounds.

She wondered if he was delaying the closets because he expected to miss the renovations once everything else was finished. "Cedar closets certainly aren't an emergency," she said. "Maybe they'll be more fun when the contractor's guys clear out."

At the park they wound their way to an area near the picnic shelters. While Alf gathered their lunch, Cathy popped the trunk to retrieve the basket she kept there with picnic supplies, including the first quilt she'd ever made with all its mistakes in plain view. It was a mishmash of colorful scraps, her learner quilt–as Helen Henry called it. Now she was always prepared for a picnic, even though she and Alf had been on few since the renovations began.

"Let's spread the quilt under the trees," she suggested. "I don't think anybody will mind."

They chose a spot some distance away under a sugar maple turning scarlet, and Cathy spread the quilt.

"It won't be too many years before getting up and down won't be easy. We need to take advantage of this while we can." She lowered herself to the ground, and Alf did the same, sitting campfire style before he emptied his bags of deli sandwiches, bottles of fruit drinks, and a large bag of the local Route 11 Potato Chips in the dill pickle flavor they both liked best.

"Here's the best part." He held up a bag from Delectable Mountain, the new bakery in Woodstock. "Dessert. They have a great selection. I knew chocolate would make you happiest."

Cathy had been trying hard not to walk into the new bakery every time she went to town, but here were goodies right in front of her. Since she hadn't bought them, how could she be blamed?

"Funny you should mention the bakery," she said. "We're working on quilts for the children of the owners. Liza Smith's rental cabin burned to the ground not too long ago, and she and her little girl, Julie, were left with nothing. Meredith, her business partner, and her daughter already had plenty of that."

Alf popped the top off one of the drinks and held it out to her. "The old log cabin? That fire?"

"That's the one. Liza and Meredith are the ones adding calories to everybody's trips into town. They opened the bakery a few months before the fire. It's pretty clear that every extra cent they had between them went into the bakery."

"Where are they living now?"

"Liza and Julie stayed with a young woman from the church until the four of them could move into a brick ranch house outside of town. It's no showplace, but it's sturdy, and it has room for everyone. Members of the bee found extra linens and cookware and added a few pieces of furniture to help. Then we decided everyone deserves something pretty, something new, and most of all, something we could make lickety split. So that's what we've been working on."

"Sounds like they're lucky the quilters took them on."

Cathy had expected Alf's eyes to roll skyward by now, but he seemed interested enough. And since she rarely regaled him with tales of quilts or quilters, she hoped her luck would hold. "We're making Julie a rail fence–like the ones I made for Matt and Mark–but in shades of peach and lavender." Matt and Mark were their twin grandsons. "Diana, Meredith's daughter, gets a quilt in mint green and yellow. One of our members is quilting them at home by machine because children are notoriously hard on bed coverings."

Alf opened his own drink. "I remember Gabe and Laura jumping on their beds whenever they thought we weren't looking."

She smiled at the memory. Gabe and Laura, their children, probably didn't have time to jump on beds now, even if they wanted to. Growing up with a father who'd been home too rarely, they had decided not to enter the high speed rat race, but they still worked hard. Gabe taught kindergarten in a Rockville, Maryland magnet school and raised their very active twins with his wife, Frankie. Laura ran a food co-op in Charlottesville, Virginia, and she and her professor husband, Rob, were pregnant with their first child. Both families lived busy lives.

She finished her story. "Liza and Meredith are next in line, and I think we're going to surprise them both with Delectable Mountain quilts. Liza had an old one from her grandmother, but it was destroyed in the fire. That's where the name of their bakery comes from."

"It's nice of your quilt group to take on that project. Is that typical of other groups? Or just yours?"

She was mystified they were still discussing the bee. "Quilters think quilts make a difference. I'd guess it's pretty standard to reach out to people who need what we love to make. I bet almost every quilt group has community projects."

"Is that why you've stayed president?"

"One of the reasons." She waited, and when it was clear from his silence that he wanted to hear the others, she went on.

"I'm a better organizer than quilter. Comes from all those years of keeping things organized at home for you and the children and working at the same time. So this is my contribution. I knew the minute I picked up a needle and thread I was never going to be a prize-winning quilter. I've never been particularly adept with my hands. Remember the gingerbread houses the children and I made together? Long on enthusiasm, short on skill?"

"You made them every year anyway."

"I had to be good at everything else in my life, but at Christmas the kids and I could cut loose and just have fun. And quilting's like that now. I knew I would never be a star, so I can relax and have fun. And I do, the way you do with your woodworking. Only you're such a talented craftsman, I'm not sure anything less than perfect would satisfy you."

"Nothing is perfect."

193

She waited because something was going on here. It wasn't that Alf didn't usually hear what she said, he did. But he was listening now, and that was different. Listening, and from what she could tell, processing her words through some unknown filter.

When he didn't go on, she hazarded a guess. "Are you feeling at loose ends, Alf, because the renovations are nearly finished? Is that why you didn't look for cedar today? You're delaying the projects that are left, so you'll still have things to do next week or the next?"

He ignored her probing. "It sounds like you have a hobby for life. One you could pursue anywhere."

"I'd like to think so."

"I wonder why you didn't join a quilt group when we lived in the city. There must be groups all over the area. Good ones."

The answer seemed obvious, and she tamped down annoyance. "I was pretty busy, remember?"

"I'm talking about after the children moved away, and you had more free time."

"After I went to a few quilt shows, I thought about it. But every quilt looked blue ribbon quality to me. And I hated to be a novice with all those experts. That's foolish. I know that now. For every quilt they displayed, there were probably fifty that weren't hung in the show. But here in the Valley it was easier to try." She managed a smile. "Everything is easier here. Driving at the top of the list, right?"

"You don't miss D.C.?"

"When I get homesick, I drive in for a day. I did that a few times this summer, remember? I met Laura for lunch, and we spent the rest of the afternoon at the Smithsonian. I tried to get you to come with us, but you were too busy with the renovations." She inclined her head in question. "How about you?"

He began to unwrap his sandwich and didn't speak until he was done. "I was happy there."

"I'm not sure that's true."

His voice had an edge to it. "You know me better than I know myself?"

"Maybe you were happy living in the city, but Alf you were exhausted and stressed all the time. The doctor said those were major factors in your heart attack." She tried not to think about those first days, Alf in a hospital intensive care unit, she and the children wondering if he would survive.

"That's why you retired early," she continued. "That and the way things were changing. You saw a long road of stress and exhaustion ahead, and wisely, you got out."

"I got out to become a farmer. Something I have no aptitude for. Only I don't find doing things I'm not good at fun, the way you do."

"You used to fantasize about it. Sometimes I thought that's what kept you going."

"Whatever interest I had has disappeared."

Cathy sat up a little straighter, ignoring her sandwich. Alf's was unwrapped but he hadn't lifted it to his lips. "I know you weren't happy taking care of the goats, and the alpaca experiment was a bust. But you enjoy the garden, don't you? You're always out there puttering unless you're in your workshop."

"I'm out there because there's nothing better to do." He looked at her. "I grow ten times more than we need."

"That's good, though. It doesn't go to waste. We pass it on to Laura for the co-op."

He shook his head. "I would probably be perfectly happy with a few pots of herbs on a balcony and cash donations wherever they're needed. This isn't me, Cathy. I'm no farmer. I miss our old life. I miss going into an office and making things happen. I miss being in charge of things that matter."

"You miss being *Ford*." Ford, a nickname for Alford, was the name by which most of the world knew her husband. Then, at some point in his childhood, Gabe had nicknamed his father Alf, after the television alien. Cathy had never known exactly why, but she was afraid the nickname had come about because to Gabe, his father *was* an alien. He appeared out of nowhere, and then he was gone again.

The name had stuck. Alf was her husband's "family" name. He was Alf instead of Dad to their children, and he'd become Alf to her. Most of the time when Cathy introduced her husband to strangers, she introduced him as Ford, although since retirement, she'd found herself calling him Alf in public more and more.

"I miss being Ford," he admitted.

She reached over and covered his hand with hers. "What brought this on? Nearly finishing the renovations? Do you need a new project? I bet we can think of one."

"I got a phone call last week."

She nodded. "From?"

"Randy Banting, at Carrollton Consulting. I worked with him on a few projects back in the day. They're opening a new division, a center devoted to testing new technologies and capabilities, and they want somebody with experience to launch it. Eventually, I'd turn it over to–"

"You? *You'd* turn it over?"

"They want to hire me to get it off the ground."

Cathy withdrew her hand. "And you told them you're retired. Right? That you got out of the rat race to protect your health. You got out because the doctors told you if you didn't, they could almost guarantee another heart attack."

"My last checkup was great. New meds, the stent, my exercise routine. I'm fit again. I can handle whatever stress comes with the job."

"The doctor told you that? You asked him specifically? You haven't seen him lately."

"He said I was almost as good as new, that I don't need to baby myself."

"New for a sixty-four-year-old man, Alf. That doesn't mean a man your age, any man, can handle putting seventy hours a week into a startup, especially a man who has health issues."

"Most of my colleagues work well into their seventies. We didn't spend our lives learning to do what we do just to drop it at the first twinge."

"Twinge?"

"Okay, it was more than that. But I'm fine now, and I still have a lot to offer."

She was biting back angry words, which never worked with Alf. He was logical and rational, and strong emotion confounded him. She'd always felt that Alf's inability to deal with his own emotions–and everybody else's–had probably contributed to his heart attack.

"No one thinks you're washed up," she said when she had herself under control. "No one. Least of all me and our children."

"I told Randy I'd come in for an interview. I want to see what he's doing and what he has planned. I don't imagine I'd stay more than four or five years. By then I'd be ready to slow down."

"You haven't slowed down, Alf. You've just changed your emphasis. You've done wonderful things at the farm and with the house. But the only pressure there is from you. And that's the way it needs to stay. You need to work at your own pace, without flights here and there, late night dinners and conferences, weekends filled with paperwork and phone calls you didn't have time for at the office."

"I know my job put an unfair burden on you."

She didn't deny it. "We aren't talking about me at the moment."

"We need to, though. Because commuting to and from the Valley might be possible if I were younger, but this will be a time-consuming position. I need to be right in the city or just over the border in Maryland. Carrollton has offices in Rockville, too, so we'll need a place on the east side to cut down on the drive. We'll be closer to Gabe—"

"And farther from Laura and the new baby."

He shrugged, as if that couldn't be helped. "You need to think about the kind of living situation you'd like. A gated community? A modern condo complex? If we plan ahead so we end up somewhere near all the things you like to do, then that's what we can look for."

She was trying hard to interpret what he was saying, although anger was swamping reason. "You're talking about a place to stay during the week? And coming back here on weekends?"

He looked away. "That doesn't make sense."

She bit off her reply. "So—what—does?"

"I had a real estate agent give me a ballpark figure on what we can hope to sell the farm for. I'm afraid we'll have to sell to find a decent place in or near the city. It doesn't make sense to hang on out here and live too simply there. I was astonished at how much he thinks it's probably worth."

"Were you now?"

"All the renovations, the soaring cost of land? We're sitting on a pile of money."

"Odd that I never thought about our home that way."

He looked just a touch chagrined. "I know you've enjoyed your time here."

"So let me review, just for clarity." She took a deep breath. "I followed you throughout your career. We made three major moves and dragged two little children in and out of schools so you could climb the corporate ladder. I did most of the parenting because you were gone. I took a job in loss control for a major insurer to fill in my time and have something for myself. I did well, too, but I refused promotions that would have taken me away from home. Because somebody had to be there."

"Do we need the recap? I know our history."

She held up her hand to stop him from speaking. "All through this time, Alf, all you could talk about was buying a little hobby farm. That was your dream, and like everything else about you, I just accepted it. When that farm became a reality, I wasn't sure how I'd feel being out here. Toms Brook, Virginia, is not the center of the universe. I wasn't sure what was waiting for me. But little by little I discovered so much that was. The church. I love that little church and Sam Kinkade's ministry. I love the quilters and our time together. I love the projects we do and preparing for the quilt shows. I love the ease of driving everywhere, the gorgeous views, watching the seasons unfold without miles of buildings in the way."

"We can find some of those things when we move. We just need to make a list and see what we can do."

She stared at him for a long moment. Then she shook her head. "No."

"No, what?"

"No, we won't find those things when we move, or at least I won't. Because I'm not moving. I've made a home here, a home I love more every day. I'm going to stay here. I'm going to be buried here."

"And what about me? What about what I need?"

"Our marriage has been about your needs. Almost exclusively."

"I didn't hear many complaints."

"That's because in so many ways it was a good marriage."

His eyebrows were suddenly one straight line over eyes flashing with anger. "Nice of you to say so. But did it ever occur to you I worked that hard so I could provide for our family, save for retirement and send our kids to great universities?"

She went on as if he hadn't spoken. "I've been willing to accommodate you, even when I needed more of your time and attention than I was allowed to have. But I'm not accommodating you this time. If you need to move to D.C. to throw yourself back into the rat race, I see two choices."

"Two choices?" He tilted his head, as if he was hearing things.

She went on. "There may be more, but the two I see on short notice? You can rent a room or an efficiency near your office and come back to see me, when you find the time. However, you might prefer to be well and truly on your own. If that's the case, you can find a comfortable apartment and stay put, and I can probably buy your share of the farm. We have a healthy investment portfolio. I think my portion will be enough that I can stay right where I am. In the meantime, your new salary will fund your new life."

When he didn't answer, she leaned forward. "Is that logical enough for you? Let me know if you come up with alternatives I haven't had time to consider." She rose to her feet as gracefully as she could manage. "In the meantime, I'm taking the car back to the bee, along with dessert." She bent and scooped up the bakery bag. "Call the garage for a ride or try a taxi."

He got up, too. "This is unbelievably childish."

She started toward the car, but she paused and faced him just long enough to respond. "It's not childish, it's training. You'll need to fend for yourself in D.C., so you might as well start now. All these years I've done most of the fending. I've certainly done all the accommodating. That stops here and now. You just let me know what you decide, okay? Whenever you get around to it."

He didn't respond and she didn't care. She was halfway back to the bee before the tears began. Resolutely she kept driving.

CHAPTER 3

Molly Lovell was a whiz with beans, although that was a dubious attribute. She would prefer baking something–anything–rather than preparing more dried beans. But beans had to be the priority.

Zach, her husband, never complained when dinner was put in front of him, even when beans were on the menu four nights out of seven. No one understood better how important it was to stretch pennies. Both he and Molly worked hard, but their jobs were low wage, and now there was a new Lovell on the way.

Out of nowhere the baby kicked so hard that Molly gasped, stepping back from the counter to rest her hand over her rapidly expanding abdomen. Her legs ached and exhaustion threatened to claim her, but she told herself all was well. The baby needed good food to thrive, and she was preparing it for supper that night. She was grateful that beans were healthy, and she could serve them with whatever fresh vegetables were linked to her rewards card at the local Food Lion. Sometimes, if she got to the store right after the day's produce had been culled, she even found discounted vegetables that were fresh enough to last until they appeared on her dinner table.

She and Zach weren't going hungry, and that was what really mattered. She'd made cornbread last night in their toaster oven, and yesterday after work, she'd found ham hocks on sale. Right now the biggest of the two was flavoring the beans in her slow cooker, along with garlic and onions. Beans were best cooked slow and steady, so that's what she was doing, and she had plenty of hot sauce on hand.

They were going to be all right.

Weren't they?

She pushed the little voice away. Too tired to stand any longer, she gave in and crossed the room the necessary steps to the recliner, falling into it and pushing it back until her feet were elevated. She had already cleaned one house that morning, and in a few minutes the owner of the cleaning service would stop by to collect her for their next job. Zach had left before dawn and with luck, his continued absence meant a full day's wages. He labored as a construction apprentice, but while his boss tried to find work, any kind of work, for his crew, everyone was suffering at the economy's whim. If Zach worked a full day today, that meant enough money to pay this month's rent on their old mobile home, along with gas for their car.

They were going to be all right.

Weren't they?

She rubbed her belly, and this time the question stayed with her. Zach refused to take help from any person, any source. She understood pride, but his worried her. Her husband didn't expect help because he'd been given so little in his life. Zach didn't understand that most people took the help they had received from birth as their due. They'd had parents who routinely took them to doctors and dentists and bought books and school supplies. Teachers who took a student's home life into consideration and offered help when needed. Grandparents who started savings accounts for college or vocational school. Friends who pitched in, and churches that reached out to give comfort and support in the name of whatever God they worshiped.

Zach couldn't see that. His mother had struggled to give him a good start, but what he remembered was how much she had suffered for it. In Zach's eyes helping was dangerous and accepting help unthinkable. Molly was still mystified that a young man so badly treated had accepted her love when he accepted nothing else from anyone.

She was grateful, though, because Zach was the finest man she knew, even if he was also the most stubborn. They might be young, but she would love Zach until the day she died.

The door opened, and the man she'd been thinking about stepped inside carrying a grocery bag. She didn't have time to get up. He took one look at her and shook his head when she pushed the recliner forward.

"You're working too hard, Moll. I told you not to take that second job today. Stay home and stay off your feet." He held out his hand to stop her from standing. "I mean it. Don't get up. How about some cold water? I got fresh bottles on the way to my next job."

The rusty water that issued from the kitchen tap wasn't safe to drink or cook with. Molly filled up gallon jugs at the closest service station, but fresh bottled spring water sounded heavenly. He fished in the bag and held up a bottle. When she nodded gratefully, he twisted the cap and handed it to her.

She sent him a smile of gratitude mixed with relief that he had more work to do that day. "I'm just resting until it's time to leave again. It's natural to get tired when you're going to have a baby. And the lady I cleaned for treated me to a glass of iced tea. She's a real sweetheart."

"She probably felt guilty she was making you work when you look like that."

She gave him her most come-hither look. "I think I look pretty amazing. You don't?"

He couldn't help but smile. "Always."

"I got supper started so I won't have to do anything when I get back from the church this afternoon."

"I thought I smelled something good."

She said a short prayer of gratitude. He'd already eaten beans three times that week without complaint. "Ham with beans tonight, and leftover cornbread. Plus a little something for dessert, too."

"I don't know how you can bake anything in that garage sale toaster oven."

"Where there's a will there's a way." For Molly baking was no struggle, not even under these conditions. The toaster oven was roomy and wide, and she could bake a pie or a cake–if she baked the layers separately. Flour and sugar were cheap, and a farmer up the road saved discolored or smaller eggs for her at a better price. She bought extras like nuts and chocolate chips when she could afford to, and in the fall, she had plucked and stored apples from a nearby vacant lot.

Zach was watching her, as if to make sure she drank the whole bottle and didn't get up. "You're cleaning at the church? You're not going to be up on any ladders?"

"No, it's easy stuff. Their sexton needed time to do an annual deep cleaning."

"I still don't like you taking extra jobs."

"The money will help a lot."

He didn't look convinced. "Reverend Sam came by my job site yesterday."

The Reverend Sam Kinkade was the man who had put in a good word--or a hundred--with Zach's boss and asked him to take Zach on. His church, where Molly would be cleaning that afternoon, sponsored a prison ministry, and somehow Zach had come to the reverend's attention. In Molly's opinion, the reverend and his church were the real deal. The church's prison ministry had already made a difference in the Lovell's lives.

Of course, Zach was suspicious of goodwill and still unhappy he'd had to accept even that much help, although Sam had explained that a job interview wasn't charity. The job needed doing by somebody. Why not him?

Molly sipped the cold spring water and thought it tasted better than any soft drink. "What was he doing at the job site?"

Zach didn't look happy. "Checking up on me, most likely."

"Zach, if he was, it was in a good way."

"He was asking too many questions about the trailer park. Like whether our trailer was going to be warm enough this winter for the baby, and if the landlord ever fixed our water supply. He said he's heard rumors somebody wants to buy this property and build a storage facility, and maybe we ought to be looking for another place."

Molly didn't know what to say. The baby was due in February. Housing wasn't easy to find, especially anything they could afford.

"Did he have any suggestions?" she asked, after a pause.

"I didn't ask. We don't need more help. We can do this on our own."

With that he turned to leave. She bit her lip. She wanted to tell him not to be so stubborn. If a better place was available, why shouldn't Sam tell them about it?

She and Zach hadn't been married a long time, but she had learned to pick her battles. This would not be the end of the discussion. But it was the end of it until she could find out what Reverend Sam had in mind.

"I bet dessert is apple dumplings," Zach said, right before he closed the door behind him.

She smiled and silently, she planned.

CHAPTER 4

The well-meaning service manager from Alf's garage was a middle-aged woman who told him all about her children and grandchildren as she drove him to the farm. By the time she dropped him off in the driveway, he also had recommendations for which local politicians to support, which Valley restaurants to frequent, and which movies to watch on television that week.

He shifted the quilt and picnic supplies under one arm and raised his hand in farewell as she drove away, grateful he no longer had to listen to her helpful suggestions–along with the details of her neighbor's gall bladder surgery.

He still wasn't used to the chattiness of people in the Valley. A trip to the barber or hardware store meant lengthy conversations about the weather and the state of the union, not to mention a blow by blow of the latest high school football game.

At first he'd been suspicious of the casual goodwill of his neighbors. Before his own garden flourished, they'd received baskets with fresh vegetables, invitations to social events, and the inevitable suggestions that he and Cathy visit every church within a twenty-mile radius. Many of the people he'd met were transplants from big cities. But they, too, had absorbed local customs quickly and were every bit as friendly. He sometimes wondered if there was something in the Valley air.

After the service manager disappeared from sight, Alf started toward the house, which sat in the middle of six rolling acres. The exterior of the Cape Cod was finished now. They had replaced aluminum siding with pale gray cedar shingles, added dark red shutters with cutout stars, and window boxes that bloomed with bright yellow chrysanthemums and winter pansies. The trim around the windows was white, which accented the gables and a new darker gray roof. Usually the front door stood open, and the custom screen door with the same decorative stars welcomed the breeze. Now the house looked deserted. Lonely.

He and Cathy had never gotten around to finding a dog. They'd discussed it, researched breeds, and tried to figure out what qualities they wanted. A working dog with boundless energy? A yappy little house dog? A dog that needed them or one that didn't? Now he was glad they'd never agreed. Whatever happened in the future, a dog would be a complication.

Merrill the Peril was going to be a problem, though. Merrill was the only remaining resident of the Adams's chicken coop, a Polish rooster with attitude. The rooster was black with a wild black and white crest that was lush and flashy enough for a Mardi Gras parade. His comb was bright red, and his maniac eyes were circles of amber. Polish chickens were so exotically beautiful they were mainly raised for show, and Alf would never have chosen the breed. Instead he'd chosen chickens that laid well, and for a while, he and Cathy had collected more eggs than their cholesterol levels would tolerate.

Then in two separate nightly raids, a fox had accomplished

what Alf couldn't. He'd been so upset at the slaughter of his chickens that he'd closed the coop.

As it turned out, closing had been premature. One of the contractor's helpers had mentioned that his chickens were attacking a rooster he'd won at a show. The young man, thin as a broomstick and strong as a bodybuilder, had sounded genuinely sad.

"Likely the rest of the flock's just jealous, because it's the craziest looking thing you ever saw. But to them, this rooster's different, so they're going to peck it to death. Guess I'll have to wring his neck, although I hear there's not enough meat on the breed to make that worthwhile."

Alf, who understood only too well how it felt to be the odd man out, had paid the worker to bring the rooster along on his next trip to the farm. At first introduction Merrill had sensed his reprieve, and since that day, he'd paid Alf back with poultry affection.

Polish chickens got lonely, so during the day, Merrill followed Alf around the garden searching for pests and promptly disposing of them to earn his keep. Sometimes when Cathy was elsewhere, Merrill followed Alf around their house, too—their little secret. Frequently the rooster vocalized in response to Alf's muttered remarks, as if he and Alf were carrying on a conversation.

Unfortunately, Merrill loved Alf, but he'd never warmed up to Cathy. Merrill didn't converse with her, and he didn't like it when she held him or combed his crest. He was more likely to peck her and screech. In her opinion the rooster wanted Alf all to himself. Alf thought she might be right.

So here he was, worrying about what to do with a rooster, when his marriage was in jeopardy.

He couldn't believe Cathy had meant anything she'd said

today. But then he hadn't believed she would leave him at the park to find his own way home, either. He'd expected her to be a little upset, after all they'd worked hard to renovate this house, and they hadn't even had time to enjoy the finished product. There was no chance they'd find another like it. A house as nice as theirs would cost three times as much anywhere close to the Capital, never mind the acreage surrounding it.

Still, he had expected her to realize that moving back to the city would offer more stimulation and opportunity. And hadn't he pointed out that there were quilt groups everywhere? He had foolishly assumed she would at least think over his new plan, maybe offer to discuss it again when she'd had time to get used to the idea.

He hadn't expected an ultimatum. He knew his wife well. Cathy considered. Cathy compromised. Cathy made the best of whatever hand she was dealt.

He grimaced at that last thought, embarrassed. They were adults with enough income to make a variety of choices. She should not be forced to make the best of *his* decisions.

He'd just expected her to understand.

After he deposited the quilt and picnic supplies at the kitchen door, he veered off to visit the chicken coop, which was one of several outbuildings. The structure built of weathered boards reinforced with stone, had stood in that spot for half a century, probably rebuilt several times but firmly planted in Shenandoah Valley earth. He'd planned to build another on the other side of the house, a miniature version of their home, with the same shingles and color scheme for Merrill. He'd started plans for a greenhouse where the coop stood now, so he could grow citrus fruit in the winter and nurture flowers and plants for his garden.

In addition to a dilapidated barn at the property's edge and a shed, the homestead, the original residence on the property, stood on the other side of a small orchard of fruit trees that Alf had hoped to revive. The homestead, part frame, part natural bluestone, had been abandoned for more than a decade. The wiring and plumbing were adequate, and most of the windows still opened, but the kitchen belonged in a museum, and Alf had hauled away the stove when he discovered that mice had set up rodent condominiums inside.

Renovating the homestead for guests was on Alf's list. He knew exactly what needed to be done to the old house and where a playhouse for his grandchildren should go. He'd hoped a playhouse would help him relate to them, maybe give them something to talk about.

His own children had grown up quickly, and he had missed a lot. Eventually Gabe and Laura had found lives that only rarely included him. He'd hoped for better with the boys and with the baby who was on its way. But somehow, he'd lost the knack for childhood conversation.

Or maybe he'd never had it in the first place.

At the coop he whistled to let Merrill know he was coming, because the rooster appreciated a warning. When he opened the door, Merrill came right up to greet him. Alf picked him up, and the rooster snuggled under his arm. They walked that way with Merrill making noises, as if he was glad to see Alf. They were almost to the kitchen door when Alf's cell phone buzzed. He set Merrill on the ground to peck at clumps of dirt and pulled it from his pocket.

Five minutes into the call he made himself comfortable on the stoop. Ten minutes later he said goodbye and hung up.

He had a meeting with the board of Carrollton Consulting on Monday. Actually, it was more than a meeting. It was the first day of a three-day intensive round of observation, questions and, at the end, interviews with everyone who had a say in hiring him. To launch the event, he was scheduled for an early dinner with the board on Sunday night in the cozy Garden Room at the historic 1789 restaurant in Georgetown.

The sun shone warm against his shoulders, and at his feet the rooster made happy noises as he found things worth pecking. From the stoop he could see the remnants of his garden, pumpkins glowing between the rows, dried cornstalks waltzing in a light breeze. In the spring he'd planted the pumpkins with Matt and Mark, one of the few times he'd come up with a project they could enjoy together. Looking at them he remembered that the boys were coming Sunday afternoon to make jack-o'-lanterns. Cathy had bought stencils in case they wanted to use them, but Alf suspected they would rather hack away with the safest knives Cathy could find—along with intense supervision. An outdoor barbecue was planned, and Cathy already had the menu in mind.

With that last came another realization.

He wouldn't be here.

If traffic was light, he could drive to the city in an hour and a half, but he would have to leave earlier to be safe. When he got there, he would check into the hotel where Randy Banting, Carrollton's CEO, planned to leave a notebook of information for Alf to look over Sunday afternoon.

Randy had admitted there was dissension in the ranks, but he was confident that Ford would know how to bring everyone together.

"Ford" knew he had a reputation for doing exactly that. As a CEO himself, he'd worked hard to make sure people could work side by side, despite differing opinions. But "Alf," the man with a rooster pecking the ground at his feet, had to admit that in the Adams family, Cathy had always been the one to bring them together, to smooth out difficulties and find common ground.

Today she'd shown no signs of smoothing anything. She had declared war, and she would use his absence on Sunday, and missing an activity the boys had been looking forward to for weeks, as ammunition.

As much as he wanted to, he couldn't blame her.

CHAPTER 5

Cathy's burst of righteous fury took her all the way back to church. But by the time she opened the door to rejoin the bee, she was picturing her husband scrambling to find a ride home. She hoped his cell phone worked in the park. In all their years together, she couldn't think of a single thing she'd done that was so spiteful.

Of course, in all those years, he hadn't set their world spinning out of control, either.

She headed for the nearest ladies' room to throw cold water on her face and collect herself, but the door was propped open and a young woman—a *pregnant* woman—was stooped over in the doorway.

Cathy rushed forward. "Are you okay? Do I need to call somebody?"

The woman straightened. "I'm fine." She looked puzzled, then she understood and gave a shy smile. "I'm sorry, did you think I'd gone into labor?"

"I..." Cathy shook her head. "I wasn't sure, but I was afraid maybe."

"Luckily that won't happen for months. I'm just cleaning today. But if you need to get in here, I'll move my mop bucket."

Now Cathy saw the bucket and the mop, and a small cart filled with cleaning supplies. She felt foolish. "No, I'm fine. There's another rest room in the basement. Are you new here?"

"Just temporary. My boss and I are doing some basics today to free up the sexton."

Cathy held out her hand. "Cathy Adams. I'm one of the quilters who meet downstairs."

The young woman took it without hesitation. "Molly Lovell. So that's what all those ladies are doing down there. I wondered."

Cathy wished she could invite the young woman to join them. She liked her on sight. Her shy smile. Her poise. And obviously her willingness to work. "We have all kinds of quilters. Beginners. Experts. Old and young. If you have time, come see what we're doing."

"Oh, I love quilts. My grandmother made me a wedding quilt." A shadow passed over her face.

Without thinking, Cathy asked, "She's gone?"

"Yes, she is."

"I'm sorry. I'm glad you have her quilt."

"I don't." Molly looked surprised that she'd answered out loud. "I mean, I should. But, well, it's complicated. When I left my parents' house, I couldn't bring it with me. But I have a photo."

Cathy couldn't imagine what was behind the story, but she nodded sympathetically. "I'm glad you have that."

Molly lifted the mop out of the bucket. "It was nice to meet you. We come to church here sometimes. Maybe I'll see you again."

"I'll look forward to it." Cathy realized she meant it.

PEONY GREENWAY SAT NEXT to Cathy and demonstrated how to turn the tip of a donkey's ear so that the point would be smooth and completely hidden. "Points are always the hardest part. Use the tip of your needle to swipe this little bit under, take a stitch and do it again." She sat back and returned the block to Cathy. "I hope that made sense."

"Sense has little to do with it. My fingers are all thumbs today." Cathy took the block and held it closer so she could admire Peony's invisible stitches.

"It's an adorable pattern," Peony said. "Your new grandbaby will love having this quilt hanging over the crib."

Twelve assorted farm creatures pieced from bright colors peeked from windows with a background of light gray wood grain, like the wood in their old barn milled from chestnut logs. Cathy was learning different methods of applique, which involved creating a picture out of fabric and sewing it to a background block. Today she was experimenting with needle turn, which was the simplest to prepare but not simple to do well. She worked on the blocks in the evening while she listened to books or watched television. So far she had finished nine. She had chosen the pattern and fabric because she wanted her new grandchild to think of their grandparent's farm when they were older and looked at the quilt.

The farm that Alf wanted to sell.

"Now you try," Peony said. When she didn't move, Peony shook her head. "Or not." She lowered her voice. "Do you want to tell me what's bothering you? Or shall we pretend nothing is?"

Cathy dropped the block into her lap. Several women were working on a quilt in the corner, and more were across the room learning how to do redwork embroidery. Nobody was listening.

"I hate to bend your ear." She looked at Peony, whose expression made it clear she really didn't mind. After a deep breath she launched in, keeping her explanation short and sweet, although she didn't recount how she had responded to Alf's news.

Peony sat back when Cathy had finished. "Well, probably not the best lunch date you've ever had."

"Not much of a lunch at all. I didn't even take a bite of my sandwich and by the time I got back here, all the tamales were gone." With no alternative Cathy had dined on the chocolate cappuccino cupcakes, both hers and Alf's, from Delectable Mountain.

She didn't feel the least bit guilty.

"So those were his choices? A modern condo or a gated community on the other side of D.C.?"

"He was kind enough to say that we can try to move close to the things I like to do. It's clear he's hoping I'll check out quilt groups and choose a location near one that sounds promising. You know, just trade this one with all my friends for another."

Peony flinched. "I see."

"Wait, I didn't tell you my response. I gave him two choices. He can find a little place to stay in the city without me and come home to the Valley if he ever has the time. Or he can make the move his permanent home, and I'll buy out his share of the farm."

"This is not good."

That was exactly the kind of understated response Cathy had known she would receive, which was why she'd trusted Peony with the story. Peony was sympathetic, but she was also content to let Cathy sort things without her input.

"I can't believe I said those things to him," Cathy said after a long moment.

"Are you sorry you did?"

Cathy considered. "No, those really are his choices. I'm not leaving here. I'm not following Alf again. My life is in the Valley now. My grandsons love coming to our farm, my daughter and her family are just over the mountains so I can see the new baby frequently. If Alf wants to be part of that life, he knows where I live."

"What do you think he'll do?"

Cathy had lived with Alford Adams for thirty-five years, but this time she couldn't predict his response. She shrugged.

Peony wound thread around a spool before she looked up. "He does have a third choice. He can forget the job and stay here with you. The question is whether you could live with his resentment."

"No good choices, are there?"

"There probably are. They just aren't clear. And with so many variables, it's impossible to move forward until you know all of them."

"That's one thing I'm pretty sure of. I'm not the one moving anywhere, not forward or backward, so none of the choices are mine. I've made my choice and it's firm. From this point on it's up to him. I will watch and wait and deal with the aftermath." Cathy gave a ragged sigh. "You know what really confounds me?"

"That this took you by surprise?"

Cathy really had chosen the right person to talk to. "You're very wise."

"You didn't know he was homesick for the life he used to lead?"

"Alf keeps everything inside, but that life almost killed him. He doesn't seem to remember how exhausted and stressed he was. Now he's just starting to establish a real relationship with his grandsons and forge new ties with his children. I thought he was fulfilled puttering around the house and garden, planning new projects. Now he's willing to let that go for a job that's going to suck him dry."

"What did he get out of his old life that he's not getting now?"

Cathy mulled the possibilities. "I'm really not sure. Attention? Respect? Intellectual challenge?"

Peony rested her hand on Cathy's knee for just a moment. "I think the answer to that question is probably the most important part."

"You could have been a marriage counselor."

"I successfully avoided anything to do with marriage for a very long time. At one time, I was very proud of that."

Cathy wanted to ask more, but one of the women at the quilt frame called Peony's name, and she stood.

"I promised I would take my turn quilting. Just remember, I'm here whenever you need to talk." She smiled, patted Cathy's shoulder, and started to cross the room to the frame. She'd only taken a couple of steps before she turned. "I just thought of something. Are you still looking for another project? That queen size quilt for your bedroom?"

After the renovations to the master suite, Alf had painted their bedroom a soft gray-green. Cathy had seen the change as an opportunity to create a new quilt to be the room's focal point, but she hadn't been able to find exactly what she wanted, despite poring over years of quilt magazines that Peony and others had loaned her.

"When I finish piecing the baby quilt," she said, "I'd like to start on the bed quilt, if I can find a pattern I like by then."

"I may have the perfect one for you."

Cathy tilted her head in question.

"I'll bring it to the next Bee."

"Is it a traditional pattern?" Peony was the unofficial quilt historian of the group, and she favored quilts women had made for decades or even centuries.

Peony looked pleased with herself. "Traditional enough. It's a pattern from the Kansas City Star. 1940s, I think. You'll like it." She paused for effect. "It's called Contrary Wife."

CHAPTER 6

Alf admired the way Cathy always stated her opinion and then moved on. In all the years they had been married she had rarely, if ever, nagged or repeated herself. She listened. Then she made sure her opinion was understood. And that was that.

In the days since the aborted picnic, she had refused to consider moving, but she had remained polite, if distant. They had both stayed busy during the day, then eaten dinner in front of the television news. But there had been no banter between stories, and after the broadcast, she had retreated upstairs to her sewing room, the smallest room in the house. At bedtime she slid between the sheets, said goodnight, and turned away from him.

He had tried just once to bring up the move again. He'd pointed out that they didn't have to decide on anything quickly, that she could look at real estate on trips into the city to be with him. They could wait until she had found exactly the right situation. She had listened and nodded.

"I have exactly the right situation," she'd said when he

finished. "I'm not willing to give it up so you can work too hard again. And I'm not willing to make another move and settle for whatever bits of you are left at the end of your days or weeks. I'm going to stay here. You have to decide how best to manage your own life."

"So you're threatening me with divorce if I don't do what you want?"

She hadn't raised her voice. "No, I'm telling you I won't move again. I think you understand the difference."

Now it was Sunday and Gabe, Frankie and the boys would be here soon for pumpkin gathering and carving. Alf should already be halfway to the city, but before announcing his change of plans to Cathy, he'd come up with a compromise. He had decided to give up just a bit of afternoon preparation at the hotel so he could be with his grandsons when they picked out their pumpkins. He had wanted to point out his sacrifice and show Cathy that he could be flexible for important family events, but he was giving up so little she wouldn't have noticed the difference.

When he came out of the house with his overnight bag, he found Cathy setting up a pumpkin carving station on a folding table in front of the house. She had politely agreed to drive the newly repaired pickup while he was away, so he slung the bag into the back of their car before he turned.

"What's on the barbecue menu tonight?"

"I have ribs in the slow cooker to finish on the grill. Frankie and Gabe are bringing salads, and I've already fixed baked beans. Dessert from Delectable Mountain."

His mouth watered. He would be eating at one of Georgetown's finest restaurants, but he probably wouldn't have time between questions to swallow more than a mouthful or two.

"Send me photos of the jack o'lanterns," he said.

"I'm sure Gabe will be taking lots of photos. I'll ask him to send them on."

"We had fun planting those pumpkins. The boys may be twins, but they approach everything differently. Mark measured the distance between seeds and Matt just threw his on the hill and stomped them in wherever they fell."

"Their jack o'lanterns will be different, too. Gabe and Frankie encourage them to follow their own paths."

"They're good parents."

"Laura and Rob will be, too."

Alf was still puzzled that neither of his children had pursued high-powered careers, but he hadn't wanted to look at their decisions too closely. They were intelligent and competent enough to do whatever they chose, but they seemed perfectly happy with their choices. When they were heading for college, he had offered to help them procure summer jobs at Fortune 500 companies with an eye to future employment, but Gabe had chosen to major in education, and Laura had studied community nutrition. By themselves both had gone on to find jobs in their chosen fields.

"I'm sorry Laura and Rob couldn't come today," Cathy continued. "But I'm planning to see her on Tuesday. She has the day off, and we're going shopping for the baby. I'll probably spend the night and take them out to dinner."

"I won't be back until Thursday. Will you be sure Merrill is inside the coop before you go?"

"I'll do my best."

"He'll be lonely."

"Can't be helped." She didn't add that she might be lonely, too, and Alf certainly wasn't going to open that particular door.

Silence extended until Gabe's small SUV turned into the driveway, and

Alf and Cathy started forward to greet them. When the car stopped, the twins jumped out as soon as they could unhook their seat belts. Now that they were seven, they had graduated from car seats to boosters and knew how to fasten themselves in place. They were identical, with shiny brown hair like Gabe's, along with their blond mother's blue eyes, but no one in the family had trouble telling them apart.

"Can we see the pumpkins?" Mark didn't wait for an answer, he streaked toward the vegetable garden with Matt in hot pursuit. Frankie and Cathy were already toting containers toward the house, and Alf was left with his son to walk sedately toward the garden.

"They haven't talked about anything else all week," Gabe said.

Gabe was tall, with his father's ski slope nose and jutting chin. In personality, though, he was more like Cathy, calm, measured in his responses, and able to express his feelings—something he hadn't learned from Alf.

Alf knew it was time to make his announcement. "I'll help them pick pumpkins, but then I have to leave. Will you mind the grill? Your mother precooked the ribs."

"You aren't staying for the barbecue? Is everything okay?"

Alf told him about the new job and that night's get-acquainted dinner in Georgetown. He finished quickly. "It's an opportunity I can't pass up."

Gabe was silent too long. When he spoke he sounded distant. "Of course you can't."

Alf wanted to take his son's words as affirmation. He wanted to believe Gabe understand his desire to be back in the maelstrom of corporate America. But even though he wasn't good at expressing his own feelings, for the most part, he did understand other people's.

He tried to explain. "I've missed working, making decisions

and watching my projects turn out well. I've missed being in the thick of things. And if I had to design a job I could do and do well, this would be the one. They came to me."

"That's flattering, I bet."

"It's not about my ego, but I'm glad I'm still remembered."

"And this?" Gabe swept his hand in front of him. "You're giving up the farm?"

Alf didn't want to involve his children in his marital problems, but he knew he had to say something. "No decisions have been made. Your mom doesn't want to leave the Valley. We're at something of a standoff. But we'll work it out."

"What kind of standoff?"

"Nothing to worry about."

"I'll make a wild guess. She's finally put her foot down and refused to move with you."

Alf stopped. "Why would you say that?"

"Because I've watched her put your career choices first for years. Forever, actually. But she's happy here. She's made a good life for herself. And I'm guessing she finally decided her needs matter. So if she stays, what are you going to do?"

"I don't think this is something we ought to be discussing."

"To be honest, I'm not surprised."

"What does that mean?"

"Work was your life. Without it? Who are you? Do you know? If you go back to working sixty hours a week, you won't have the time to ask yourself inconvenient questions, will you, Dad?"

"Work was not my life."

"Then you fooled the rest of us." Gabe turned so he and Alf were almost face to face. "But you're right, this is between you and Mom. I'll find a way to explain to the boys how busy you are. And I'm sure you'll make whatever time you can for them and for Laura's new baby."

Alf knew some kind of apology was needed, and reassurance, too. "I'm sorry to miss the pumpkin carving, but I'll do everything I can not to disappoint the boys again. This opportunity came up suddenly, and I couldn't reschedule tonight's dinner."

Gabe searched his face. Then he shrugged. "You know what? Eventually they won't be disappointed. They'll know what to expect, and while they're still little boys, they'll be grateful for every bit of attention you give them. Kids are like that. And you? Maybe you can squeeze in enough time with them to be happy. I guess you won't know if that will satisfy anybody until you try."

He turned and started toward the vegetable garden where the boys were already laying claim to their favorite pumpkins. Alf didn't even try to keep up.

CHAPTER 7

Molly was reaching the point of no return on living in their trailer. She knew the more appropriate term was mobile home, but there was nothing homey about this one. She'd seen more spacious models in campgrounds, and every day she found something new to worry about. This morning's problem was the hot water tank, located in their bedroom closet, and it seemed to be leaking. Zach had called their landlord, but the old man had insisted that with the weather turning cooler, the water heater was probably just sweating. The fact Zach had been able to talk to Mr. Gibson at all was surprising, since usually, he didn't bother answering calls. From what she knew, he and Zach had talked for a while, and whatever else was said remained a mystery. She doubted any of it was good news.

Before leaving that morning, she had removed everything from the closet floor and set it on the bed. She hoped the heater didn't burst while they were gone.

Today she was going to talk to Reverend Sam and find out if there really were better housing alternatives than the trailer. Even if water was lapping at their ankles when she went into labor, her husband wouldn't ask for help. Zach had to be dragged to church, and they never stayed long enough after a service to speak to anyone. But Reverend Sam had been so kind the day she cleaned the church, interested in how she and Zach were doing and clearly available to help if needed.

Her husband wanted the best for them, but she suspected he was scouting for alternatives on his own. Unfortunately the Lovells wouldn't look good to a potential landlord. Neither of them had job security, and once the baby was born, Molly would be out of the job market for the foreseeable future. She hoped to find work on nights when Zach was sure to be home, but so far nothing had materialized.

Today she had called the church twice from a client's house, but Reverend Sam hadn't been in. She'd been reluctant to leave her name and phone number in case Zach was at home when the minister returned the call. She wasn't going to lie, but she wanted that conversation out of the way before she talked to her husband.

Right now she was at the grocery store trying to choose between cans of tomatoes or a jar of olives to use up the little that was left of their grocery money. Normally she wouldn't even have looked at olives—one of her favorite foods—but these were marked down because the "best by" date had almost arrived. Tomatoes were practical, but oh, the glamour of olives perched on top of a salad made from the lettuce already in her cart.

She was still trying to decide between good sense and fantasy when somebody came up to stand beside her.

"Molly?"

She turned and found Reverend Sam staring at the canned goods, too. She couldn't believe her luck.

"Yes." She turned her best smile on him. "Molly Lovell. Zach's wife."

"He's a fine young man."

Tears sprang to her eyes. "He has every reason *not* to be."

He nodded gravely. "I had an uncle who grew a garden on a mountain side. Nothing there but rocks, but he said that the plants that didn't know better and fought their way toward the sun bore the best fruit."

"Although at least half his seeds probably gave up without trying," Molly said.

"More, I'd guess. Which is why Zach is worth fighting for."

She felt comfortable enough after that introduction to tell him that she'd been calling. He listened as she explained, ending the story with the leaking water heater.

"My secretary told me about the calls. I had a feeling they might have been from you. I saw you come in here to shop, so I thought I'd check."

"I guess you don't really need olives." She managed a sad little laugh.

"I think maybe you do."

"You're right." Molly reached for the jar and tucked it into her cart. "I need canned tomatoes, too, but they'll be here next time."

Sam lifted his hand into the air, as if he just thought of something. "Tomatoes. Do you need some? There's a woman in the congregation who puts up a million quarts every summer and gives a fair share of them to us. It's not that Elisa and I aren't grateful, but we've run out of room to store them. Will you please take some off my hands? You'd be doing me a huge favor. I'm giving jars to everyone I can think of."

She sniffed because she only half believed the minister was wallowing in home-canned tomatoes. "That's so kind, but then Zach will ask where I got them, and I'll have to explain."

"And he'll know we talked?"

She gave a slight nod.

"Molly, he's going to know anyway, because I'm going to tell him. I won't go behind his back. That's the last thing he needs. But you have to find a better place to live. It's not charity. I just have more access to people who might know about one."

She chewed on her bottom lip. "Give me this evening to talk to him first. Then maybe drop by with the tomatoes in the morning? I'm pretty sure he isn't working tomorrow unless he finds day work on his own somewhere."

"Tomorrow then." He left. She stared at the shelves as she asked herself if she'd done the right thing. Questioning herself lasted only seconds. For the rest of the afternoon, she formed her battle plan.

IN THE END, no battle plan was needed. When Molly walked into the trailer with a bag of groceries, Zach was already inside mopping up water.

"Let me put this down and I'll help," she said, setting the bag on the counter beside the stove.

"I've been at it for an hour. There's nothing left in the heater to leak. I drained what I could, and I'm mopping up the rest."

"It's just sweating, remember?"

He straightened. "I know we can't live like this, Moll, and Mr. Gibson isn't going to replace the water heater. He's planning to sell the property. He's ready to close the deal. We'll find another place. I've been looking."

She put her hands on her hips. "I'll tell you what we're going to do. We're going to let Reverend Sam look, too." She held up her hand when he started to speak. "And do not tell me we don't need help. I don't agree, and I won't listen. We are going to ask for help looking for new quarters, not for a hand-out. We aren't from here, so we don't have many contacts. Reverend Sam has hundreds. And that's all there is to it!"

She turned and went outside to retrieve the second bag. But she knew, when she went back into the trailer, Zach wouldn't yell or argue. She had taken a stand, and she was not going to back down. Before marrying him, she had taken a stand against her parents, who had threatened to expel her from the family if she married an ex-con. She had said goodbye to her comfortable life, to her bedroom filled with sweet mementoes, packed one small suitcase and married Zach anyway, because she had known it was the right thing to do.

Now she was standing firm once again. Zach was too smart not to see the truth. Molly would follow through this time, exactly as she had before.

CHAPTER 8

O
n Thursday afternoon Cathy was in her sewing room staring at the half square triangles she had cut from new fabric, when she heard Alf drive up. She peeked out the window to make sure the car was theirs and then settled back to work.

She'd bought the fabric on her trip to Charlottesville to see Laura and shop for the new baby. She hadn't expected Laura to accompany her on that part of the shopping trip, but not only had her daughter volunteered to come along, she'd been entranced by the fabric. Cathy thought maybe another family quilter was emerging.

With the intention of finding fabrics for the Contrary Wife quilt, she had taken a sample card of the paint she and Alf had chosen for their bedroom. Laura had listened as Cathy discussed the merits of a quilt using different shades of green or choosing a print and then using those colors as guides for the four other fabrics she intended to buy. In the end, that's what they'd decided.

The patterns in the print they'd both fallen in love with

were subtle. Pale blues and greens predominated, so she and Laura had chosen pastel colors to accent them. A pale yellow like the sunshine. An ivory fabric with brighter white scroll work. Laura had been determined to find the right accent color. In the end she'd held up a soft green, with designs sketched in a darker teal. Cathy had known she would love working with it. The colors blended beautifully.

Laura had absorbed the best of both parents. Her hair was the soft fawn brown that Cathy's had been before it began to turn gray, and her hazel eyes were like Cathy's, too. But her slender figure and taller than average height had come from Alf's side of the family. The baby was due in three months, and Laura was glowing with good health and excitement.

As they'd stood in line to have the fabrics cut, Laura had tackled the tension between her parents. While Cathy hadn't planned to involve her, Laura and Gabe had been in touch and come up with a few suggestions.

Now Cathy heard her husband's footsteps on the stairs and wondered what Alf would say when she passed those suggestions on to him.

"How was the traffic?" she asked, when he was standing on the threshold of her tiny sewing room. Asking was polite, although the answer wasn't really important since, whatever the tie-ups, he'd made it home.

"Not bad since it's the middle of the day," he said.

"And your meetings?"

"Long. If there's a question they didn't ask me, I can't imagine what it is."

She glanced up. Alf looked tired, but she knew better than to point it out. If she did he would head right outside and chop firewood, just to show he was the same man he'd been when their children were growing up.

"I didn't know when you'd be home, but I have an enchilada casserole ready to go into the oven for dinner. There are plenty of vegetables for a salad if you'd like to make one. I picked lettuce from the garden. I think it will produce another few weeks unless we have a heavy frost."

"If I cover the row at night, it might survive until Thanksgiving."

She didn't point out that he probably wouldn't be home to cover rows or harvest whatever survived. He might not even be home to enjoy a salad on Thanksgiving Day.

"How did shopping go with Laura?" he asked.

"If the baby came tomorrow, she'd be fine."

"She's still not saying if it's a boy or girl?"

"She and Rob are very clear they don't want to know."

"Do you care?"

"No, and besides, I might have another chance at a grand-daughter down the line."

"I got the jack-o'lantern photos from Gabe. Scary."

"Not as scary as watching those little boys hack away at our pumpkins."

He was silent a moment, then he cleared his throat. "I'm sorry I missed seeing that. I bet it was something."

She was working hard to keep her voice and expression neutral. "The boys carved a little pumpkin to give you. It's supposed to be your face. I wouldn't take that too seriously."

He smiled. Alf had a great smile, rare enough to notice every time it peeked through. It was his smile that had first attracted her to the serious young man in the office where both had held summer jobs, hers between her junior and senior years at Temple University in Philadelphia, and Alf's from Wharton, where he was pursuing his MBA. Over the summer she learned he had spent his childhood and adolescence trying to help his mother cope with his father's gambling. Until the day he died, Alf's father had been sure he would win back all his money and more on the next bet.

Alf came by his desire to work hard and establish a strong financial base honestly. She had loved him for his dedication–and for a lot more besides.

"I wish we could see them in their Halloween costumes." Alf was still smiling.

She saw her opportunity and grabbed it. "You know, we could. Gabe invited us. We could drive up the morning of Halloween and spend the night. I bet Frankie would love to have us there giving out candy while she and Gabe take the boys trick or treating."

She watched the smile settle into resignation. "I'm sorry, but I can't. I'm flying to Tulsa that morning to meet someone on the board who couldn't be in town for my interviews this week. He's important enough that they don't want to decide without him. So they're sending me to him."

Cathy put down her rotary cutter and took a deep breath. "Are you going to take the job if you get an offer?"

"If it's a good offer."

With a Herculean effort she maintained her neutral expression. "If I go to Rockville by myself, I'll take photos. You can add them to the ones of the jack-o'lanterns that Gabe sent you. You can make a Halloween album to enjoy in your hotel room."

If he heard the note of sarcasm, he didn't react. "If I get the job, I'll have more say over my own schedule, Cathy. But during the interview process, I'm at their mercy."

"I don't remember you having much control in the past, Alf. The job made your decisions."

"I don't remember it that way." He paused. "Just don't drive to Rockville at rush hour, okay?"

"You may want to trade our pickup for a second car."

"We don't have to decide right now. I'll take the pickup to

the airport this time. I asked them to try to get me a flight from the regional airport if possible."

"Good."

He disappeared and after a little while, when she was calmer, she folded the fabric she'd been cutting and placed it on a small stack. Then she went to put the casserole in the oven.

She was setting the kitchen table when Alf came in to make the salad. He had never been much of a cook, nor had time to try, but since his retirement he'd become an extraordinary salad maker. He was probably tired, but he was determined not to show it. The casserole had plenty of vegetables, but she'd mentioned salad, and now, he was going to make sure salad was on the menu.

If it killed him.

He opened the refrigerator and began to pull out everything in sight. "I had a little time off on Tuesday, so I drove around Capitol Hill. Remember telling me how much you would like to live in a rowhouse so close to everything? The Eastern Market's right there. We'd never lack for fresh vegetables."

"We don't lack for them here."

"But I'm not going to have time for a garden, Cathy."

"There's a perfect area for a kitchen garden outside the back door. That's all I'll need. It won't be hard to make that happen."

"There's nothing there now except grass and weeds. I won't have time to dig up and make a garden *there*, either."

"I'm fully aware how busy you'll be. I can do it myself. I'll get a landscaper to design and prepare one. I've wanted to do that anyway."

"This place is too much for you to manage. You don't see that?"

She couldn't believe he'd left an opening wide enough for her to guide a team of horses through. "I do see it." She took a deep breath. "Gabe and Laura see it, too. I've talked to them about it."

He didn't exactly slam the lettuce on the counter, but it did thunk against the granite. "You've talked to them about what? How impossible it will be to stay here while I'm living in D.C.? They're planning to come out every week to help you?"

"Of course not, but they've suggested I find somebody who will exchange rent in the old homestead for helping. I'd like to find somebody with broad skills, so if something goes awry, like the pump or the furnace, they'll know how to get it running again. I think it's worth a try."

Alf looked stunned. "You don't even know if the job with Carrollton is a go, and you and the kids are already planning to replace me?"

She stared calmly at him. "Does leaving me here alone to cope sound like a better plan?"

"You can come with me! I'm willing to compromise. If you really want to hang on to this place, then we can rent it to somebody who will take care of it. Then we can use that money to rent a place in D.C. We won't be able to afford Capitol Hill, and whatever we get won't be fancy, but we can manage something. Then we can figure out what to do with the farm once–"

"Once I've stopped being homesick? Once I start making new friends and forget the old ones? Once we live your life instead of mine and I realize how important yours has always been and how small and unimportant mine is?"

He was clearly stunned. "I have never thought about a move in those terms."

"You might need to." She started to move past him to leave the kitchen, but Alf put his arm out to stop her.

"Where do you expect to find somebody willing to trade

rent for odd jobs? Do you think that's something you can ask in a want ad? How will you know that whoever answers the ad is honest and reputable?"

"It's a lot easier to check people's credentials than it used to be, Alf. And, of course, I'll check. But I don't think I'll need a want ad. I'm going to ask Reverend Sam to help me find somebody. He knows all the parents who have children at La Casa Amarilla."

Alf might not go to church often, but he did know about La Casa, a house on the church grounds where Spanish-speaking children were tutored by church members. Practicing English was a big part of every afternoon.

"How can you be sure they'll be able to stay in the country?" he asked. "You would trust Reverend Sam to come up with somebody who won't be whisked away in the middle of the night? That seems like a good idea to you?"

Cathy met his gaze. "That's one idea, yes. But there's another possibility."

Alf dropped his arm, as if he didn't want to hear her second suggestion. She gave it anyway.

"Reverend Sam is always looking for places to settle the men he works with in his prison ministry once they're released." When Alf continued to stare without speaking, she nodded. "I like the idea we can help whoever he suggests as much as that person can help us."

For once Alf's feelings were easy to read. "No. Absolutely not. I won't let you."

She tilted her head. "Since it's pretty clear you won't be living here, Alf, I don't think your opinion counts."

She left him to think that over. She hoped when the timer went off, he knew enough about food preparation to take the casserole out of the oven.

CHAPTER 9

When he'd proposed renting out the farm, Alf had been certain Cathy would be satisfied with the compromise. He saw himself at Carrollton for three years, maybe four. By then the new program would be running smoothly and he'd be ready to retire.

Again.

He couldn't predict exactly what he might want to do at that point. Maybe he would be ready to come back to the Valley and resume his status as gentleman farmer. Or maybe by then, Cathy would be so delighted with city life, they could sell the farm and settle down in D.C. for good.

At dinner he had explained again what a good solution he'd come up with, throwing in a bonus. "And you can drive back here for your quilt meetings if you want to," he'd said.

Cathy hadn't even looked up from her plate. "If anybody commutes, Alf, it's going to be you."

The rest of the week had passed with little conversation. He'd worked in the garden, more to stay out of the house than to prepare soil that would produce nothing but weeds in the spring. With no more than a wave of her hand, Cathy left for town when the construction crew arrived to finish their work on the living area. He had no idea what she was doing or with whom, but he wished he could have gone with her, maybe had lunch out or gone for a hike together.

Instead he pulled into the lot of the Shenandoah Valley Community Church where he had an appointment with Sam Kinkade. He knew a little of Reverend Sam's history. He had been a minister in a large, wealthy Atlanta megachurch until he took one too many steps over a line during a social justice protest. Then he had spent time in prison and again later, after marshals had come into this very church to remove a young woman and her brother who had been given sanctuary there.

That story had a happy ending. Reverend Sam had married the woman, Elisa, and while not everyone in the church had wanted him to stay on after he served out his prison sentence, more had committed themselves to helping Sam make needed changes in their community. The church was involved in various projects, most notably work with immigrants and prisoners. It was also a church where people enjoyed spending time with each other.

Alf wasn't sure how he felt about Sam or what he had done, but he did recognize a man of principal, as well as one who was perfectly happy where he was.

The building itself was white brick with a steeple rising gracefully over a shining tin roof. Today the parking lot held only a smattering of cars, which was unusual. The church was normally bustling with activity. Alf had chosen a good time for a conversation with Sam.

Inside the church smelled of lemon and pine and something recently baked in the parish hall kitchen. He followed signs to Sam's study, where nobody was behind the desk in the reception area, but Sam's door was open. When Alf came to a stop in the doorway, Sam rose and greeted him.

"You found your way. Good. I'm more or less here by myself today, at least for a while. There's a wedding scheduled for later, so before too long, the place will fill up with florists and caterers."

Alf joined him in the study. A leather couch was positioned in front of two windows that looked over a rose garden bearing a few end-of-season roses. He sat on one end after Sam motioned for him to take a seat, and Sam sat on the other.

"The garden looks like a success," Alf said. "Your doing?"

"Pulling weeds is the way I work out stress. And when I can open the windows, the garden pays me back. Most of the roses are old varieties chosen for scent."

Alf thought of the roses blooming beside the old homestead, some former resident's pride and joy. On his long list of chores, refurbishing the rose garden had landed at the bottom.

Sam was dark-haired, with startling blue eyes that were examining Alf as he waited for him to explain why he was there. Alf had heard the man speak. If he'd been inclined to attend church on a regular basis, he couldn't have chosen one with a better preacher.

"Cathy tells me she's going to contact you," Alf began. "Maybe she already has?"

Sam didn't confirm or deny. He just continued to look receptive.

Alf capsulized Cathy's idea about finding a renter for the homestead who would take on farm chores as payment.

"Do you mind backing up a little?" Sam asked. "I seem to remember you've done a lot of work on your place. Cathy's shared some before-and-after photos with the Bee, and I know some of our members have been there. Has it just become too much for you to handle?"

Alf knew that if he didn't explain, Cathy would detail her version when she talked to Sam–if she hadn't already.

He summarized Carrollton's invitation to apply for an important new position, and how they seemed to feel he was exactly the right man for the job.

"The interviews have gone well. There's one more, then we'll all decide," he finished.

He expected Sam to nod and then explain why he might be exactly the right person to help Cathy find a renter. After Sam finished that, Alf planned to explain why *any* renter was a bad idea, but particularly one that Sam selected from his work in the community. Instead Sam leaned toward him.

"This is a big change for you."

"Not really. It's exactly the kind of work I do best."

"I'm sure it is. But it's definitely a change from retiring out here and making the farm your home."

From that, Alf guessed that Cathy had already complained about him. "I miss the city. I miss working at something I'm really good at, something that makes a difference."

"What kind of difference?"

Alf considered. "The new initiative will help Carrollton expand their holdings and move even more aggressively into the marketplace."

"It's a company you respect. It must be."

"Carrollton consults with clients–private and governmental–and helps them develop solutions to ensure their future success."

Sam nodded. "And that feels worth such a big change in circumstances?"

Alf found himself saying things he hadn't expected to. "I have a lot of skills and talents that aren't being used here. And I'm still young enough to use them."

"Of course. That makes sense. How about living this far

from your former stomping grounds? You're looking forward to moving back to the city? It's a great place, no question, but it's very different." Sam leaned even closer. "Won't it be a little like leaping between riders on a fast-moving escalator and hoping you survive to make it to the top?"

Alf tried not to wince, because it would be exactly like that. "I'm up to it."

"I gather Cathy isn't. It doesn't sound like she plans to go with you."

"I didn't come to talk about that."

"Well, yes. On the other hand, if she wants me to find someone to help her while you're gone, that means she's planning to stay."

Alf rubbed his forehead until he realized what he was doing. His hands landed back in his lap. "I think she's making a big mistake. I want to sell the farm and find a place in the city where we can both be happy."

"She's not happy here?"

"She claims she is."

"And you doubt her?"

Alf considered that, and finally shook his head. "No, she's doing what she wants to, and apparently that's more important than coming with me."

"Did you move a lot in the earlier years of your marriage?"

Alf wondered how they had gotten so far off topic. He was here to let the minister know he would not tolerate him finding a tenant who might be in trouble with the law. Instead they were talking about his marriage, and still, he couldn't stop himself from answering.

"Cathy knew moving was part of meeting our goals. She was willing."

"Willing is an interesting word. I'm willing to pay my taxes, do in fact, but I'm never happy about it. I pay them because I'm contributing to something bigger than myself."

"Cathy knew we were making a life together and making certain we'd have enough income to put our children through school and then enjoy ourselves in retirement." Suddenly those final words were magnified in his head, like somebody was shouting them through a megaphone.

"If you don't mind me asking, did you achieve the financial security you hoped to? Because from what I can tell, both of you were successful in your chosen professions."

"I see what you're doing," Alf said. "I see where you're *going*."

"You would because you're an intelligent man. But also one who's ambivalent about his future. Or am I wrong?"

Alf ignored the question. "I do not want an ex-con or an undocumented immigrant living on our farm. I don't want Cathy to be subjected to problems with our sheriff or with immigration while I'm working in D.C."

"Consider this, will you? You may be trying to remove all her choices. I don't think you want her staying here alone, either. It sounds like the only real solution in your mind is for Cathy to go with you."

"If she would, we could find enough compromises to be happy."

"It sounds like the original deal was for the two of you to work together to meet mutual goals. Now you've set new goals, and you want her to put your goals first, even though you've met all the ones you were working toward through the years. I imagine you both gave up a lot to get where you are today. Unfortunately every man and woman has a saturation point."

Alf knew all about saturation points. Market saturation. Advertising saturation. He'd seen employees pushed beyond their saturation point when it came to learning new things or working overtime. Yet hearing the problem with Cathy stated so clearly made him uneasy. He'd been sure if he let her choose an area to live in, she would settle in quickly and be happy.

The idea of a saturation point, one where compromise was no long possible? Despite what he knew, he had assured himself that didn't exist.

Sam got up and went to his desk, returning with a file folder that he placed on the table in front of Alf.

"I recommend you check out this young man. Zach Lovell went to prison four years ago for stealing his stepfather's service revolver. The stepfather was a violent alcoholic, but unfortunately, he was also a deputy in another Virginia county, and he used the gun to threaten Zach's mother whenever he'd had too much to drink—which was just about every night. One of those nights, after his stepfather passed out, Zach took his gun and threw it in a lake."

"Surely the law understood his reasoning."

"A boy just finishing high school isn't much of a match for the sheriff's department when they're protecting one of their own. He was charged with grand larceny and sent to prison. His stepfather continued to threaten his mother, and eventually he nearly killed her in one of his drunken rages."

"Wasn't that proof the boy had been telling the truth? Was Zach set free?"

Sam grimaced. "The law doesn't work that way. The stepfather went to prison. Zach's mother moved out of state, and eventually, Zach was released a little early for good behavior. He married his high school sweetheart, and they're expecting their first child in the spring. Unfortunately, they're barely scraping by. Molly cleans houses, and Zach is a laborer with a construction company, but the salary is minimal, and he's the first to be laid off when a job is finished. He's good with his hands, and he works hard. But two years in prison isn't what employers most want to see on a resume."

"Has he been in any trouble since he got out?"

"No. He and Molly are trying to make the family Zach was cheated out of as a kid. Everything you need to know is in the folder, including references from his employer, a few people he works with, some of his high school teachers. But financially the Lovells are in trouble. So if they don't have to pay rent, their future will be rosier. I worry that when the baby comes and Molly stops working or has to pay for childcare, they're going to get so deep into the hole they won't be able to dig their way out."

"If you were out of town and your wife was alone, would you let them live in a house on your property?"

"If I had an extra house, I would move them into it tomorrow."

Alf scrambled to find another reason not to agree. "The house isn't in great shape. Nobody can live there at the moment."

"At the moment they're renting a mobile home with no hot water. They will do almost anything to move out, and they aren't looking for a mansion."

Alf couldn't lie. The team in charge of his renovations were still coming and going and would probably agree to take on this project, too. "It's going to take two, maybe three days of hard work by a crew just to get it up to minimum standards."

"Zach and Molly can help get the house in shape. It will feel more like it's theirs if they're given that chance."

"You're requiring me to take your opinion on faith. Isn't this a lot for you to ask?"

Sam got to his feet, a sign the conversation was finished. "A lot for me to ask or for you to receive? I think in this case, it's more the latter. You and Cathy will be the winners. And now

I'm afraid I need to look over the wedding service for this afternoon. Take the folder if you're not already set against the idea
and give the whole thing some thought. But if Zach doesn't
work out, I can find someone else. It's up to you—or more real-
istically, Cathy."

They shook hands and Alf left. In the parking lot he tossed
the folder on the seat beside him. At home he got out and
started toward the front door, but on the stoop, he turned, and
then, with a sigh, headed back to the pickup to stare at the
folder through the side window.

In the end he carried it inside.

CHAPTER 10

Halloween was now just a memory of two adorable ninjas with jack-o'lantern sacks overflowing with candy, and Thanksgiving was tomorrow. Cathy had invited her children and their families to celebrate the holiday together at the farm, since there was plenty of room and places for the twins to play. One of the workmen who had helped with the renovation had helped her move furniture and set up two extra tables in the great room dining area. Frankie's parents were coming for dinner, too, along with Rob's brother and his wife. She was in charge of the turkeys and stuffing, and everything else would arrive with the guests.

Cathy just hoped her husband would arrive, too.

Alf had taken the job with Carrollton and moved into a temporary sublet in the city near the Metro line. In the past month he had come home twice, once for a day, once for a weekend. She hadn't liked what she saw. The vacant expression in his eyes that meant he was thinking about everything he had left undone. The slump in his shoulders. He'd gone to bed early and gotten up late, as if sleep had evaded him in the city, or he hadn't indulged. Of course when asked, he'd claimed everything was fine, and he was settling into the new routine as if he'd never been away from a desk.

Now Cathy's watch told her it was three o'clock, and Alf was supposed to be home. In a few minutes the Lovells were coming to meet him and take a look at the house.

Cathy had been delighted when she realized that Molly Lovell, the lovely young woman who had been cleaning the church, was the feminine half of Sam's recommendation. Cathy had met Molly's husband after last week's service. Zach, tall and lanky, was probably the most serious young man she'd ever met, as if he were afraid a smile would prove he was no match for what life had thrown at him. Molly, on the other hand, bubbled with enthusiasm.

The young couple were clearly in love, but even more visible was their mutual determination to move beyond Zach's years in prison, years when Molly had never given up on him. They clearly wanted to make something better out of the rest of their lives. Three weeks ago they had moved out of a broken-down trailer and were temporarily living in a cheap motel, but they needed help fast.

Her cell phone rang, and Cathy lifted it out of her jeans pocket without glancing at the caller I.D. "Are you coming? Because we are not going to reschedule."

"I'm an hour away." Alf paused. "Maybe a little more."

She filed the comment she wanted to make. She had an entire file in her head titled "Opinions That Might End Your Marriage." Instead she spoke slowly and carefully. "I can't imagine the Lovells will want to wait for your grand arrival, Alf. Both of them worked today, and they're probably exhausted."

"I'm really sorry."

Alf rarely apologized, although he always made it clear he

was sorry in other ways. So, for a moment, she didn't know what to say.

"I'm sure whatever kept you was *important*," she said stressing that last word to make sure he knew what she really thought.

"Apparently everybody in the world is traveling for the holiday. Traffic is a nightmare. I hope the Lovells will still be there, but I'll understand if they aren't. There'll still be time for me to meet them before we decide."

She filed away her answer, too—before long she would need a real file cabinet to keep track of all the things she didn't say—and slid the phone back into her jeans. They were new jeans. In the weeks since Alf had been staying in D.C., she had decided if she couldn't change her husband, she could change herself. She'd gone on a strict diet, and without another person to cook for, pounds had peeled away. The momentum had stopped, as it usually did with a diet, but she had lost enough to move down a size and planned to lose more. She'd gone to a better hair stylist and gotten a new cut and even submitted to blond highlights to blend in the gray. She refused to look as depressed as she felt.

The construction crew had already taken care of a few things at the homestead to make it more acceptable, and that morning she had spent two hours inside, sweeping and clear-ing, to get ready for the visit. All the moth-eaten upholstered furniture had been hauled to the dump, and she had a good lead on replacements from a State Department family who preferred selling to storing for the years they would be away. She just had to find out what her renters might be bringing with them.

As she'd worked, she'd opened the front and back doors and immediately a breeze had swept through, as if whoever had built the house had planned it that way. Mentally she had added new screen doors to the work list for the crew because doors would be a bonus in the summer, even though she planned to add window air-conditioners in the bedrooms.

The foreman had made his own list. The kitchen needed the most renovation. Replacing the missing stove was tops, but he'd also added a new refrigerator and cabinets for the near future. She hoped if the Lovells wanted to move in, the foreman and Zach would figure out who would do what else and when. From things Sam had said, Zach wanted to have a hand in both making choices and renovating the house. The young man did not want charity, and from her own observations, he wanted to make a real home for his family, preferably with his own two hands.

Fifteen minutes later a small rust-dotted sedan pulled into the driveway, and Cathy walked to the parking area to greet Zach and Molly. They were dressed up, as if they'd showered and changed after work to make a good impression. Zach wore neatly pressed khakis and a tucked-in shirt. Cathy wore a loose-fitting green dress that didn't disguise a baby bump. They were holding hands.

Molly was the first to speak. "It's like a piece of heaven out here, isn't it? Do you wake up every morning just brimming over with excitement and thanks because you're living in this beautiful place?"

The young woman's eyes were shining, and Cathy thought she saw tears, as if she was afraid that this blessing might not actually be granted to them.

Sometimes decisions were easy. A woman saw something that needed to happen, and she made sure it did. Simple, no fuss. Cathy reached over and took Molly's free hand. "That's how it's going to be for you. You're going to like living here, and we're going to like having you. Let's go look at your new home. If you decided you want it, that is."

"You and your husband already decided you want us to move in?" Zach asked. Cathy heard everything he didn't say. *Don't lead us on. Don't make promises you aren't going to keep. Don't dangle heaven in front of Molly's eyes and then snatch it away.*

She met his eyes. "The job and the house are yours, if you want them."

"We want them." Zach visibly relaxed and even managed a ghost of a smile. "We sure do, but only if we can work off our rent. We aren't looking for charity."

Cathy smiled, too, and tried to keep her own eyes from brimming over. "Then welcome home."

WHEN ALF DROVE in there were no unfamiliar cars beside the house. Not surprisingly he had missed meeting the Lovells, and now he would have to call them himself and see if they could meet another time over the holiday weekend.

He had done his best to get home in time, but just as he was about to leave, Randy Banting had dropped by his office to go over a long list of discussion points. Randy had claimed that he wanted to be sure when they geared back up on Monday, no significant time would be lost. Of course, as CEO, he hadn't felt it necessary to make an appointment or find out if Alf was in a hurry to drive home. He was fully aware that Alf had been a CEO himself, and Randy was probably trying to remind him who was boss now.

By the time Alf had finally escaped to the car he'd leased, he'd suspected he was going to be late getting back to the Valley. Then, when getting out of the city took three times as long as it normally did, he'd been sure of it.

There was no point in regrets. He had three days before he

had to drive back on Monday, and while he did have work to do, at least he could relax on Thanksgiving Day and enjoy his family. He felt as if he hadn't had a real conversation with Cathy in decades.

When he got out of the car, he resisted the urge to check on Merrill. He knew better than to visit the rooster before seeing his wife. Inside, the house was silent. He thought Cathy must be home since their car was parked outside, but he called her name and didn't get an answer.

He thought about all the things that could happen to a woman living alone, and his heart sped a little faster.

She wasn't in the kitchen, where he stopped to stow a bag in the refrigerator, and she wasn't in the master bedroom. He found her upstairs in the smallest bedroom, most likely created as a nursery when the house was built. Cathy had made the space her sewing room, and she was bent over her machine, which sat on plywood between two sawhorses.

Alf stood in the doorway and watched a moment. "Hey, I was getting worried. I should have known to look here first."

She stopped stitching and looked up. Then she rose and edged her way around the table, a maneuver that was complicated by the narrow aisle beside wooden shelves on concrete blocks. The shelves were filled with baskets of supplies and fabric.

She stepped into his arms for a quick hug. He hadn't been sure he would get one, considering. When she stepped away he examined her more closely. "Hey, you look great. I like your hair, and you look–" He realized he'd better stop right there.

She grinned. "Thinner? Younger? Go ahead and say it. I worked for it."

"Beautiful." He put his arms around her and pulled her close again. She didn't resist, but she didn't quite snuggle, either.

"I obviously missed the Lovells," he said. "I'll call them and see if they have any time to get together this weekend. I can meet them wherever they'd like."

She broke free and took a seat at her machine once more. "You'll meet them tomorrow. They're coming for Thanksgiving dinner."

"You invited them? Isn't that getting their hopes up?"

"I invited them to live here, too."

Alf took a deep breath and then another before he spoke. "Without consulting me?"

"Without letting you micromanage. Yes. You weren't here, and they loved the old homestead. They're so excited about moving in. Zach already has a couple of great suggestions for fixing it up, and he wants to do the work himself when he can. Zach is pretty buttoned down, like a dog who's just waiting for the next kick, but Molly was like a kid at Christmas."

"I see." And he did. He managed to swallow his anger because he'd set himself up for exactly this, and a man reaped what he sowed. "So by coming home late, I had no voice in the decision."

Cathy was gnawing on her bottom lip, which meant she was working hard to say what most needed to be said in a way he would hear it.

"You had a voice," she said after a moment. "I've lived with you a long time, Alf, and when you were away while the children were growing up, I had to make decisions on my own. I learned to consider your opinion, even when you weren't there to give it. So that's what I did today. I know you, and I know you'll like them. You'll be happy you could help them get on their feet. Of course, if I'm wrong, we'll find a way to put things right. But I wasn't going to multiply their worries any more than I had to. Both these young people have had a very hard row to hoe, and it's time somebody gave them a tractor. Or at least a rototiller."

He couldn't help smiling, and he felt his whole body lighten. "Country metaphors?"

She smiled just a little, too. "Those young people have had a very hazardous interstate to cross, and it's time somebody gave them a traffic light."

"I think I like hoes and tractors better."

"I want to finish what I'm doing, and then I'll come downstairs, and we can rummage for dinner." She looked up. "I thought we'd just have sandwiches. There's so much cooking to be done tomorrow, I didn't want to do anything much tonight."

"I'll take care of dinner."

She looked surprised. "Really?"

"You don't think I can make a decent sandwich?"

"I just thought you might be too tired after your trip home."

"Not too tired for what I have in mind."

"Are you taking me out?"

"Better."

Her eyes lit up. "Did you bring home dinner?"

"You'll see."

She smiled again, and he was reminded how many times that smile had soothed away whatever was bothering him. He didn't want to leave. He liked watching her too much.

"So what are you working on now?"

She looked surprised he was still standing there. "A quilt for our bed."

"That sounds like it has to be pretty big. How do you quilt something like that?"

"You can either do it by hand or on a machine. I haven't decided. I might have to send it out to be quilted by somebody else or get in line at the bee to have it quilted by the group. I don't have a longarm machine, and if I had one, it sure wouldn't fit in this room. And I don't have a quilt frame, either. But right now, I'm trying to figure out what's wrong with what I've done so far in piecing it."

He walked a little closer and looked at the pile of fabrics cut into pieces to the right of her machine. "Why do you think something is wrong?"

She looked even more surprised. "You don't want to talk about quilts, Alf. Why don't you go downstairs and put your feet up? I'll be down before too long."

Instead he picked up some of the fabrics and held them together. "They're beautiful fabrics. I don't know a thing about it, but I can't imagine these fabrics making anything but a pretty quilt."

"There's so much more to it than pretty fabrics."

He liked solving puzzles, and since this one involved the woman he loved, it was genuinely interesting to him. "What kind of things?"

"How well it's sewn. You know, if the seams are straight and not crooked, and the right width. That kind of thing."

"So is that the problem? You weren't careful enough? Or is this quilt too complicated that you're bound to make mistakes?"

"No, it's not complicated and everything's the right size. But look up there." She nodded her head to the wall to her right. He hadn't paid attention when he came in, but now he turned a little and looked at the wall while she talked. She'd hung something white and fluffy from the ceiling down, and it took up most of the small space. Patches of fabric were sticking to the fluffy surface.

"That's a design wall," she continued. "The blocks stick to the batting, and I can move them around and decide how best to place them in the quilt. This pattern has lots of different ways to turn blocks so I can make different designs."

He moved a little closer, but it didn't help.

He stared a few more seconds. "So, the fabrics are beautiful. They go together beautifully. But when you put them up there, they kind of merge together."

He looked back to her, hoping he hadn't made a mistake. "It's kind of like a watercolor. Soft swirls. That's not what you want?"

"Can you see a pattern?"

"Pattern?"

"Lines, stars, anything?"

He tried and failed. He stepped back a little farther, into the hall. "I think I can see one from here."

She got up and joined him, standing in front of him. He rested his hands on her shoulders and waited.

"Great," she said in a tone that meant it wasn't great at all. "If a spider crawls across our bedroom ceiling, he might be able to see the pattern I intended."

"It's still pretty in its own way."

"It's too much work to just be kind of pretty."

"The fabrics are beautiful." He pulled her back against him. "Let it sit in your imagination a little and see what some distance does for you."

"I'll be downstairs in a little while."

Alf went to the kitchen to prepare.

By the time she arrived, he had food waiting on the counter. Wine—a very good Pinot Noir—had been opened to breathe. Two kinds of cheese were sitting on a cheese board he had made for Cathy years ago, perfuming the room. He'd chosen her favorites, an English farmhouse cheddar and a French brie. The Pinot was from Italy. He supposed this was an international event considering that the wafer crackers he'd piled on the cheese board were from Australia.

"Oh, doesn't this look wonderful," she said, peering down at the cheese.

"There's a great little gourmet shop down the road from my sublet. I'll take you there when you come to stay some weekend." Most weekends had been filled with work since he'd started at Carrollton, but she held her tongue and didn't point that out now, for which he was grateful.

"I'm going to feel guilty eating all this good cheese the night before Thanksgiving," she said. "We should be fasting."

"Do you want to fast? I can put it away."

"Touch that cheese and I'm asking for a divorce."

Actually the wine and cheese had been intended for tomorrow, Alf's contribution to the festivities. Altogether there were two pounds more of assorted cheeses in the refrigerator, but he'd had his reasons for serving these two tonight, despite having a full dinner to come.

"I'll pour the wine. Will you cut me a piece of each?"

"Gladly." Cathy took the knife he had set out and began to slice. "We've had this cheese board just about forever. Remember when you made it for me?"

He remembered that Christmas well. He had wanted to make her something with his own hands, and the basement in their little rental house had provided room for a table and the assortment of carpentry tools his father had passed on to him—most likely to keep them from being sold to pay debts.

"It was my first attempt," he said, "and not my best. I'm surprised you've kept it all these years."

"I'll be clutching this cheese board when I go to my grave."

He laughed. "I bet that's a sight no undertaker has seen before."

"You never thought it was good enough. You're a perfectionist."

He couldn't believe the conversation had moved to this so quickly. "I remember when I made it. I had all these scraps of wood. I'd figured out a design and put it together as carefully as anything I've made in the years since. And when I was done, it was..." He paused for effect. "Blah. The woods were just a few shades apart and my design got lost. Age hasn't helped."

She took the wine he handed her. "You think I don't see what you're trying to tell me?"

He was relieved to see she was smiling. "We're talking about my cheese board. What could I be trying to tell you?"

"I realized after you came downstairs that I fell in love with my fabrics and let them guide me on the new quilt instead of guiding them. There's so little contrast between them no pattern can emerge. I should have known."

He tried to sound surprised. "So that's the problem?"

"Alf!" She laughed. "Subtlety is not your strong suit."

"What are you going to do?"

"What every quilt maker dreams of doing. I'm going to buy more fabric. I'll use the fabrics that don't work in something else."

He held up his glass in toast and they clinked.

"I miss you," she said simply. "You don't say a lot, but you always know the right thing to say."

He felt something like tears prick the back of his eyelids. "I miss you, too."

They stared at each other a long moment. She was the first to recover. "So what's on our menu besides this amazing cheese?"

"Crab cake sandwiches and peanut butter pie. And sweet potato fries, which I'll warm in the oven for a few minutes when we're ready."

"You went to the Old Ebbitt Grill?"

He had known she would recognize the menu. When they'd lived in the city, they had loved eating at the restaurant together. "I had it delivered to the office. I thought you might like a taste of some of your favorites. And I was sure the last thing you needed tonight was to cook."

"You must have planned ahead. I'm assuming you did this from love, not guilt you were late coming home."

"I ordered it the moment they opened this morning."

"How many times have you eaten there since you started your job?"

"Not once."

She tilted her head in question.

"It's *our* place. I'll wait until you find a weekend to join me in town, and we can go there together."

"When your weekend is completely free, I'll come up."

He didn't assure her he could find a weekend like that because that would be a lie. Even now, even here over the holiday, he had a briefcase filled with work he had to complete.

"Why don't I set the table," she said. "Then I'll tell you more about the Lovells while we eat. By the way, Merrill loves Zach and vice versa."

"The best possible reference."

"I knew you'd think so."

CHAPTER 11

As she drove toward the farmhouse parking area, her backseat filled with Christmas shopping bags, Cathy waved at Zach, who was taking a break from repairs inside the homestead to putter in Alf's vegetable garden, clearing old plants and debris to add to the compost pile. He and Molly had only been living at the farm for three weeks, but he was already busy making plans. Next fall he wanted to sow a cover crop to further enrich the soil, and he had already attended a local seminar to learn what would work best. The young man was a born farmer, and she knew if she looked harder, she would probably see Merrill strutting along behind him.

She had spent the afternoon at the Tysons Corner mall. She already had Lego sets and rockets for her grandsons, and plenty of pre-baby gifts for both Laura and Molly's little ones. The two women's due dates were just a month apart, first Laura in late January, and then Molly in February. Cathy had finished the wall hanging quilt for Laura and Rob's baby and was almost finished with a pieced quilt for Molly and Zach's.

But she hadn't let homemade quilts stop her from buying more gifts.

Fall and early winter were filled with celebrations. After Christmas, which was now just around the corner, things might naturally slow down, but not with two babies on the way. There would be plenty left to celebrate at the farm and in the family.

All the planning and decorating had helped her keep busy, although she missed Alf just as much. He hadn't been home since Thanksgiving, and while they talked most evenings, conversation was a poor substitute for living in the same house and sleeping in the same bed. He assured her he was fine, that the job was going well, and he would be home between Christmas and New Year's Day. But she didn't believe him. He sounded tired and preoccupied, not to mention busy. She knew she would be lucky to have him at home for even a long weekend over the holidays.

Every night she worked harder on the Contrary Wife quilt and wondered if Alf's health would improve if she moved into the city and stopped being a real-life contrary wife. She could make sure he came home at a decent hour, cook healthy meals, insist he take walks with her.

And afterwards, every night she realized that moving to please him was not the right solution for either of them.

Now she pulled into her space, then backed up and around so she could make a quick getaway that evening. Several of the quilters were meeting at Helen Henry's house to figure out how to quilt the Peaks and Valleys quilt now that Helen had announced she had finally put the top together. As she got out to start toward the house, she heard a car slow on the road and then turn into their drive.

She watched until she realized the visitor wasn't someone using the driveway to turn around. The car pulled in just beyond her and stopped, and she realized the newish sedan was the car Alf has leased. She waited as he got out.

Cathy didn't know what to say. It was only Tuesday, so Alf wasn't home for the Christmas break, which came next week. She met him halfway and hugged him before she spoke. "This is a major surprise."

He stepped back to look at her. "I figured if I called to tell you I was on my way, you might not believe it."

For a moment she was mute. All the possibilities flashed through her mind, including the two worst. He was too ill to work, or maybe, because she had refused to move to the city, he had decided to call their marriage quits and wanted to tell her in person.

She forced herself to speak. "Are you okay? Is anything wrong? Come inside and sit down."

"No, it's nothing like that, Cath." He sighed so long and hard she was afraid drawing air back into his lungs was going to be a struggle.

Afraid of what he would say, she waited until she was sure he could speak. "Are you home for the day? The night?"

"Till next year."

She waited, knowing from experience that he was looking for the best way to explain.

In the end he did it in few words. "I just needed to be here, so I came."

"Just like that?" It was the last thing she'd expected to hear.

"The top executives and some of the board are flying to Bermuda for meetings tomorrow and not coming back until the 23rd. Hotel space opened unexpectedly, and Randy grabbed it, so it was short notice." He took another long breath. "I decided not to join them."

She knew enough about corporate politics to realize how that decision must have gone over. "And you still have a job?"

"Last I heard. He wasn't happy, but I told him I have plenty I can do here, and if they really need me, we'll arrange a video conference."

She waited, but he didn't go on. She knew better than to push. "That must have made you feel good, to know you could choose your own path that way."

"They know I'm doing a good job."

She couldn't help herself. "Are you here because of things I've said?"

He looked surprised. "Of course not. You know better."

"I guess I don't."

He put his arms around her and pulled her close. "I'm here because this is where I want to be, with you and the kids, not sitting at a conference table at Christmas time looking over a pink sand beach while Randy Banting drones on and on about process improvement and shifting budget priorities. If I want to go to Bermuda someday, I'll go with you." He was clearly done with that part of the conversation. "I have stuff to bring in. Let's go inside."

"Let me carry something."

Inside she deposited the two canvas bags stuffed with toiletries and clothing upstairs in their bedroom, then she went into the kitchen to make tea while he made one more trip. He still looked harried, and she suspected refusing to go to Bermuda had taken something out of him. She resisted pouring a shot of restorative bourbon into his tea.

Ten minutes later he came down and dropped into his favorite chair in what was now their great room. He looked as if he'd driven from California instead of D.C., but she suspected it wasn't the drive that had drained all his energy.

"First, how are the Lovells working out?" he asked, once he was comfortable.

She hadn't considered how Alf's return might affect Zach

and Molly, who were just settling in. Both young people were already so worried that they would do something Cathy didn't like. Pleasing Alf would feel even harder to them. Maybe impossible.

When she didn't answer he continued. "I saw Zach out in the garden. Getting it ready for winter? Did you ask him to do that?"

"Zach loves that garden, and, of course, it's big enough to supply them and us and the food co-op, too, next summer. He's just cleaning and clearing to take debris out to the compost piles. It was his idea." She paused. "That's a good example of how they're working out. I hope you aren't thinking of asking them for a report."

He looked surprised. "Do you really think I would do that?"

"I don't know what to think anymore. I wasn't even sure you'd come back for the holiday. Of course, I didn't think you'd go back to work, either." The hurt she'd felt for weeks was spilling over.

His answer was surprisingly insightful. "Sometimes I don't know myself anymore, Cath. I used to know who I was. Before I retired. Before I had the heart attack."

"Are you trying to find that person again?"

He managed a smile. "Is that what you think?"

She lay her hand on his knee. "I should have asked that question a long time ago."

"It wouldn't have helped."

She sat back and waited. He didn't have to tell her he was in turmoil and that the job was not the magic cure he had hoped it would be. She wanted to ask if he could be happy here now, but she knew better. Alf didn't know. She wondered what an answer would look like for him, and how soon one would appear.

Instead, she said what he needed to hear. "Carrollton's loss this week is my gain. I'm so glad to have you home again."

"And I'm glad to be here."

He hadn't touched the mug of tea she'd made him. Now he gestured to it. "Maybe I can warm this up later? I think I need a nap. Do you mind?"

She wondered if he would really sleep, or if he just needed to be alone. She stood when he did and picked up the mug to take it back to the kitchen. "I'll make that shrimp stir fry you like so much for dinner. You have to get used to home cooking again."

"I dream about your cooking. I'll help if you need me." He bent over and kissed her, then turned toward the stairs.

Cathy watched him go. Her job was to fix things in their family, but this time, she knew the best she could do was to support and comfort. Alf had to figure out the rest of his life by himself. She just hoped that whatever he decided was good for both of them.

She didn't know how long she could continue to be a contrary wife.

CHAPTER 12

Merrill was delighted to have Alf home for a while. Alf thought Cathy was delighted he was home, too, although she was not as outwardly rapturous as the rooster. He had given her enough hints about his internal struggles that like a prize fighter tensing for the next blow, she was holding back and waiting to see what happened next. Since he was still feeling his way, reassurance was hollow.

Randy Banting had obviously seen the last-minute trip as a holiday perk for his executives and board, and he and Alf had clashed over his decision, far more energetically than he'd told Cathy. So far there'd been an ominous silence from Bermuda, but Alf had no regrets. He had missed Halloween with his grandsons, and he hadn't been home since Thanksgiving to help Cathy decorate the house for Christmas. Randy, who was divorced without children, didn't give a lot of thought to families. But Alf's own family was rarely out of his thoughts.

And right now, he wasn't thinking about Randy or Carrollton. He was just glad to be home.

Merrill pecked lightly at his hand, more a love tap than anything else. Alf scratched the rooster's head. Zach and Merrill were friends, too. The young man had made repairs to the coop that, at one time, Alf had planned to do himself, and Cathy had said that Zach always had the rooster with him when he worked in the garden.

Zach was an enigma. Since his return, Alf had engaged in a couple of uncomfortable conversations with the young man. Neither of them was good at small talk, and both times Zach had looked as if he were waiting for Alf to toss him and pregnant Molly into the cold—never mind the Christmas story.

Alf had tried to reassure Zach that even when he was home, there was still enough to do around the property to keep them both busy. He'd made a lame joke about the way the farm was now covered, A through Z, but Zach was clearly not somebody who trusted jokes or platitudes. He'd learned the hard way that people in charge weren't always fair or honest.

Today, with two days until Christmas Eve, Alf and Merrill were finishing a morning stroll around the property. With the holidays and dropping temperatures, construction jobs had slowed, and Zach had admitted he would be home for a while until the construction company got more work. He had offered to do projects around the farm. There was still a lot to do inside the homestead, but Alf could tell Zach didn't want to feel like a charitable endeavor. So he had started a list of things that needed to be finished soon, things he wouldn't be here long enough to finish himself.

He was about to put Merrill back in the coop when he noted a small SUV pulling into the driveway. With Merrill still in his arms, he started in that direction and was halfway there when Sam Kinkade slid out of the passenger side of the car while his wife, Elisa, got out of the driver's side, brightly wrapped gifts tucked under one arm. Alf knew Elisa from gatherings at the church, but he didn't remember either Kinkade visiting the farm. He wondered why, but the answer came quickly. Alf hadn't been enthusiastic about entertaining, or, for that matter, making friends in the Valley. He'd found excuses every time Cathy suggested having company.

Now he wondered why.

"Who's this?" Elisa asked, after he reached them, smiling down at Merrill, who stretched a little taller to stare at her.

"This is Merrill the Peril, and he's not always friendly." By the time the warning was out of his mouth, Elisa, a lovely woman with black hair and a slender body, was scratching Merrill's head, and the rooster was preening.

"But apparently I can't tell when he's going to be friendly or not," Alf said.

"I'm an old hand with roosters. There were chickens in every village where I worked in Guatemala."

He answered questions about Merrill and Polish chickens in general and laughed when Elisa informed Sam that raising Polish chickens might be part of their future.

"I should have told you we were coming," Sam told Alf. "Zach and Molly are expecting us. We're just here to see their new home and pass on a little Christmas."

As if on cue Zach stepped out of the small orchard that separated the two houses. He shook hands with Sam and smiled self-consciously when Elisa kissed his cheek. "Molly's making coffee." He turned to Alf. "I'd like you to see what I've done inside, sir, you know, to be sure you're okay with it? Will you come, too? I mean if you have time..."

Alf knew when he was trapped, and he followed the others through the trees to the homestead. He'd already seen what Zach had done outside. The young man had reset the stones in the walkway up to the house and used more to line a flowerbed beside the path where Molly had planted daffodil bulbs. She had planted them the week they'd moved in, which said a lot about their hopes and dreams. Zach had cleaned out dead foliage and heavily mulched the roses, explaining in his serious way that he'd read up on them, and he couldn't really prune until February. He was hoping he hadn't done any damage.

The door opened and a very pregnant Molly stood in the doorway. She was a pretty girl, straight brown hair past her shoulders, and eyes the color of chestnuts in a heart-shaped face. She might be a knockout in nicer clothes with more attention to her appearance, but her smile made up for the lack of either. "I'm so glad you're all here." She focused on Alf. "And Mr. Adams, welcome to your own house."

"Yours now," Alf said, feeling like he ought to add more but didn't know what. "The outside is looking great."

"Zach's going to give it a fresh coat of paint when the weather's warm again, and I'm going to plant flowers along the porch just as soon as I know what's already here and what's not. A woman I clean for said she has lots of flowers she can divide for me."

Alf couldn't imagine Molly cleaning at this stage of her pregnancy. Were cleaning products harmful to the baby? Was she bending over to scrub floors? He wanted to insist she stop, but, of course, he couldn't. Maybe Cathy could help him come up with the best way to proceed on that.

Molly stepped aside as they filed in. Alf could smell coffee brewing and something spicier, probably dinner, simmering on the stove. He tried not to look as if he were taking inventory. He knew that Cathy had purchased furnishings at a moving sale because the Lovells had little to bring with them. There was a comfortable-looking sofa in the living room and one narrow armchair. Now Zach brought two straight-backed chairs from the kitchen table, so they all had a place to sit. The room was newly painted and warmed by an area rug, but the fireplace, which would have added cheer and warmth, wasn't in use. Alf seemed to remember one of the construction crew telling him that the stones had to be repointed and the chimney cleaned and checked before it would be safe to light a fire inside.

"Can we have a tour first?" Sam asked.

Alf could see improvements already, although not everything had been done to his standards. The most noticeable change was that Zach was building bookshelves on each side of the out-of-commission fireplace. The shelves weren't exactly level, and the cheap pine boards were full of knots. There were gouges on their surface, as if a possessed belt sander had done the work.

"The wood is discards from our last work site. I borrowed a sander from our foreman, but it's not right for wood this soft," Zach said, as if he'd read Alf's mind. "I'll have to smooth it by hand."

"Won't they be great, though?" Molly was beaming. "I have a box of children's books to put there when Zach is finished. I've been looking at garage sales since I found out about the baby. We made shelves a priority." Her eyes widened. "Of course, if you don't want them here..." She looked at Alf. "I mean Zach's making them so they'll be easy to remove, in case..."

Alf smiled at her. "I think shelves are a good addition."

They walked through the downstairs. Alf noticed that Zach had ripped out the warped and discolored kitchen cabinets and installed more shelves with concrete blocks and boards for a meager number of canned vegetables and boxes of rice and pasta. The new stove that had replaced the mouse condo was the star in the room. While far from being top of the line, compared to everything else, it gleamed with importance. The refrigerator, which had been in the house for years, was just a generation or two newer than an ice box.

New kitchen cabinets, a modern refrigerator, and the fireplace. Priorities. Immediately.

By the time they returned to the living room after viewing the upstairs with its outdated bathroom and two small bedrooms, Alf's list had grown. Seeing the problems before anyone lived here had been a different experience than seeing it with the Lovells in residence. Now all he could think about was the baby who would soon be living in the house. Yes, it was safe–he'd seen to that. Yes, rooms would be warm enough because of the furnace in the dirt floor cellar, and the well that served the homestead was sanitary and sufficient for their needs. Everything was sparkling clean, and Molly had arranged what she could as attractively as possible. She'd added potted plants here, candles there, scarves draped over the back of the sofa. A two-foot artificial Christmas tree decorated with glittering pinecones and paper chains stood on a table with a few small gifts beneath it. Elisa added the two she'd brought to the pile.

Molly deserved better.

Zach? Had nobody ever taken this boy under their wing? He knew about the outlaw stepfather, who had doomed Zach to incarceration when he had tried to protect his mother, but hadn't anybody with morals and a warm heart tried to help? He could feel anger rising inside him. Sam had told him Molly and Zach were good people, but he'd been doubtful. Now he was only doubtful he could find the right way to make up for their poor start.

"Where do you do your woodworking?" Alf asked, keeping his feelings out of his voice.

"Downstairs."

Alf knew what "downstairs" looked like. The cellar ceiling was so low that Zach would need to stoop while he worked. Nobody had been down there in years except to check on the furnace, nobody but varmints, most particularly mice. Even when the furnace was running, the cellar was damp and moldy. It was far from being a suitable workshop.

Elisa asked Molly to show her what she had collected for the baby, and Sam and Alf were left alone with Zach.

"Has work stalled over the holiday?" Sam asked Zach.

"More than I'd like."

"With the holidays so close, our sexton could use some help getting the church ready. Moving the rest of the decorations up from the basement and later back down. I told him I'd find somebody." He paused when Zach didn't respond. "I'm not inventing jobs, Zach, this is a real one. We pay better than minimum wage, and it's maybe three days of work. If you can't, I'll have to find somebody else."

The noticeable tension in Zach's shoulders eased. "Any time, sir. Thank you."

"I'll see if we have other possibilities, too." He went on when Zach started to shake his head. "Look, son, I'm required to lend a hand. My board will fire me if I don't."

Zach stared at him, his eyes narrowing. "I'm not your son..."

Alf stopped breathing, but Sam clearly knew how to repair what he'd said. "I guess that was wishful thinking. I'm sorry that slipped out, but, you know, I wish you were." He reached out and touched Zach's arm.

Zach looked torn, and Alf was still expecting an explosion. Instead he finally said, "Me, too." He quickly looked away.

Sam moved on. "Have you heard from your mom?"

"We're going to take the baby to see her if we can next year. She's up in Tennessee, starting over and trying to make a life."

"She has help?"

Zach nodded and looked at Alf. "Like Molly and me."

Alf swallowed. Hard. "You know, what, Zach? I have an idea, and I hope you'll help."

"You know I will."

"I want to make a woodworking shop in the old shed by the barn. I'm not sure what it was used for originally."

"It might have been a smokehouse. When you walk inside it still smells like hickory."

Alf hadn't bothered worrying about the shed because there had been so many other outbuildings that had needed to be looked after. "Do you think it's big enough for a workshop?"

"Plenty big enough."

"Then let's make a deal. You help me renovate it when you have time, and in turn you can use it, too, along with all my tools. And I'm embarrassed to say I have a lot of tools. It's kind of my hobby."

Zach looked as if he was trying to separate charity from need. "You really want to do that?"

"Right now I'm set up in our basement, but Cathy needs a sewing room. So if you and I fix up the shed, then I can make a real studio for her downstairs. When we bought the house, the basement was already half finished, so there's electricity, a roughed-in bathroom, windows and a door to the outside. It won't be that hard, and the change will make everybody happy."

"I don't know about using your tools. Honestly, I don't know what I'm doing half the time."

"They helping with that at work?"

"Not much. Mostly I carry stuff and clean up. Sometimes somebody will show me how to do something small."

"Low man on the totem pole. That's how we all start. But my father was a cabinet maker, so I learned a lot as a kid."

"I've seen your work. You really know what you're doing."

Alf wondered if he did. He was making a commitment to this young man. A big one. He glanced at Sam, who was smiling. Suddenly Alf knew he'd been set up.

The odd thing? He wasn't one bit sorry.

CHAPTER 13

A few minutes after their guests left, Zach still looked as tired as he did after a full day of hauling boards and cleaning up job sites. Molly understood why. When most teenagers were learning how to relate to other people, Zach was learning to stay as far away as possible. Something as basic as meeting his stepfather's eyes might result in a punch or a kick–until he'd grown old enough to fight back. Then prison had been worse.

She had met Zach as a high school sophomore in a small group assigned to write a paper together on the three branches of government. They were the only ones who had taken the paper seriously, and despite making it clear he wanted to talk as little as possible, eventually he had dropped his guard. He was bright and creative, and he found ideas in the texts they investigated that she'd never considered. By the time he'd begun to seek her out for more than class, she'd already been hopelessly in love.

The love hadn't dimmed, and her faith in their marriage grew brighter every day. So now, even though Zach looked as if she could knock him flat with an index finger, she squared her shoulders.

"That went well, didn't it? The Kinkades were so pleased that we're here now and not in that awful trailer. And Alf seemed happy with everything we've done to the house."

Zach looked as if answering might cost his last fragment of energy. He gave a short nod instead.

She pretended he was as enthusiastic as she was. "Isn't it a great idea to set up a shop in the old smokehouse? And for you to be able to use all those fantastic tools? It helps you both. It's perfect."

"Something could happen, Moll. Don't count on any of this."

"Look around, Gloomy Gus. Things are only getting better. Reverend Sam has more work for you. Cathy and Alf need us here, and they're happy with all the contributions you're making. Today we entertained our first guests, and they were happy to be with us."

"Uh huh."

She shook her head. "You look like you're going to drop over. Why don't you take a little nap."

He looked stunned, as if a man taking a nap was impossible to fathom. "I'm going to check out the smokehouse. Alf asked me to."

"Okay. The fresh air will do you good. Only don't be gone all afternoon. I'll probably need help getting dinner on the table."

He looked puzzled. "Aren't you making chili?"

"You were listening."

"Ears and nose. I can smell it. It's driving me crazy."

"That's what I hoped."

"What's hard about getting chili on the table?"

"Just that we want to do a little fancying up around here before we do."

"Why?"

"Because when I walked outside with Alf, I invited him and Cathy to have dinner with us tonight. And he said they would come."

~

CATHY WAS BEGINNING to have just a touch of pride in her revised Contrary Wife quilt. She had taken the focus fabric to a quilt shop and invited Peony Greenway to join her for an afternoon of shopping. Together they had looked for new fabrics that would still work, while providing much needed contrast.

She had hated to start over, but Peony claimed that not only was Cathy a contrary wife, but a contrary quilter, too, the very best kind.

From her sewing room, where she'd been making the last of the new blocks she needed, she heard Alf coming up the stairs. In a moment he tapped on her sewing room door and stepped in without waiting.

"Got plans for dinner?"

She looked up. "Leftovers. Unless you're cooking?"

"We've been invited out."

She could feel her eyebrows shooting up like rockets. Over the course of their careers, she and Alf had entertained and been entertained frequently. But when they had retired, most of the time he had managed to find reasons not to do either. She had figured he was recovering, so instead she'd poured her energy into family celebrations, renovations, and the bee.

"We've been invited somewhere, and we're actually going?" she asked.

"You sound stunned."

"I'm just hoping..." She cleared her throat. "We're not driving into the city for some social obligation you forgot to tell me about?" She looked down at her black jeans and chunky knit sweater. "I'm hardly dressed to impress your colleagues."

"As far as I know, my colleagues are finishing their last rum swizzles in Bermuda before they head home. This is closer." He savored his next words. "Molly's making chili and cornbread, and she asked if we'd like to join them for dinner. You don't have to change your clothes."

"The Lovells? Feeding us? Shouldn't we be feeding them?"

"Cathy..."

She held up her hand. "You're right. I'm sorry. This is lovely, but..."

"But?"

She shrugged. "I want to be helpful, not helped."

"Tonight we'll be *helped* by two young people. This will mean the world to them, and because it will, it will be *helpful* to them to do it."

She was surprisingly moved. "This is so kind and so unexpected." She paused. "And did they happen to mention dessert?"

"Why, do you have something to take over?"

She laughed self-consciously. "Honestly? I'm hoping Molly baked. Remember the black forest cake she made for Thanksgiving dinner?"

"I remember a fabulous cake. I thought it came from Delectable Mountain."

"No, Molly made it. And that was back when she was living in a derelict motel with nothing more than a toaster oven. She loves to bake, so hopefully we'll have dessert. Wednesday I bought a dozen tamales from one of the La Casa moms, so we can take those."

Alf didn't answer. He was standing back now, looking up at

Cathy's design wall. "Wow. What a change. The design just pops right out. It's wonderful."

She got up to stand beside him. "It does, doesn't it? And I can change the direction of some of the blocks and it's an entirely different pattern, so I'm still deciding." She didn't point out that his own contrary wife had changed a few blocks in their marriage, too, twisting and turning them with no end design in sight. She hoped that the marriage turned out as well as the quilt.

"Have you decided how to quilt it?" he asked.

She was still surprised–and pleased–when he asked quilting questions. "By hand, I guess, or maybe I'll send it to someone with a longarm machine."

"Would you like your own? A longarm machine, I mean. There are a lot of different kinds. You'll need to choose, but I've been researching them online."

She slipped her hand through his arm. "You've been looking online? On quilting sites? Have you really?"

"I want to get you a longarm for Christmas, but I didn't know anything about them. These days my eyes roll back in my head when I turn on the computer, like they know torture is ahead."

She laughed, delighted. "I should make you buy me one, just to torture you some more. But honestly? What I really want is much simpler."

He looked hopeful. "One of those new sewing machines that does everything except cook dinner? You could pick out one yourself."

"Thanks, but my machine is complicated enough. No, a quilt frame. A sturdy one that's not unsightly so I can set it up in a corner of the great room and work on the quilt in the evenings."

"You're not going for the cheaper alternative just because that's what a good wife does?"

"You're kidding right? What's the name of my new quilt?"

He laughed uneasily. "Right. Of course."

"No, I really want a quilt frame that looks like it belongs in the great room." She moved into his arms to kiss him. "Thank you so much for worrying about this and trying to plan the perfect present."

He pulled her closer. "We don't even have mistletoe."

"The mistletoe did its job a long time ago. But I know where some is growing behind the barn. Let's see if we can reach it and take it to the Lovell's house. They're so young they might still need it."

"I don't think so," Alf said. "Those two are so in love my heart hurts when I see them together.

"I wish we could do more for them."

"I don't know what I can do, but you can."

She kissed him again and then stood back. "What?"

"Zach mentioned that Molly wants to quilt, but she doesn't know how."

"And you said?"

"I said I knew somebody who would love to teach her."

Cathy hugged him hard. "Best Christmas present ever."

CHAPTER 14

Through the years the Adamses had always eaten their Christmas Eve feast together, followed by a midnight candlelight service and opening presents early the next morning. This year their celebration had been at Laura's house, because this far into her pregnancy, no one had wanted her to travel. By nine Christmas morning, Gabe's family had taken to the road to see what Santa Claus had left at home in Maryland, and by ten, Cathy and Alf had said their goodbyes and driven across the mountains home.

"It's harder to get together now," Cathy said, as they pulled up in front of their house. "In the future we may have to change the tradition to fit two growing families. They may not want to leave home."

"Maybe we can start a new tradition and have them all come here on Christmas night. We have enough room for everybody, and someday we could add that playhouse I've talked about. Bigger, maybe, with pull-out beds and a bathroom so grandkids could sleep there when they're older."

Cathy didn't look at him. "You've talked about that before."

He realized that he'd just admitted he was still thinking about improvements for the farm. And since coming home for the holiday, he hadn't once mentioned the possibility of Cathy moving to D.C. She was surely aware of both, but luckily for him, wasn't trying to discuss this turn of events.

She changed the subject instead. "The boys loved the presents you got them."

Before coming home for the holiday, Alf had gone to the Air and Space Museum and bought each grandson an astronaut suit, along with a talking space tablet to share. He'd never seen anything cuter than early that morning when the boys had put on the suits and pretended they were visiting the moon. They had refused to remove them for the ride home. Frankie had texted from the road to say that according to the twins, the family wasn't going to Maryland, they were flying to Mars.

"Laura packed up a ton of leftovers from last night's dinner," Cathy said. "Let's take some over to Zach and Molly after we settle in again. We can bring their Christmas presents, too."

She and Alf had collaborated on what to give their "renters." They hadn't wanted to overdo because anything too elaborate might seem like charity. So for Molly, Cathy had cleaned and oiled her former sewing machine, which while neglected, now that she had a more versatile machine, was still in excellent condition. She'd also packed up a handmade fabric bag filled with sewing supplies and promises of quilting lessons when Molly was ready. Alf had cleaned and oiled the smaller of his two circular saws and purchased a new belt sander so that Zach could finish his bookshelves in style. He figured that when he showed the young man how to use both pieces of equipment, he could slip in a few carpentry lessons, too.

Outside the car Alf stretched. "Want to take a little walk to shake off the drive?"

Cathy was already rummaging through a bag on the back seat. "I want to get the leftovers in the fridge. You go ahead."

He started around the house and inevitably toward the chicken coop to check on Merrill. Even though he knew Zach was keeping a close eye on the rooster, he was sure Merrill missed him when he was gone–not that he would ever say such a thing out loud.

Closer to the coop he heard what was best defined as a ruckus. He sped up, wondering if a fox had somehow made its way into the structure, despite all their efforts. Once there, he stopped and leaned forward. Merrill was not alone, but the intruders were feathered, not furred.

He heard footsteps behind him and turned.

"Hey, I thought you'd be home later." Zach stood with his hands in the pockets of worn jeans, looking too much like someone who expected a slap or a punch.

By now the squawking from the coop had reached epic proportions. Alf had to raise his voice to be heard. "What's going on?"

Zach cleared his throat. "Well, see, the girls are your Christmas presents, if you want them."

Alf turned and examined the wire cage just inside the door containing two beautiful Polish hens. "Where on earth did you get these little beauties?"

The hens *were* beautiful. One was a golden beige with a white pom-pom cluster of feathers on her head. The other was black with a white crest. Both were small, and Alf thought they were probably still growing.

"I saw them online. Somebody was moving and selling all his chickens. I managed to snag these two. See, I think Merrill's lonely. I take him with me whenever I can, but they're kind of sociable birds, you know? And being alone out here was too much like solitary confine–"

He stopped. Alf closed his eyes a moment, thinking of the young man, guilty only of trying to save his mother. Zach never talked about his experience in prison. Alf knew he'd been in a minimum-security facility, but that was all.

"You weren't in..?" Alf didn't go on.

"Me? No. They don't call solitary confinement that anymore anyway. But the idea? It kind of hangs over your head the whole time you're inside, just waiting for somebody to haul you off and isolate you. And even with people around, I missed having somebody I could talk to. I think Merrill does, too."

Alf didn't find it odd the boy was ascribing human emotions to a chicken. "This is just so..." He cleared his throat. "So kind. More for you to do, though, when I'm gone."

"Yeah, but good stuff. I've been reading about poultry management, and Polish chickens. Want to let the girls out now and see what Merrill thinks? I put them inside this way so he could get used to them. But every time I've come out here, he's had his beak inside their crate. I think they like him, too."

"Let's give it a shot."

Alf opened the door to the coop, and Zach opened the cage. Then they stood back.

At first none of the chickens moved. Then one of the hens waddled toward the opening and stuck her neck out, pom-pom first. In a minute she was outside, and Merrill was right beside her, checking her out. They both started to vocalize as the third chicken made her way into the coop.

Alf watched as the chickens marched after each other, feathers fluffed and heads bobbing. They didn't get close, as if they had a detailed plan they were following, but eventually they formed something like a circle and began to chatter.

"I think they'll be okay now, don't you?" Zach waited for Alf's nod, then slid the cage outside and closed the door to the coop.

Alf put his hand on Zach's arm. "Thank you."

Zach didn't move away. "Before she married my stepfather, my mom used to take me to church. I remember being in a living Nativity when I was maybe six, a shepherd with a staff a lot bigger than me. Somebody put live chickens in the stable with us. I remember one kept pecking my ankle and I cried. I'm guessing the real stable in Bethlehem had chickens, too. So I figured a little bit of the Nativity scene was a good Christmas present."

Alf realized that was the longest speech he'd ever heard Zach make, and certainly the most revealing. "I'll make a deal with you. We'll keep the chickens with great pleasure, but let's get Molly to the hospital when her time comes. We don't need a Nativity re-creation any more genuine than this."

Zach looked at him and grinned. "Now that's the truth."

CHAPTER 15

The holidays had been over for two weeks, and Alf was back in D.C. Cathy knew he had a lot to catch up on and probably wouldn't make it back until the end of the month—in time, he promised, for Laura's due date. Cathy missed him more than she told him when they spoke, but she found ways to keep busy. Among other things Molly had been thrilled with her Christmas present, and so far, Cathy had given her two sewing lessons. The young woman was a quick study, and she'd already made potholders for practice. Now Cathy had decided it was time to introduce her to quilts.

Friday after lunch they trooped upstairs to Cathy's sewing room, which was just big enough for two if neither of them breathed deeply. Molly looked around with delight while Cathy watched from the doorway. "It's snug," Cathy said, "but I don't have to pack up the machine so I can serve supper on the table at night. Some of the members of my quilt group have to work that way."

"That's the quilt group at the church?"

"It is. We call it the bee. Would you like to come with me sometime?"

"If I'm not cleaning houses that morning I'd love to." Molly trailed her fingers over the neatly folded fat quarters of fabric piled high on the closet utility shelf that Cathy used for storage. "I don't know how you can cut this up. It's so beautiful, every single piece. Aren't you afraid you're going to make a mistake?"

Cathy understood because she had felt the same way at the beginning, and sometimes still did. "You have to take chances, even if they don't work. I've made a lot of mistakes in my time. Some big ones recently."

Now Molly moved out of the closet and stared at the Contrary Wife blocks on the design wall. "You sewed all these blocks yourself?"

"And a lot more." She explained about her first attempt at making blocks and then admitted the sad truth. "I had to replace at least two dozen that just weren't working."

"Two dozen? Why?"

"The fabrics weren't providing contrast, like they were supposed to. But I think I'm on the right track now."

"It's going to be the most wonderful quilt ever. But all that work on the ones you aren't using?"

"You have to be willing to make mistakes and move on, but I didn't throw them out. I keep every block I don't use, just in case." Cathy stepped in to shuffle the plastic boxes on the shelf to pull out the right one. She held it out. "I call this box my infirmary, but really, it's more like a graveyard. Blocks go in, and they don't come out."

Molly took the top off the box and began to thumb through them. "These are beautiful, too. Can you really let them just sit here?"

Cathy was delighted at how easily this was falling into place. "Well, no, I have a plan. Even better, it involves you."

"Me?"

Cathy lifted the box out of Molly's hands. "Let's go downstairs where we can spread these on the table."

Downstairs Cathy removed the candles adorning the great room table, and she and Molly began to lay out the blocks from the infirmary box. Cathy was surprised there were so many. Before long the box would be too full for more. Not just a home for the rejected Contrary Wife blocks, the box also contained sample blocks for other quilts that she'd decided against, beginning attempts at applique that hadn't been bad enough to discard or good enough to use, and patterns that had been too complicated or easy. Also included were three blocks for the Peaks and Valleys quilt that hadn't, in her opinion, been good enough to get past Helen Henry.

"They don't all go together, but this is practically a quilt already," Molly said.

"Do you want to play a little?"

"I love to have fun."

Cathy smiled, because she had come to understand that while Molly's life wasn't easy, she was a woman who appreciated every little thing that came her way, things most people took for granted. Molly was blessed, a woman who made her own world brighter.

"I have to do some things in the kitchen," Cathy said. "In the meantime, while I'm working on that, why don't you rearrange these? Play with the ones you like best. Maybe so you can make a small quilt to practice on?" She gestured at the blocks. "Possibly a baby quilt?"

Molly looked thrilled. "You're sure? You don't have plans for these?"

"It's my infirmary, remember? Or better yet let's call it my orphanage. You adopt the ones you want to use."

Molly laughed and Cathy left her to organize the blocks any way that pleased her. Cathy knew how it felt to spend hours playing with fabric, twisting and turning and sometimes trimming orphaned blocks into different shapes and sizes. If Molly enjoyed doing that, she was already a quilter at heart.

Twenty minutes later she joined Molly at the table again. A number of the blocks had been separated into color groups and were neatly piled along the table's edge. In the center of the table, Molly had taken some of the orphaned Contrary Wife blocks and twisted and turned them. A design was forming, soft and restful, but there weren't enough of the right blocks to finish it. She was trying to incorporate half a dozen that just didn't work.

"I'll be right back." Cathy left and returned a few minutes later with fabric that was left from making the blocks that graced the table.

Molly was delighted. "You have more."

"You came up with a great idea there, but you don't have enough blocks to finish it. It doesn't matter, though, because this is perfect. If you want, I can teach you to make some of the same blocks with the same fabrics to finish it. Then I'll help you sew it together and finally I can show you how to quilt it. The perfect beginner project. And the design you've made? It's soft and sweet. I didn't see it before, but it's perfect for a baby quilt."

"I love all the greens. No matter whether I'm having a boy or a girl, green works perfectly."

"Plus I have some animal fabric here." Cathy pulled from the bottom of the pile. "See? I think there's enough to back a baby quilt. It has the same color palette."

"It's going to be so beautiful." Molly brushed her fingertips along the new fabric. "But you're sure? I mean the blocks, the fabric, and all the lessons? It just feels like so much."

"There's nothing a quilter likes better than to teach somebody else to quilt. I'm as excited as you are."

Molly looked up. "Every quilt has a name, right?"

"Almost all."

"These blocks? Like the quilt you're doing upstairs? They have a name?"

"Contrary Wife," Cathy said.

Molly stared at Cathy, then at the blocks, and then back. Her smile was a yard wide. "Then I picked the perfect blocks, didn't I? Zach would sure say the name fits."

Cathy laughed. "Let's just hope it's not a contrary baby."

CHAPTER 16

Cathy wasn't home when Alf arrived. Today was officially Laura's due date, but the doctor thought the baby was stalling to arrive in early February instead. He unpacked his car alone before he strolled out to the coop to see the chickens. Merrill was delighted at his arrival, and the hens examined him thoughtfully, as if somewhere in their tiny brains, they remembered seeing him before. Everything looked tidy, as if Zach had been out recently to care for them.

He was just closing the coop door with an indignant Merrill demanding to join him outside when Zach appeared.

Alf shot him a smile. "Merrill wants to come, but I was going back up to the house. He's hard to reason with."

"He's probably feeling..." Zach paused for effect. "*Henpecked*."

Alf laughed. He couldn't remember Zach making a joke of any kind. He was glad to see this new side of him. "Well, I know that feeling. How about you?"

"When she's on a roll, Molly can peck with the best of them."

Both men laughed. Alf was still smiling when Zach spoke again. "Since you've been gone, I started fixing up the workshop. If you have time, we could go look at it together. I mean, whenever you want to. I know you're not here for long, and you probably have things that are more important."

The young man would be shocked if Alf told him he was wrong and why, but he knew better than to confide in Zach before he had spoken to Cathy. "Nothing more important than seeing what you've done," he said. "Have time now?"

"Nothing but."

They started toward what had been the old smokehouse, and even from a distance, Alf could see the changes. New boards covered gaps in the original structure. The old boards had been thoroughly cleaned and the ground cleared around it.

"I can already see some major improvements. If you have nothing but time, does that mean things have slowed at work?"

"It's up and down." Zach hesitated then shrugged. "Honestly, more down right now. We've got some major jobs coming up, but right now they don't need me much. I'm working a couple of nights a week at the feed store, cleaning up once everybody's gone. They've got a guy out sick so it's temporary, but it helps until the construction jobs start up again."

"That's a tough way to live. You ever thought about college?"

Zach seemed surprised. "That's not something guys like me think about much."

"Molly told Cathy you did really well in high school."

"Don't ever let Molly in your vegetable garden. Every snail and slug will be worth saving."

Alf wanted badly to point out that Zach was worth so much more than a snail or slug, but he restrained himself. "So you didn't do well in high school?"

"I did okay."

"You're smart." Alf held up his hand when Zach started to interrupt. "I can see you're smart, Zach. And you're a hard worker. You're loyal and your values are strong."

"Not exactly what they said at my trial."

"I'm sure." Alf expected Zach to stop there, but the young man surprised him.

"Molly left college to marry me. She was there almost two years before her parents stopped paying her tuition because of me."

"They were that upset?"

"Her father. He told her if she chose me over his rules, she could pack and leave. Molly's mom always let him decide things. That's how she was brought up, but she wasn't happy to send Molly away."

"They know about the baby?"

"Molly writes her mom, but she doesn't write back. Molly's not even sure she gets her letters."

"That's a shame."

"Molly wants to finish college someday so she can be a teacher. She should."

"What would you do, if you could?"

"Me?" Zach gave a short laugh. "I don't think about a future. I think one day at a time. Safer that way."

Alf was sure the young man was right, and it was safer, in his position, not to dream. But "safer" was a high wall to scale. Even though his own childhood and adolescence had been difficult, Alf had never been physically abused and never watched his mother beaten by a maniac with a badge. He knew he couldn't decide for Zach.

"You like to grow things," he said instead. "That's obvious. You like working with your hands. What about academics. What classes did you like best?"

"I took some computer classes in prison for college credit. What else was there to do?"

"Did you like them?"

"I liked them fine, but I don't want to work in an office. I'd rather be outdoors."

Alf imagined many former convicts chose to be outside whenever they could. Fresh air and freedom were vastly underrated by people who always had access to both. "You can use computer skills with any job, so it's good you have some."

"I don't need them carrying lumber or cleaning up job sites."

"You won't be doing that the rest of your life."

Zach smiled a little. "Put in a good word with the man upstairs for me, would you?"

They stopped at the door, and Zach unfastened the rope looped over a peg that kept it closed. He stood back to let Alf enter first.

Alf was delighted immediately. Zach had scrubbed and aired the room and covered the dirt floor with inches of sawdust which he explained he had carted home from a construction job. One wall was adorned with tools hanging neatly in rows for an efficient use of space, and a carpenter's bench sat along another, just plywood on sawhorses for now, but the young man had aspirations he didn't mind explaining.

"I've been looking at plans on the internet. We could build a few mobile stands for the table saw and other things we could move out of the way when we need more space. I saw some ideas for stands with casters if we ever put in a hard floor of some kind. And there are all kinds of ideas online for making more surface space with shelves that flip up and down."

"Everything looks great so far."

"Well, not everything's been moved out here yet. I had to do some work on the roof first, but now it's nice and tight, and we can move things in as you figure out where you want to put them."

"I really like the brackets by the ceiling for storing long pieces of wood." Alf pointed to the spot where a few boards were already stacked.

Zach couldn't quite hide how pleased he was. As they walked back to the house they talked about options, about what still needed to be moved into place, what they wanted to build for storage and more workspace.

"Cathy's birthday is coming up in March," Alf said as they reached the yard. "I promised her a quilt frame but couldn't even start before Christmas, so I'd like to go gung ho. Since you have time, want to help me turn the basement into her sewing room, now that we have a good place to put all the tools?"

Zach looked pleased. "Sure. You can show me what you want, and I can even send you photos. Then you can check on the weekends you come home."

Alf nodded. "I don't think that's going to be a problem. We'll work on it together."

"Do you have plans for the frame? Or is that something you know how to make already?"

"I promised her I'd make a frame she can be proud to show off. So I'll have to do some research." Alf realized how much he was looking forward to that, to designing and creating the perfect frame, maybe designing a display rack to go with it, shelves downstairs and a real table for Cathy's machine, a place for her to cut fabric, drawers for all her notions.

There was so much to look forward to. He felt a weight lifting from his heart. "Did anybody ever tell you that before you can look to the future, you have to let go of the past?" Alf realized how Zach would interpret that. "I don't mean you, Zach, believe it or not. I'm talking about myself."

Zach was silent.

"I'm sorry," Alf said. "It sounded like I was continuing our earlier conversation."

"Maybe you weren't, but you could have been."

"I guess letting go of the past is something all humans wrestle with."

"Sometimes there's a lot to let go of."

"More for some people than for others," Alf said. "And for some of us, just figuring out all of this is hard enough."

Zach made a sound that Alf could swear was a chuckle. "Well, some of us have wives that make sure we do."

Alf clapped him on the back. "Right there I'd say we're two of a kind."

CHAPTER 17

Cathy had never been so proud of the bee. They'd called a special Friday afternoon meeting to start quilting the Peaks and Valleys quilt, or so they'd said. Truthfully, though, the meeting had really been planned as a surprise baby shower for Molly, who had only been to one other meeting and had already endeared herself to her fellow quilters.

Now Cathy stood to one side with Peony Greenway and watched the young woman cooing over every little gift that had been wrapped and presented. The bee knew Molly's situation, so members had been practical with flair. Bags of diapers packaged with handmade burp cloths, knitted hats and booties, and several quickly made quilts peeked out of gift bags filled with onesies, rompers and bibs.

"I'm so happy for her," Cathy said. "Molly deserves so much and asks for so little."

Peony, who had helped Cathy set up chairs and refreshments, was obviously pleased everything was going so well.

"She's a lovely young woman and I have a feeling she's going to be a wonderful quilter. She'll be a joy to have around."

"Zach's a fine young man, too. They're so in love." Cathy looked at her watch. "I guess it's time to head home. She'll want to get supper on the table."

Peony took her arm to stop Cathy as she started to move toward Molly, who was exclaiming over a set of appliqued burp cloths Kate Brogan had made for her. "Have you looked at the quilt yet?"

Cathy realized she hadn't. Helen and several others had set it up on the frame here in the Beehive, because getting together elsewhere had been too complicated. "With the holidays and everything else, I haven't even seen it since Helen finished the top."

"Why don't we go look at it together."

They started toward the corner where the quilt was now in place. Peony stood back as Cathy moved forward to examine the quilt. The ends were rolled up so the center could be quilted first.

She leaned over and squinted, wondering if she was imagining what she saw.

Her block was right in the center.

Peony came to stand beside her. "Surprised?"

"My block's right there for everybody to see. And there were so many better blocks. When we laid it out, mine was way off on an edge, where nobody would notice it."

"Helen redid the layout before she sewed the blocks together. She said that since you're the heart of this group, your block had to be the heart of the quilt. We all agreed."

Cathy felt tears filling her eyes. "It actually looks good there. Helen worked her usual magic."

Peony draped an arm over Cathy's shoulders. "It looks good because it is good, not because of anybody's magic.

You've made a lot of progress since you started quilting. But more important, it's a small way to let you know how important you are to us, and how grateful we are."

"I have so many things for the baby now!" Molly was bubbling over with enthusiasm. Cathy couldn't have been happier, too. Molly loved the bee and had said she would come to their meetings every chance she had. In return the other quilters loved her. Cathy knew how important it was to feel as if you were part of a group that cared, a group that was there to share your joys and sorrows. Molly had Zach, but both Lovells needed the support of the wider community to really begin to feel at home in the Valley.

"You will have such fun putting everything into the dresser you refinished," Cathy said.

Molly had found the dresser by the roadside, somehow gotten it into her car, piece by piece, and carried it home. She and Zach had sanded and painted the scarred pine a lovely pale yellow.

"I'm going to paint the bassinet that Kate gave me to match. She said she definitely doesn't want it back." Kate Brogan had passed on several items to Molly and Zach that she'd been happy to part with. Now the baby had a place to sleep, at least until it was a few months old.

Cathy and Alf had discussed furnishing the Lovell's nursery, but in the end, they had decided against it. Molly and Zach already felt the Adamses had done too much to help them. And the couple were finding ways to take care of the furnishings themselves. The top of the refinished dresser was exactly the right height for a changing table and already had a thick foam pad covered with leftover fabric from Molly's Contrary Wife quilt-in-progress.

"Everyone is so kind to me," Molly said.

"They should be. You deserve kindness, and you give it back in full measure."

"After my parents..." Molly shook her head. "I just started to believe I wasn't worth much."

Cathy knew that Molly wrote her mother regularly but never received a reply. The way other people's families worked was always a mystery, and Cathy struggled not to judge. But she couldn't imagine turning away a child, just because she wasn't following the life path the parents had set out for her.

Especially when she was about to give birth to their grandchild.

"Your parents must have been very angry," Cathy said. "I hope someday they'll realize their mistake."

"My father never will. He holds on to a grudge like it's a medal he won in a war. But my mother?" Molly cleared her throat. "That was the worst of it. I thought she would understand."

"But she didn't?"

"She's not afraid of being hurt, not the way Zach's poor mama was. My father's not a violent man, he's just rigid and old-fashioned. I think she's afraid if she crosses him and does what she knows is right, he'll send her away, too, the way he did me. They've been married for a long time, and Mama's never had a job or much say on decisions. I think that was why she was so set on me finishing college. She wanted me to have something to fall back on, if I needed it. She never did."

"I'm glad young women today are better able to make their own way in the world. You can be proud, Molly. You're doing what you think is best and doing it well."

"I wouldn't mind a little more security." Molly said as they pulled into the drive. A delivery van had arrived before them and parked in front of the footpath through the orchard to the homestead.

A man wearing jeans and a flannel shirt was standing beside the truck where the side panel of a baby crib leaned against it. As they watched he hefted it under one arm and started toward the Lovell's house.

Molly turned. "Did you and Alf buy that for us?"

Cathy wasn't sure Molly was going to start crying with joy or humiliation, but there were tears in the girl's eyes.

She put her hand on Molly's arm. "No, no we didn't. We thought about it, I'll be honest. But we thought you might not approve. This must be from somebody else."

They parked behind the van and got out of the car. Cathy grabbed a handful of tissues from the backseat and handed them to Molly. "Sweetie, obviously somebody loves you. Let's go see who."

They met Zach coming out of the house, followed by the delivery man who nodded as he skirted them to go back to the van.

"What's going on?" Molly demanded.

Zach swallowed hard. "Your mother."

"Mama's here?"

"No. But she sent the crib. Here." He held out his hand, and Molly took a small gift card and opened it. "And another package came earlier with another note. It's the wedding quilt your grandmother made you." He moved a little closer, as if he were afraid she might need his support. "Your mother's coming to visit once the baby's here, if you still want her."

Now Molly was holding the card to her chest, crying openly. "She says...it was wrong to cut me off, and no matter what happens, she's not going to let my father...decide what she can do about me and the baby."

Zach put his arm around her shoulders. "She's brave," Zach said. "He's not an easy man to stand up to."

"But she did! She did!"

Cathy knew better than to say what she was thinking, but despite her best effort, she knew she was smiling. The world seemed to be filled to overflowing with contrary wives. She was thrilled straight down to her toes that she'd just witnessed another one in the making.

CHAPTER 18

The delivery van wasn't the only vehicle parked in front of the Adams's house. As Cathy pulled around it to park after unloading Molly's presents, she realized that Alf's car was parked beside their pickup.

Alf was home already. She hadn't expected him for hours. In truth, she hadn't really expected him today at all. Something usually came up just before he was scheduled to drive home for the weekend, and if she was lucky, he finally made it in time for Saturday supper.

Inside the house she went in search. She found him, of all places, in the basement, and she wondered if he was checking to see which tools Zach had moved. He stood on the concrete floor, gazing at cinder block walls as if they held the answers to universal mysteries.

"Alf?"

He turned and smiled. He looked tired, but not exhausted, as if despite a long work week and drive home, he was happy to be here. He'd already changed into jeans and a fleece pullover, and of all things, he was holding a measuring tape.

She went to greet him with a kiss, delighted to have him home and glad she'd dressed in a pretty blue sweater and skirt for Molly's shower. "I didn't expect you so early. Can you stay for the weekend?"

"I'll be here."

"I just got back from the church. I put spaghetti sauce in the slow cooker before I left, just in case you got here." She explained how well Molly's shower had gone. "And now there's a crib! Did you see the delivery van? Molly's mother sent it. Molly's over the moon."

"That sounds like a new beginning for them." Alf put his arms around Cathy and pulled her close. "Any news from Laura?"

"Not yet. Any day now you'll be a grandpa again. And an honorary grandpa to Zach and Molly's baby."

"I can't wait. I want to enjoy both of them."

Cathy wondered how Alf was going to manage that, since the babies would probably arrive when he was back in D.C., and he was able to get home so rarely. He released her, but he took her arm to hold her there.

"Stay a minute. I need advice."

There was no place to sit, and she was tired. "Here? It's a lot more comfortable upstairs."

"This is basement advice."

She faced him. "I hope you don't mind, but Zach's been taking a lot of your tools over to the old smokehouse. He'll give you a tour. He's been working hard, and I think you'll like the results."

"I've seen it. He's doing a great job. We'll have fun finishing it. But when all my tools are out of here, this will be your new sewing room. Unless you don't want it here."

Cathy stared at him. "Are you kidding? It's a wonderful space. Lots of light. The plumbing for a bathroom. But that's the problem, isn't it? It's still just, well..." She turned up her hands. "A basement. It would need a lot of finishing to make it comfortable...attractive. I think I'd rather stay where I am."

"Well, you need to, of course, for now. Until this is finished. But since we're going to start putting up the wallboard or paneling in the next week or so, now's the time to put in your order. What do you need? What do you want here? Do you have friends who can advise you on what you need most? There's plenty of room for almost anything you might want. I've already seen a few plans online—"

She stopped him. "Why?" She was having trouble wrapping her head around this. "Why are you looking online? Alf, you hardly have time to breathe when you're home, and Zach's handy, but not handy enough to tackle a big project like this on his own. He would need help, and you and I are still paying for all the other renovations, so we can't afford to hire a skilled carpenter. We don't need additional bills, even if you are working again. I'll be fine where I am—"

She stopped a moment and thought about what he'd said. "What did you mean you're going to start finishing the walls in the next week or so? What are you talking about? How can you do that from D.C.?"

He took a deep breath and launched in. "I have all the time I'll need to work on it now. I resigned from Carrollton right after Christmas, and I've spent the past month getting things set up for my replacement."

Cathy wasn't sure she'd heard him right. "You resigned a month ago? Without telling me?"

"Why? Did you want to stop me?"

"Of course not! But why did you keep something that important to yourself?"

He spoke slowly, as if he was thinking the answer through, one word at a time. "I completed a cycle, I guess. I took the job without consulting you, and so I knew I had to leave the same way. More important, though, I didn't want you to wonder if I was going to change my mind or do something even more foolish, like take another job somewhere else. And I didn't want you thinking I was quitting just to please you and needed applause for being a good husband. I did it because I wanted to."

Cathy didn't know what to say. She had adjusted to not having Alf at home, but she had never grown to like it. There were compensations, like being able to eat or not eat at regular mealtimes, not having to leave notes explaining where she'd gone or debating what to watch on TV. But she had missed those things a little, too. She had friends. She had commitments. She had plenty of opportunities to stay busy.

But she didn't have Alf.

"Why did you want to?" she asked, as his words still rumbled in her head. "Why did you quit? You said you didn't want to be a farmer anymore. You missed going into an office and making things happen. You missed being in charge of things that matter. You missed being *Ford*."

This time he answered even more slowly. "The job with Carrollton only took care of one of those, Cath. I did go to an office every day. In fact I practically lived in one after the job started. Only I discovered that being office-bound was never the best part of what I'd done before. And whether I'm Ford or Alf, I'm the same guy."

She watched as he smoothed his hair, something he only did when he was thinking out loud. "And yes, I was making things happen again, and successfully, too. But they weren't things I cared about anymore. I finally realized that whatever I needed, I wasn't going to find it doing the things I used to do."

"How are you going to be happy here? You're not saying you want to be a farmer again?"

"I'm going to leave most of the gardening to Zach and Molly, although I do like the idea of making a kitchen garden behind our house to putter in. Zach will help with the digging, I'm sure. He needs work right now, and there's enough to do around here to keep him busy until construction starts up again."

"So what are you going to do?" Cathy realized her impatience was showing in her voice. "Alf, you must have thought this through. Are you going back to square one? Are you going to be bored? Are you going to miss having challenges to solve?" She couldn't help herself. "Are you going to come up with another hare-brained scheme to uproot us?"

He took her hands. "We're here for the long haul, at least until we can't manage such a big place anymore, if that time ever comes. And I'm sorry. I really am, for putting you through all this. Thank you for hanging in with me. And thank you for being..." He laughed a little. "A contrary wife?"

She grabbed and hugged him again. "You're serious about making this a quilt studio for me?"

He put his arm around her shoulders and guided her toward the stairs. "We have a lot to talk about. Let's do it over wine."

CHAPTER 19

Cathy held Susannah May Lovell in her arms. March had arrived, and the weather was slowly warming. Before too many more weeks, Zach would be pushing aside garden mulch and tilling in his cover crop. He already had a list of seeds to plant first and seedlings of broccoli, cabbage and cauliflower preening under shop lights he and Alf had installed near the basement furnace.

Cathy and Molly were in the basement now, looking over the latest improvements. Zach and Alf were at the workshop, and Sam Kinkade was with them to see what they were doing.

"Such a beautiful baby," Cathy crooned. "A smart baby. A kind baby."

"Such a wide-awake baby." Molly yawned and closed her eyes a moment. "She doesn't seem to need much sleep."

"What about Mom and Dad?"

"Tons. We need tons. She doesn't scream, exactly. She just demands we pay attention. And she's not hungry or wet. She just wants to be held and walked. Circles are good. She likes walking in circles."

"Someday you'll be ready to let her fuss a little. But it's hard."

"Not there yet." Molly smiled. "But it's nice to have somebody else holding her for a change. Zach's so busy he's not at the house much during the day. Either that or he's avoiding us. He knows if he's there, he'll be on walking duty."

"Not avoiding. He's busy here or in the workshop. I don't see much of Alf either, except at mealtimes. And any time you want me to babysit so you can nap, I'm here."

Molly leaned over and kissed Cathy on the cheek. "I'm so lucky."

"I'm the lucky one. I have Susannah right here and Jillian not far away. They're going to be great friends." Laura's baby had been born less than a month before Susannah and looked the way Cathy remembered Laura at the same age. Cathy and Alf were in love with both little girls.

"How are Jillian and Laura doing?"

"I'm going back to spend a few days next week. Laura's hanging in there, but Jillian isn't much of a sleeper, either. Unfortunately, she's fond of car rides. At two in the morning."

"I think both babies are just excited to be here. They don't want to miss a moment."

"What do you think of the studio so far?"

"I think it's going to be wonderful. It's already wonderful."

Together Zach and Alf had walled in a large room, which was connected to what was now a functioning bathroom. The floor plan was still hard to discern, since so much was yet to come, but Zach had envisioned much of it, showing real talent for design. Alf was encouraging him to take night classes to get an associate degree and become a draftsman.

Together they had built shelves, and cabinets were in progress in the workshop, with Alf patiently teaching Zach what he needed to know as they went. Alf had insisted they start with simple cabinets for the Lovell's kitchen, good practice for the sewing room, and with that project nearly completed, they were moving on. Alf was pleased with the speed the young man had improved. These days Alf seemed pleased with just about everything.

As a bonus, when Zach's expanded skills became apparent on the job, his boss had moved him up a pay grade, apprenticing him to his top carpenter. Zach was learning valuable skills and bringing home a larger paycheck.

"Do you see that space over there?" Cathy nodded toward the corner because her hands were too occupied with Susannah to risk pointing.

"What are you going to put there?"

"A table for your sewing machine, so you can come over and sew whenever it suits you. We'll put in more shelves at the end for anything you want to leave here. This way you won't clutter your house with quilting supplies unless you want to."

"Really? You won't mind my company?"

"I can't imagine anything nicer than having you and Susannah here. There's room for a Pack 'n Play right there." Cathy nodded again. "I'll need to buy one for Jillian's visits anyway."

"My mother liked to sew. Clothes, mostly. I used to help her. She made my prom dress." She laughed a little. "My father made her cover the neckline with lace because he said it was too low, which ruined the whole dress. She attached it with snaps so I could rip off the lace once I left the house."

Cathy laughed. "How is she, do you know?"

"She's not backing down about spending time with me and Susannah. And I guess Dad has figured out she'll walk out the door for good if he tries to stop her. He'll have to make a choice, and since nobody else would put up with him, it won't be a hard one. She's planning to come next week."

"Any chance he'll come, too?"

"Not a one. His loss.

"Definitely that."

"I think the hardest part of marriage is figuring out when you have to take a stand and when you have to compromise."

"You've caught on to that early."

"How do you know? How do you figure it out?"

"If you can't live with the compromise, you can't make it." Cathy thought about the stand she had made herself. "I guess your mom knew she couldn't live without you, so she stood up when she had to."

"Is that what it's like to be a parent? Choices all the time?"

"Lots of them. I'm afraid you can't just be a contrary wife, you have to be a contrary mother, too."

Molly made a face. "At least we're bigger than they are."

Cathy held out Susannah, who looked like she might just take a nap now. "Enjoy it while you can."

ALF HAD JUST BEEN WAITING for Sam Kinkade to show up. From what he could tell, Sam kept his finger on the pulse of everything important in the community, especially when it had to do with someone in his congregation or one of the programs he supported. Alf had known it would just be a matter of time before Sam came calling.

"I can't believe what the two of you have accomplished," Sam said, walking around the workshop area. "What a great place to work on your projects."

He had already stroked the first polished cherry cabinet that would go into Cathy's quilt studio, as if his fingers couldn't believe how perfect the wood grain was. Alf and Zach would put the pieces together at the house, but everything was ready to assemble, and there were many more pieces in various stages.

"What do you suppose cabinetry, or a whole sewing studio like this would cost somebody who wanted one built in their own home?"

Alf knew Sam wasn't asking an idle question. Nothing about Sam was idle.

"Thousands," he said.

"That would be my guess. And it would depend, right, on how much you did from scratch, or how you incorporated ready-made cabinetry and did the finishing touches yourself. How big the studio. Lots of variables."

"These were almost free. Alf had the wood, and we worked around that," Zach said. "We didn't need to buy anything ready-made."

"And this." Sam fingered a leg of the quilt frame that Alf had made for Cathy. In the end, and after research, Alf had used a design like one a local Mennonite family had shown him. He had carefully crafted the frame from maple, using pegs instead of nails and hand carving on the feet–something he'd always wanted to try. The frame was fully adjustable, collapsible if needed, and if he did say so himself, a beautiful piece of furniture, to boot. He was undeniably proud.

"Cathy hasn't seen that yet," Alf said. "I'm going to set it up while she's visiting our daughter tomorrow."

"She's a lucky woman. She'll be the envy of her friends. And this?" Sam gestured toward a matching piece.

"It's a quilt rack. To display the quilts she makes."

"I can't help thinking there's a market for these."

Alf and Zach exchanged glances. They had discussed this. They knew what was coming.

Zach cleared his throat. "Yeah, it's too bad we don't have more carpenters to make them. There's all kind of things we could add. Contraptions to hold thread and other notions, for a start. We could make a little business. Nothing fancy, but it would be a good way to train a few men or women to work with their hands. It's too bad we can't find people like that, but Alf and I, we're pretty busy. We'd need somebody to help us do that part."

Sam's eyes were shining. "And I bet if somebody *did* help, you'd turn this little home business into a going concern. You two would be perfect to run one. Zach, you know how it feels to start working at something you've never done, and Alf, it's not like you don't have the carpentry and business skills to turn a business like that into something extraordinary."

"Yeah, we'd need a bigger workshop," Alf said, "something like the barn that's sitting at the edge of my property doing nothing right now. If we just had men and women who were willing to help. People who need jobs and are eager to learn new skills."

"You saw me coming a mile away, didn't you?" Sam asked.

"Let's go up to the house and talk it over, but don't get ahead of yourself. We'll want to start small with just the right people. And you'll need an introduction to Susannah Lovell, while you're there." He finally glanced at Sam who was grinning. "By the way, you're gloating."

All three men laughed.

"I'll put Merrill up, and I'll join you," Zach said, scooping up the rooster who had been pecking the sawdust on the other side of the workshop.

Sam and Alf walked toward the house as Zach started toward the coop.

"That's one fine young man," Alf said. "I don't know what · we'd do without the Lovells around here."

"I don't know what they'd do without you. You're happy?" Sam asked. "Feeling fulfilled in the Valley at last?"

Alf didn't have to think. He already knew the answer. "Every relationship has its dark moments. It takes one person, usually the one who sees most clearly, to lead the way into the sunshine."

"It sounds like you're speaking from experience."

"In the end I was dragged back into the light by a contrary woman." He hesitated then laughed. "I guess that's the best kind to be married to."

Sam clapped him on the back. "You're exactly right."

THE CONTRARY WIFE QUILT

Contrary Wife is a traditional quilt block introduced in the Kansas City Star in the 1940s. The Star began publishing quilt patterns in 1928 and continued until 1961. During that time they published more than a thousand patterns.

Contrary Wife is a nine-patch quilt, like Steps to the Altar, but easier for a beginner because each block has fewer pieces. Like that quilt, it can be assembled numerous ways.

Are you interested in making your own quilt? You'll find patterns for all the traditional quilts in this story online. Just type the quilt pattern into your search engine and see what comes up. Or you might want to start with these two sites: allpeoplequilt.com and quilterscache.com, where lots of patterns are available.

Happy quilting!

EPILOGUE

FOR PEAKS AND VALLEYS

The Shenandoah Community Church had taken a big chance scheduling the prison ministry fundraiser so early in the spring, and scheduling much of it outdoors, on top of everything. Everybody knew that April weather in the Shenandoah Valley was as likely to cause frostbite as sunburn. Helen Henry was pretty sure she'd seen snow in April a time or two herself, but Reverend Sam had been confident the weather would cooperate today.

Helen's mother Delilah had always said that some men were such numskulls, if they threw themselves on the ground, they would miss. But Helen had been wrong to doubt the minister. From the moment the sun had come up that morning, the sky had been as bright and the air as warm as the prettiest summer day.

Maybe the perfect weather was due to global warming, like her daughter Nancy always insisted, or maybe it was due to the reverend's prayers. She didn't know, but when she'd gotten out of bed and seen sunlight pouring through her windows like honey through honeycomb, she'd known that most everybody in Toms Brook and beyond was going to stop by the church at some point today to see what was what.

Now she was standing in the churchyard while a crowd surged around her. Fairs and festivals were favorites here. Maybe these days local people had cars and could drive toward the city to find more sophisticated entertainment. But the people who'd chosen to settle here, to live this more rural life-style and gaze at mountains more frequently than computer screens? They were the same folks who were here today, throwing darts at balloons and taking kids for pony rides. They were the same people eating the burgers and hot dogs that the men's group was grilling, the very same that were buying wall hangings and pillow tops from tables the quilters had set up in a tent by the church's front door.

Simple pleasures or simple-minded? She wasn't sure. She'd never lived anywhere but the Valley, not in all her nearly eighty-nine years, but then she'd never had the chance. What did she know other than how to grow food, and years ago how to run a vegetable stand so she could keep herself and Nancy fed?

Of course, she did know quilts. What else could she do on those cold winter nights huddled by the wood stove or the breezy spring evenings on the front porch? And maybe quilting had been where she'd found her pleasure. She'd worked too hard every day to find anything but a sore back in their garden. But at night, with nothing between her and the stars above to tend to, she'd stitched pieces of fabric together any old way it pleased her. And now that she was too old to do much of anything else, she'd found friends with the same interest.

And look what they'd done together.

Reverend Sam came up to stand beside her as she gazed at the Peaks and Valleys quilt. "I didn't expect anything like this," he said. "It's stunning. No other word for it. And different from what the bee usually does, isn't it?"

"Paper piecing. Even a bunch of old biddies can learn something new if they have to." Helen didn't take her eyes off the quilt, which was behind a makeshift stage just a foot off the ground on cinder blocks. Even she had to admit the bee had outdone itself. The result was more art quilt than traditional. The paper-pieced mountain peaks and the sunsets behind each one fairly twirled in the air. They'd chosen not to create a border, and she was glad. This quilt was all about freedom and things that weren't hemmed in. She supposed that was right for a quilt meant to help prisoners start a new life when they got out of jail.

"Don't look now, Helen," Sam said, "but the bee's getting younger and younger. Elisa when she has time, Kendra and Jamie. The La Casa moms, Rebecca O'Keefe, Molly Lovell and Cathy's daughter Laura." He glanced at her. "The Beehive's fairly buzzing."

"Just so's you know, we spend more than a little time down there trying to figure ways to make your life difficult."

He laughed. "Don't I know it?"

"I checked a bit ago," Helen said. "Cathy Adams insisted we had to sell enough tickets to wallpaper the Taj Mahal. Turns out, she was thinking the right way. Could be a lot of folks will benefit from this quilt."

"How many tickets did you buy?"

Helen slapped her hands on her ample hips. "You think I need another quilt in my house? Nancy and Tessa would just give it to charity." Helen's daughter and granddaughter kept an eye on her tendency to "collect," and she had to admit at one time, that tendency had gotten a little out of hand. Of course they had already come and gone for the day, both of them carrying raffle tickets in their own handbags.

"Not a chance they'd give this away," Sam said. "How many?"

"How many did *you* buy?"

"How many should I have bought?"

"Six at least." The bee was selling the raffle tickets for five dollars a piece or three for ten dollars. Nobody with any sense would buy less than a multiple of three. Cathy had said that people always wanted a bargain, so they would buy more with a discount.

"I bought fifteen tickets." Sam paused. "And then Elisa bought fifteen more."

"You already have plenty of quilts at your house."

"And every one of them beautiful."

She harrumphed. Of course he had to say as much, since most of them had been given to the minister and his wife by the bee.

"Your turn," he said. "How many did you buy? And I happen to know you already have a few quilts yourself."

"I figured if the Good Lord wants me to have this quilt, he'll give it to me with one ticket or a hundred."

"How many?"

"Six." She peeked at him and saw he was grinning. "Five tickets for the Lord, one for me. Just to stay on His good side."

He laughed and clapped her on the back. "You'll be sitting right beside Him," he said before he headed toward the pony rides where Bejoy Clayton, Kate Brogan's twin sister, was leading Kate's son Rory around the circle. Bejoy was one of the younger women to take up quilting. If some things were harder for her than for most people, quilting wasn't one of them. Together she and Kate had produced a bright folk art wall hanging for sale today, and Helen happened to know it was the first item that had sold that morning.

Cathy Adams came to stand beside Helen. "With all the

tickets we sold ahead of time, I think we'll make at least a thousand dollars on this quilt, maybe more if we're lucky. And another three hundred for the wall hangings and pillow tops for sale today. Then there's that the sculpture Harry O'Keefe contributed. That's going to go high."

The sculpture was part of a silent auction of fine art pieces, with results to be announced tomorrow morning at the church service, so that bidders had the whole night to worry and increase their offers. Helen was pretty sure that Cathy was keeping tabs, and she looked pleased. When it came right down to it, Helen couldn't see what the fuss was about. At least she could tell what the figure was, a man with his arms outstretched, but all rough edges and hard lines. Peony Greenway, apparently an old friend of Harry's, had asked him to create it. Helen guessed that maybe for some people, the sculpture, like the quilt, symbolized freedom.

"It's been a long day," Cathy said. "You're doing okay? We kept you busy."

Helen wondered how many more of these fundraisers she would see. She'd lived longer than she ought to, and every morning when she woke up she was surprised. Little things pleased her most since she didn't really expect to see them much longer. Little Reese bringing her hot tea in the morning when Helen was sitting on the porch, or her great-grandson Ian riding a bike with training wheels down the front drive on a summer evening when the MacRaes were visiting. This year she expected the training wheels to come off, and then nothing would hold that little 'un back.

Today she'd spent a majority of the afternoon teaching the church youth group and their friends how to sew a straight seam on machines donated for the day by bee members. She still couldn't believe that for most of these young people, this was the first time they'd sat behind a sewing machine. On top of that, she couldn't believe that the boys had enjoyed her lesson as much as the girls. In fact, before she could tell him not to, one of them had taken apart the machine he'd been using and fixed whatever had been ailing it so that it stopped skipping stitches.

"Somebody had to show those silly teenagers a thing or two," she said.

"If you can do one more thing, we'd like you to draw the raffle winner. Will you still be here at five o'clock? That's just half an hour more."

Helen was pleased at the honor, although she tried not to show it. "Cissy's coming to get me about then. When she gets here, she and Reese will want to look around anyway. I reckon she'll wait for me."

"I'll take you home if she doesn't want to. Alf and I drove separately, so it won't be any trouble. He and Zach are inside taking orders for quilt racks."

Now that she'd gotten to know him a little better, Helen liked Cathy's husband. She'd even given a little thought to buying one of those racks he and Zach Lovell were making. The men were donating twenty-five percent to the fundraiser, so, in a way, the price was a charitable donation. Maybe it was conceited to have her quilts displayed where they could be admired, but she didn't expect to go to hell for such a small sin.

Then she thought of something. "What if I don't like the person whose name I draw?"

Cathy shook her head. "Helen..."

"We can't let just anybody have that quilt. Why some people are so..." She shook her head while she tried to find an adjective more polite than the ones she wanted to use. "So *uneducated*," she said at last, "they'd take a quilt like this to the beach and spread it on the sand."

"We aren't letting just anybody have it. Whoever wins it

had to buy a ticket. And the tickets aren't cheap. Five dollars is not a whim. It will be fine."

Helen couldn't very well argue. What was she going to do? Grab the quilt from behind the platform where it was displayed and make a run for it?

Cathy wandered off, and Helen realized she had exactly enough time to go look at the quilt racks again. In the end she ordered two, because she couldn't choose between maple and cherry. She figured it was still only one sin, whether she ordered one rack or a hundred. The Lovell boy actually smiled at her, and if she was lucky, that would be a mark in her favor when she tried to pass through the pearly gates.

When she emerged into the sunshine, Cissy and Reese were just walking up from the parking lot, Cissy in jeans and a bright green blouse, Reese with her strawberry blond hair in pigtails. The two looked so much alike nobody would doubt they were mother and daughter. Reese spied Kate's daughter Bridget and ran off to see the ponies with her. Cissy came up to join Helen.

Cathy was already on the platform thanking everybody who had worked so hard on the event, particularly those who had created items to sell. Without speaking Helen pointed, and she and Cissy headed that way.

By the time they wormed their way to the front, Cathy was praising the quilters for all the hours they'd put into the quilt and explaining a little about the way it had come to be. A large crowd had gathered, and Helen saw quilters from the bee who she hadn't seen that day. She imagined some of them had come hoping they would win the quilt.

Cathy told those who had gathered how thankful she was for their attendance, and then, because undoubtedly, she knew that her audience was getting restless, she gestured to Helen.

"This is Helen Henry, who created the pattern based on the gorgeous peaks and valleys right here in the Shenandoah Valley, where many of us are lucky enough to live. But the pattern also symbolizes those peaks and valleys we all go through in our lives, and the way the deepest valley eventually gives way to a peak if someone extends a hand to help us climb. That's what we believe will happen with the money we raise today."

Cathy stepped toward the front of the platform as people politely applauded. Helen heard rustling, as if the onlookers were getting their raffle tickets out of pockets or purses so they'd be ready to take possession of the quilt if they won.

"Helen has agreed to draw the winning name," Cathy said. From some local charity or another, the bee had borrowed an acrylic drum on legs that could be twirled to scramble the tickets. Cathy held out her hand to help Helen up on the platform. Helen had just enough time to regret needing help before she was standing beside the drum.

"Spin it a few times, Helen," Cathy said. "For good luck."

"Good luck for somebody." Silently Helen made a wish that whoever won the quilt would treat it right. She nudged the drum and it revolved lethargically, but not for long since it was heavier with tickets than she'd guessed. The second time she gave it a bigger push, and it spun enthusiastically enough that the crowd applauded.

"Reverend Kinkade, will you come up, too?" Cathy said. "We'll let Sam check the ticket stub just to be sure Helen and I read it right."

"Been reading since my mama taught me my letters from our family Bible." Helen sniffed, but she wasn't really sorry they'd have another set of eyes on the ticket. You couldn't be too cautious.

"Okay, here goes," Cathy said. The drum had stopped spinning, and now she unlocked the door where they'd been depositing ticket stubs for most of the past month. "Helen?"

Helen knew a bit of drama was called for, and how often did a woman as old as lead paint get to exploit it? She reached into the drum, and began to feel around, digging deeper, moving sideways one way than another. Finally, afraid she might foment a rebellion, she took one of the tickets between her fingers and slipped her hand free.

She looked down, and for a moment, she couldn't believe what she read. Then she looked up, searching for the winner in the crowd. "You'd better read this, too," she told Cathy. Cathy took it and smiled. "Sam?" She passed it to him. "Why don't you read that out loud for us?"

Sam grinned. "The winner is Mr. Harry O'Keefe."

Applause was mixed with disappointed groans, which were quickly drowned out.

Helen searched the crowd for Harry. After a moment she spotted him at the edge of the crowd. She wasn't surprised to see him, but she was surprised at what he did next. In fact, she was stunned. Harry scooped up Peony Greenway, who was standing next to him, and kissed her. And from what Helen could tell, that kiss was anything but perfunctory.

Harry O'Keefe and Peony Greenway?

"You didn't suspect?" Cathy said in a low voice, smiling at her.

For once Helen was speechless.

"Maybe Peaks and Valleys will be a wedding quilt," Cathy said.

That did seem possible. Helen had to agree that every marriage was full of both.

As the crowd drifted away, Harry, who had already fielded dozens of congratulations, came up to claim the quilt. Peony was right beside him. "I'm giving it to Peony," he told Cathy, nodding to include Helen. "She deserves it."

Peony looked delighted but not surprised, as if the matter had already been discussed. "We're still going to hang it at Harry's, though."

"I'm doing some redecorating," Harry explained. "This will be perfect on the wall of my living room." He turned to Peony, who was wearing a pretty rose-colored dress, and dangling pearl earrings. "Right?"

Peony didn't look the least embarrassed. "We'll have to paint the room a neutral color so the quilt won't get swallowed up."

"Not much neutral about my house, that's for sure." Harry reached up to help Alf, who'd come over to take the quilt down, and together the two men and Reverend Sam worked on unfastening it from the frame where it hung.

"I waited a lot of years for that man," Peony said in a low voice, as if in answer to unspoken questions. "Since I was a girl."

Cathy draped her arm along the other woman's shoulders. "Worth waiting for, I'd say."

Helen knew something was expected, something profound. When faced with that kind of devotion, that kind of extraordinary patience, any woman who was standing there had to say something.

She cleared her throat. "You and Harry come over to my house someday, and I'll show you right where the idea for that quilt came from. Mostly peaks from the top of a hill behind my house. Peaks, like when..." She ran out of words, or else she couldn't say anything as sentimental as she was thinking out loud.

"Peaks like when somebody is truly loved?" Cathy asked.

327

Helen wouldn't have said it quite that way herself, but she supposed that was as close to truth as anything ever could be.

Peony hugged her and Cathy joined in with a laugh. Helen felt her arms going around the other two for a squeeze. Maybe she wasn't much for hugging in public, but just this once, it was probably all right.

PEAKS AND VALLEYS QUILT

Helen Henry, who stars in or visits every Shenandoah Album novel designed the Peaks and Valleys quilt described in this collection of novellas herself. While Steps to the Altar, Woven Paths, and Contrary Wife are all traditional quilt blocks, Peaks and Valleys is Helen's own paper-pieced design.

If you're a quilter who hopes Helen's pattern for Peaks and Valleys is available, it isn't, at least not exactly. But even Helen admits the idea was inspired by, among other quilt designers, Leila Gardunia, who offers several different sized patterns for Scrappy Mountain and Scrappy Mountain Range paper-pieced blocks. Enjoy Leila's beautiful patterns at her website: www.leilagarunia.com.

Etsy is a great place to find quilt patterns, and they have many mountain peak quilt patterns including Leila's, to inspire you, too. Just search for "mountain quilt pattern" on the Etsy site to jump start your imagination.

If you make your own Peaks and Valley project, why not

share photos of your creation on Emilie Richards Readers Page on   Facebook: https://www.facebook.com/authoremilierichards.

A NOTE FROM EMILIE

Through the years I've received so many pleas for more stories in my Shenandoah Album series about quilts and quilters in Virginia's Shenandoah Valley. While my publisher wanted me to move on to other ideas, many of you did not. And truthfully, I wanted to write more.

Endless Chain, the second in the series, introduced a church quilting bee and many of the women who met weekly to pursue their favorite craft. Most of these women were minor characters, appearing only occasionally in *Endless Chain* and subsequent novels in the series. But these women were real to *me,* and I decided it was time to share some of their stories.

Steps to the Altar reintroduces the church bee, whose name, over the course of *Endless Chain,* gradually changed from the *Shenandoah Community Church Wednesday Morning Quilting Bee and Social Gathering* to the *SCC Bee,* because these women, like all quilters, had too much to do to waste time. They didn't need a lengthy name. They knew exactly who they were.

The two major characters of that novella, Connor and Rebecca, are new to the series, but you'll find others who are not, and they play a handcrafted version of Cupid to help this young couple find each other.

Kate Brogan, of *Woven Paths*, was introduced in *Endless Chain*, along with her children, Rory and Bridget. I was particularly drawn to Kate, a young woman trying to find a little time and space for herself around the demands of motherhood. As the mother of four myself, I could relate. Kate's twin sister, Bejoy, is a new peek into Kate's life, as are Kate's husband, Mickey, and oldest son, Cormick. Kate and Bejoy's adventures driving from Florida to Virginia were absorbing for me to write, as I reimagined a trip I've taken numerous times. I fell in love with Bejoy. I think you will, too.

Cathy Adams, of *Contrary Wife*, was never intended to star in her own story. She was the president of the bee, a hard working, no-nonsense retiree who could keep the quilters focused on what was important. And yet after I decided to title a story after the evocatively named traditional quilt block, Contrary Wife, Cathy began to emerge from the shadows. Among other reasons, she had a husband who may or may not have needed a "contrary wife." I needed a mature, energetic heroine, and I knew from previous books that Cathy was married to Alf, who had retired to become a gentleman farmer. All the makings of a good story were right there, so how could I resist?

Are you wondering about the timeline for these novellas? After all it's been quite some time since the last Shenandoah Album novel. The Shenandoah Album series began with *Wedding Ring*, set in 2002 and finished with *Sister's Choice*, which ended in spring of 2008. I wrote a short story, *Nine Patch Christmas*, for my newsletter readers, and set it in 2008, as well.

When I decided to write the three books that became *Peaks and Valleys*, thirteen years had passed in real time since 2008, but I knew I couldn't let that much time pass in my series. Age all my characters thirteen years? Impossible. Helen alone would be over a hundred years old, and while I fully expect Helen to live and quilt that long, for this volume, I wanted to pick up right where I had left off. Because of that, *Steps to the Altar* begins in spring of 2008, and the epilogue ends in spring of 2009. If you wonder why Alf didn't call Uber or Kate didn't buy Bejoy a digital camera? That's why.

Many thanks to my Krewe of Review for their careful reading of this manuscript and for their enthusiastic reviews. Special thanks to Terry Guerra, Marjorie Baus Roberts and Michael McGee for taking up the copy editor gauntlet.

I hope you enjoy this addition to the series. I welcome your reviews of *Peaks and Valleys* wherever you care to leave them. You can also email me through the contact page of my website: www.emilierichards.com. To enjoy my monthly newsletter and occasional free content like the story *Nine Patch Christmas*, along with frequent giveaways, you can sign up on my website or on my Facebook Reader's Page: www.facebook.com/authoremilierichards

I look forward to your comments.

ABOUT EMILIE

USA Today best selling novelist Emilie Richards is the author of eighty novels with more than 15 million in print world-wide. She currently writes women's fiction, but she started in the romance genre where she won the Romance Writers of America RITA award, as well as a life-time achievement award from Romantic Times magazine. Her women's fiction has received starred reviews from Publishers Weekly and Library Journal.

Find out more about Emilie Richards at www.emilierichards.com.

BOOKS IN THE SHENANDOAH ALBUM SERIES

You can find all of Emilie's books on her website: emilierichards.com.
The novels in her Shenandoah series are:

Wedding Ring

Endless Chain

Lover's Knot

Touching Stars

Sister's Choice

Peaks and Valleys (A novella collection.)

Peaks and Valleys

A Shenandoah Album Collection

Cover by Karri Klawiter.
Cover photos by Linda Yolanda and Digidream
Print ISBN: 978-1-950365-12-8
Ebook ISBN: 294-0-160735-64-1

❀ Created with Vellum

Made in the USA
Monee, IL
17 December 2022

22113002R00187